# A Matter of Timing

## A Pride and Prejudiced Variation

### Linda C. Thompson

A Matter of Timing - A Pride and Prejudice Variation
First Edition

Copyright © 2017 Linda Thompson

All Rights Reserved. No part of this book can be reproduced in any form except in the case of brief quotations embodied in critical articles or reviews, without permission in writing from the author and publisher.

This is a work of fiction. Names, characters, businesses, places, events and incidents are either the products of the author's imagination or used in a fictitious manner. Any resemblance to actual persons, living or dead, or actual events is purely coincidental.

For information, please contact:
Linda C. Thompson Books
1700 Lynhurst Lane
Denton, TX 76205

Cover Design and Graphic Flourishes: Karin Bench

ISBN-13: 978-1548298838
ISBN-10: 1548298832

# DEDICATION

Two of my dearest friends showed up in my life at a time of great change. They helped to ground me through the changes I faced. They also helped me grow into a more confident adult and were instrumental in preparing me for the future that would one day be mine. Melodie and Michelle, you are both more like sisters than friends. It is staggering to think this friendship has now lasted for forty years, and I look forward to many more!

# TABLE OF CONTENTS

| | | |
|---|---|---|
| 1. | Visiting Derbyshire | 1 |
| 2. | Showing Off Pemberley | 15 |
| 3. | Introductions | 23 |
| 4. | New Friends and Old Foes | 39 |
| 5. | Understanding Before Disaster | 53 |
| 6. | Making Arrangements | 63 |
| 7. | The Quest Begins | 73 |
| 8. | Unexpected Results | 85 |
| 9. | A London Interlude | 101 |
| 10. | A Surprising Homecoming | 121 |
| 11. | An Unexpected Occurance | 131 |
| 12. | Tales of Wickham | 147 |
| 13. | The Doctors' Diagnosis | 157 |
| 14. | Preparations | 169 |
| 15. | Excursions | 181 |

| 16. | Laughter is the Best Medicine | 203 |
| 17. | Home Again | 215 |
| 18. | The Big Day Arrives | 229 |
|  | Epilogue | 235 |
|  | End Notes | 239 |

# VISITING DERBYSHIRE

A SMALL, ELEGANT CARRIAGE CLIPPED ALONG the road at a spanking pace. The golden sun shown down hotly on the passengers, but the breeze kept the heat from being overpowering. As the carriage pulled into the quaint little village, an exclamation of delight burst forth from the youngest of the passengers, sparking a smile from the older female in the party.

Traveling with the Gardiners was always the highlight of the summer for twenty-year-old Elizabeth Bennet. This year, her relations had planned to tour the Lake District, but business constraints had made a trip of that length impossible. Consequently, Elizabeth, along with her aunt and uncle, Helen and Edward Gardiner, traveled in a leisurely fashion from Elizabeth's home, Longbourn, in Hertfordshire to the village of Mrs. Gardiner's youth, Lambton, in Derbyshire. Along the way, they had stopped to tour many great estates and other sites of interest. They had visited Wimpole Hall and grounds in Cambridgeshire, Boughton House in Northamptonshire, and Carlton Curlieu Hall in Leicestershire.

After several days of traveling, they were to stay at the Chestnut Tree Inn in Lambton, for the next se'nnight, perhaps even longer. Upon their arrival at the inn, the innkeeper, Mr. Burton, greeted Mrs. Gardiner like an old friend. He ushered their party to the finest rooms the inn had to offer and quickly arranged for both baths and refreshments for the visitors. As the trio had stopped to tour Chatsworth earlier in the day, they were quite tired upon arriving and retired early after a pleasant meal.

On this, their third morning in the area, Mrs. Gardiner suggested they apply to tour Pemberley. Elizabeth, however, was very reluctant to do so. The owner of Pemberley was Mr. Fitzwilliam Darcy, with whom Elizabeth claimed an acquaintance, but they had argued violently and parted on extremely bad terms. Wanting to correct the misinformation Elizabeth had flung at him during their argument, Darcy had dared to write her a letter and personally deliver it before walking out of her life. Elizabeth had read Mr. Darcy's letter countless times since receiving it and longed for an opportunity to apologize to the gentleman. Elizabeth regretted her extremely rude behavior when she had refused his unexpected proposal. Due to her injured vanity, a result of hearing Darcy call her "tolerable but not handsome enough to tempt him," as well as the lies of the nefarious Mr. Wickham, Elizabeth had accused him of the worst kind of conduct, and the memory of the event and her behavior haunted her.

"Aunt, my acquaintance with Mr. Darcy is very slight. I would feel uncomfortable intruding upon his family in his home."

Before Mrs. Gardiner could answer, a knock sounded on the sitting room door. It was the young servant, Hannah, arriving with their breakfast. "Hannah, do you know if the Darcy family is currently in residence at Pemberley or if the estate is available for a tour?" Mrs. Gardiner inquired.

"No, ma'am the family is not 'ere at present, but they be 'spected in the next day or two, says me brother, who is an under-gardener at the estate" was the maid's reply.

## A Matter of Timing

Mrs. Gardiner turned to her niece. "There, Lizzy, that should put your mind at rest. Shall we tour Pemberley this afternoon?"

"All right, Aunt. If it pleases you, we will visit Pemberley," Elizabeth replied reluctantly.

After dining, they spent the morning in visits to a few more of Mrs. Gardiner's childhood friends who still resided in Lambton. Elizabeth tried to focus on those she met, but she could not dispel a feeling of concern about visiting Pemberley.

---

So it was that an hour after luncheon found Elizabeth and the Gardiners in the carriage for the five-mile journey to the Darcy estate. Elizabeth could not help but enjoy nature's beauties as they rode through the Derbyshire countryside. The rocks and hills were a sharp contrast to the more pastoral setting surrounding her home. When they turned in at the gates to Pemberley, Elizabeth anxiously looked for the house. More than half an hour later, it finally came into view. The driver stopped the carriage at the top of a rise, affording the visitors the best view of the manor house. Elizabeth gasped at the sight.

Before her, nestled into a valley, sat an enormous house built of a soft beige stone. A great expanse of green lawns led down to a lake on whose smooth surface glimmered a perfect reflection of the stately mansion. Rising behind the house was a steep hill of dark woods. Elizabeth 'had never seen a place for which nature had done more, or where natural beauty had been so little counteracted by an awkward taste. (1) Eventually, the carriage began to move again and within twenty minutes it had stopped before the door of the great house.

The Gardiners applied for a tour of the estate. A short time later the housekeeper, Mrs. Reynolds, greeted them. As she guided the guests through the house, Mrs. Reynolds could not contain the expressions of approbation she liberally bestowed on the master of the estate. The Gardiners and Elizabeth toured several drawing rooms (each more beautifully decorated than the preceding one). They also saw the large dining room (with a table that could seat close to one hundred people). The music room included a magnificent new pianoforte Mr. Darcy had purchased for his sister. The Pemberley ballroom was the largest Elizabeth had ever seen, and, finally, the gallery.

It was here where the housekeeper stopped before a picture of the current master. Elizabeth was breathless at the sight of him. He appeared as she remembered him, stately, handsome, and with the intense look in his eyes that she had always mistaken for dislike. As the others moved on to view a recent portrait of Miss Darcy, Elizabeth remained before Darcy's portrait. *Had I not been so foolish and vain, misjudging you as I did, of all this, I might have been the mistress. You did not deserve all of the anger and disdain with which I treated you. If only I could see you once more and apologize for my poor treatment of you.*

With one last lingering look, Elizabeth moved away to join the others. Upon departing the gallery, Mrs. Reynolds moved towards the main staircase. She would escort the group outside and the gardener would continue with the tour, showing the family the beauty of Pemberley's grounds.

Before they descended the steps, Elizabeth turned to Mrs. Reynolds. "Would it be possible to visit the library?"

"That is not usually included on a tour of the house, Miss." Her tone was a little frosty.

"I understand. I only asked as I have heard much about it from Mr. and Miss Bingley, as well as Mr. Darcy."

The housekeeper looked intently at the young lady before her. The visitor was lovely, with dark curls and bright eyes. Mrs. Reynolds had been impressed

## A Matter of Timing

with the young woman's kindness and the appreciation she had shown for the estate. She was so different from the detested Miss Bingley, who had spoken of the changes she would make to the stately and elegant interior of the home. "You know the master?"

"I was so fortunate as to make his acquaintance when he visited Mr. Bingley at his estate in Hertfordshire. Mr. Bingley's estate, Netherfield Park, borders that of my father."

"Well," said Mrs. Reynolds, hesitating only a moment, "if you are a friend of the master's, I am sure he would not mind me showing you the library."

"I thank you for your offer, Mrs. Reynolds, but I would not want you to go against Mr. Darcy's wishes."

"Are you quite sure, Miss? I am sure he would not mind a friend seeing the room."

"Well, perhaps if we only look in from the hallway," suggested Elizabeth. She dearly wished to see if the room was as magnificent as she had heard.

The housekeeper led the way to the library and opened both of the double doors, then stepped aside. Elizabeth stood in the center of the opening and inhaled the comforting scent of parchment, leather, and furniture polish. Light flooded the room from a bank of tall windows opposite the door. The furnishings were navy, burgundy, and hunter green, with several settees and plush chairs set about for reading. Two large tables stood before the window. Floor-to-ceiling shelves lined the walls, and it appeared that a balcony wound around the room, creating a second story. There were also display cases containing rare pieces and other artifacts. In one corner of the room stood two globes, one obviously much older than the other.

Elizabeth was astonished by all she saw. "It is, indeed, the most amazing room I have ever beheld. I am sure it would take more than a lifetime to read all the treasures contained therein." She turned to the housekeeper. "I thank you very much for showing me this spectacular sight. I doubt I shall ever see another room anywhere that can match it." Reverence and awe filled her voice.

"I am pleased you found the room to your liking." Mrs. Reynolds closed the library doors and turned to lead the guests downstairs. She took them through a hallway that led to a terrace on the back of the house. Here they met the gardener, who led them through the formal gardens.

Elizabeth wandered quietly, not fully listening to the information the elderly man shared with her relations. Her mind was too full of the master of the house. Elizabeth had long since come to realize she had been immediately attracted to Mr. Darcy, and his overheard comments about her 'tolerable' appearance had hurt more than she was willing to acknowledge. As a result, she had gone out of her way to be disagreeable to the gentleman. If she were honest with herself, she had to admit that she had enjoyed their verbal sparring. Few men in the environs of Meryton could equal her sharp intellect, and it had been a pleasure to match wits with such an intelligent gentleman.

As her relatives followed the gardener deeper into the formal gardens, Elizabeth took a small path to the right that led to a walled enclosure. The arched door was locked, so Elizabeth found a bench against the wall in the shade of a large oak tree and sat looking at the beauty around her. She closed her eyes and tilted her face to the sky. Elizabeth loved the warmth of the sun on her skin. Opening her eyes, she gazed about, taking in the incredible beauty of the gardens of Pemberley.

Elizabeth's gaze eventually drifted to the stable. She noted that the complex was larger than her family's home. Suddenly her cheeks flushed with color. She jumped up from the bench and wrung her hands. Striding towards her was the man on whom her thoughts dwelt. In spite of the unsettled feeling he roused in her, Elizabeth could not fail to notice his handsomeness. Darcy carried his jacket and hat, and she could see the water sparkling off his messy curls.

The lawn shirt he wore was damp and emphasized the broadness of his shoulders. The tight pants Darcy wore showed off his strong, shapely legs. It was evident he had not yet seen her, and she wondered what his reaction would be upon discovering her presence.

---

Fitzwilliam Darcy's massive black stallion clip-clopped along the dusty road. Truthfully, he was relieved to have had a reason to leave his party behind at the inn a half day's journey from Pemberley. Darcy needed time to think and to overcome the troubling thoughts that had plagued him since April. His disastrous proposal to Elizabeth Bennet while she visited at Hunsford near the estate of his aunt, Lady Catherine de Bourgh, had cost him the good opinion of the only woman he would ever love. Darcy determined to put the loss behind him and find a way to move forward. However, he could not picture a future without Elizabeth. Darcy could recall her appearance as easily as if she stood before him. Her unruly dark curls and sparkling eyes stirred him as no other woman he had ever known. It was more than her beauty that drew him to her, however. Darcy had never met a more intelligent, well-read woman, and he was aware that life with her could never be boring.

Darcy's unrelenting thoughts of Elizabeth Bennet were not the only reason he was glad to leave the rest of his party behind. He needed separation from Caroline Bingley. Darcy enjoyed having his best friend, Charles Bingley, visit his estate, but his patience with Charles' sister, Caroline, was wearing thin. She had set her cap at him upon their first meeting several years earlier. As a result, Darcy was careful to never show her any particular attentions. Unfortunately, his consistently distant behavior did not deter Miss Bingley from pursuing her desired goal. In fact, with each year that passed, her efforts to impress him with her worth intensified, significantly increasing his discomfort in her presence. Darcy knew she had no genuine affection for him, but she desperately wanted to rise to the first circles of society. One would think their long acquaintance would have made Miss Bingley realize Darcy's dislike for society, but she could not see past what she wanted to comprehend how incompatible the two of them truly were.

Try though he might, Darcy could not banish the thought of Elizabeth Bennet from his mind. Her loveliness was breathtaking. Elizabeth's dark eyes and unruly curls were often Darcy's undoing. She had a quick, intelligent mind and a sharp wit. Darcy recalled each of their encounters, from his first seeing her at the Meryton assembly, to his disastrous proposal, to his last glimpse of her as she accepted his letter before leaving Rosings. He often wondered what her reaction to his missive had been. Did she still hate him, or was she able to accept his explanations and grant him some measure of forgiveness? Darcy wished with all his heart that Elizabeth was a member of the upcoming house party. He had often imagined her in his home and regretted that it would most likely never happen. Wallowing for a month after her rejection of his proposal, Darcy eventually realized that many of her criticisms about him were true. As a result of his epiphany, Darcy spent the next month trying to improve his behaviors. He promised himself that should he ever be privileged enough to meet Elizabeth again, he would apologize for his poor proposal and demonstrate to her that he had taken her reproofs to heart.

Pemberley was only a few more miles. Veering from the road, Darcy allowed Beowulf to have his head, and the stallion soared over the fence that separated the road from Pemberley's land. Darcy gave the horse a gentle kick and they raced across the fields, headed for the stables.

When Darcy arrived, he jumped from the saddle and patted his horse affectionately before turning him over to a groom. "Rub him down well and give him an extra scoop of oats. I rode him hard all the way to Pemberley."

Stripping off his jacket, Darcy stepped up to the pump, giving the handle a pull or two. He ducked his head underneath the water to cool himself after the hot ride. Retrieving his hat and coat, Darcy settled them over his arm and moved in the direction of the back terrace to make his entry into the house. He needed to clean up quickly and meet with his steward.

Darcy looked out at the gardens as he approached. They had been his mother's pride and joy, and their maintenance was a priority for him in honor of her memory. A flash of color in his peripheral vision caused his head to turn. The sight that met his eyes stopped him in his tracks. There, before him, sat Elizabeth Bennet. Assuming the heat was causing this most pleasant illusion, Darcy closed his eyes for several seconds. Elizabeth was lovelier than he remembered, with several strands of hair curled around her sun-kissed face. When he opened his eyes, the vision was still there, but it had changed. With the sun behind the green and white striped gown she wore, Elizabeth's figure, including her shapely legs, was clearly visible. Darcy caught her eye and noted the expression of shock on her face. The shock quickly changed to discomposure, as her face flushed with embarrassment.

Darcy had often envisioned Elizabeth enjoying the gardens at Pemberley and became momentarily lost in the illusion. The sound of Elizabeth's voice quickly drew him from his dreams. "I beg your forgiveness, Mr. Darcy. I should not be here. I would not have joined my relatives for a tour had I known you would be here." Elizabeth twisted her hands nervously. "Please excuse me. I will await my relations in the carriage; you need not be bothered by me." Elizabeth looked about in confusion, wondering which way she should go. The look of fear and distress in her large dark eyes reminded him of a doe he had once seen in the forest.

As she moved towards him, in the direction of the stables, Darcy realized he needed to stop her or she might walk out of his life again. He put out his hand to halt her motion and quickly bowed to her in proper greeting.

"Please, Miss Bennet, there is no need for you to leave. I am happy to see you again. What are you doing in Derbyshire?"

Mr. Darcy's words were a shock. He was happy to see her? How could that be after the way she had treated him when last they met? Elizabeth looked at him carefully, but his expression betrayed no anger. What she did see in his face was pleasure and, perhaps, hope. Hesitantly, Elizabeth answered. "I am touring the countryside with my aunt and uncle. Mrs. Gardiner grew up in Lambton and very much wished to see Pemberley again."

"Again?" asked Mr. Darcy.

"Aunt Gardiner indicated her family once toured the house during the holiday season."

"I see. I hope your aunt is enjoying her day, then." Darcy looked around, wondering where these relatives might be. He saw an older couple across the garden in company with his head gardener. "Would you be so kind as to introduce me to your relations, Miss Bennet?"

Elizabeth felt her mouth drop open in surprise. She quickly closed it. "I would be happy to do so, Mr. Darcy."

Darcy was about to offer his arm when he realized the current condition of his attire. He quickly returned his hat to his head and, with difficulty, shrugged into his jacket. Realizing that dust covered his coat sleeve, he spoke sheepishly. "Please forgive me for not offering you my arm, Miss Elizabeth, but I have just arrived and I fear the dust of the road is still upon me."

Elizabeth gave him a tentative smile as he extended his arm for her to step onto the path. Walking beside her, he quickly navigated the walkways

## A Matter of Timing

that would bring them to where Elizabeth's relations stood. When they stopped before the couple, Darcy turned to Elizabeth and waited for her to make the introductions.

"Mr. Darcy, please allow me to present my uncle and aunt, Mr. and Mrs. Edward Gardiner of Cheapside. Aunt, Uncle, this is Mr. Fitzwilliam Darcy, the master of Pemberley."

While Elizabeth made the introductions, Darcy studied the couple before him. Both were fashionably dressed in well-tailored clothing. Their faces showed interest in him, but no sign of the usual fawning he would have expected from members of the trade class. They spoke in cultured tones and with obvious manners and intelligence. He had made another error in prejudging the Gardiners based on their address.

Elizabeth watched Darcy carefully as she gave him her relations' address, but his response contained not a flicker of surprise of hint of hesitation.

"It is a pleasure to meet you, Mr. and Mrs. Gardiner. How are you finding Pemberley?"

"It is everything delightful, Mr. Darcy," Mrs. Gardiner responded with a happy smile.

"Indeed, Mr. Darcy," added Mr. Gardiner. "I believe it is the finest estate we have seen during our travels."

"I am pleased to hear that. Have you seen the house yet or are you starting your tour here?"

"Mrs. Reynolds was very kind in showing us the house. We thought to spend some time in the gardens before returning to the inn in Lambton," Mrs. Gardiner answered. "It is as lovely as I recalled."

"Yes, Miss Bennet mentioned you were from Lambton."

"You would not remember it, sir, but we frequently met in the past."

Darcy cocked his head to the side and looked at Elizabeth's aunt thoughtfully. As he stared, a smile grew on the lady's face, and she immediately saw when recognition appeared in his gaze.

"Would your family name have been Thompson, Mrs. Gardiner?"

Helen Gardiner gave a soft laugh, and her smile increased as she nodded.

"Your father was Mr. Thompson, owner of the bookshop," Darcy stated confidently.

"Yes, he was."

"As I recall, it was you who made sure I always received a treat when I accompanied my father to the bookshop."

Helen Gardiner nodded again.

"It was a sad day for me when you left Lambton, as there were no treats to be had after your departure. I still visit the shop often, but my sweet tooth goes unsatisfied these days."

Elizabeth marveled at Mr. Darcy's expressive countenance, as she could easily see his happiness at the memory. In the past, he had always worn an inscrutable expression in every situation in which Elizabeth encountered him.

Darcy continued. "I have only just arrived, but would love to join you on your tour of the park if you would permit me a few moments to refresh."

"We would be gratified to have you join us if it would not inconvenience you, sir. Shall we continue to wander here while we wait?" asked Mr. Gardiner.

Looking at Mrs. Gardiner, Darcy asked, "Are you a great walker, like your niece?"

She gave a small laugh and exchanged a look with her husband before answering. "I fear there are few who profess to be as great a walker as Lizzy."

Darcy wished to laugh with her but would not risk offending Elizabeth. However, when he noticed she, too, was laughing, he felt safe in agreeing. "I was fortunate enough to have her company on a few rambles in the past. She is a very intelligent young lady and has an uncanny knack for seeing the truth in most situations. I have learned much by my association with her."

## A Matter of Timing

Elizabeth was startled at his words and immediately thought he was referencing their time in Kent in an attempt to embarrass her. However, she reined in her anger and looked at him to determine his meaning. In his expression she saw only sincerity, though deep in his eyes there appeared to be something more. What it was, she could not be sure.

Darcy turned to his gardener. "Mr. Greenwood, would you please ask the stables to ready the landau for a tour of the park." The man immediately moved to carry out his master's instructions.

Mrs. Gardiner was quick to demure. "That will not be necessary, Mr. Darcy. Though I am not a great walker like Lizzy, I am sure I can manage a tour of your park. There is no need to put yourself to such trouble."

"It is almost ten miles around the park here at Pemberley, Mrs. Gardiner, and I would not wish you to tax your strength in this heat." All three of his companions looked shocked to discover the size of Pemberley's park lands. "Now, if you will excuse me, I shall return to you as quickly as possible."

# SHOWING OFF PEMBERLEY

Elizabeth watched Darcy walk away, a bemused expression on her face. Mr. and Mr. Gardiner shared a look after noting their niece's visage.

"What a very pleasant young man," remarked Mrs. Gardiner. "I saw nothing that would lead me to believe him capable of the behaviors you described upon first meeting him, Lizzy."

"Mr. Darcy was very gracious in his greeting to us and his offer to show us the park," agreed her husband.

In a subtle tone, Mrs. Gardiner added, "Perhaps he is somewhat shy in company and feels free to be himself when at home. Many people are more comfortable in such a setting."

Though Elizabeth heard the remarks addressed to her, she was unable to formulate a coherent reply. *Towards me, Mr. Darcy behaved with such consideration, and he was not angry to find me here. Could it be he took heed of my reproofs regarding his behavior? Would he do this for me?*

"Elizabeth, are you well?" Her aunt's worried tone finally broke through her confusion.

"I am quite well, only very surprised. Mr. Darcy was more cordial than I have ever seen him." She knew her aunt had quickly seen to the heart of the matter in suggesting that Darcy may be shy. Had he not told her so himself? Aloud she said, "You must be correct, Aunt, about what could cause such different behaviors in the gentleman."

Mrs. Gardiner was very perceptive, and she knew Elizabeth very well. There was more to this story than her niece had yet shared. Perhaps with some gentle coaxing, she could persuade Elizabeth to confide in her. For as Helen Gardiner saw it, Mr. Darcy appeared to be attracted to Elizabeth, and it would certainly be an outstanding match for her dearest niece. She would have to pay close attention to the couple's interactions during the remainder of the afternoon.

---

Once in the house and out of sight of his visitors, Darcy could not hide the smile on his face as he raced up the stairs to his suite, startling his staff by shouting orders as he went. Taking a few minutes to arrange a surprise with Mrs. Reynolds, he placed himself in the competent hands of one of the footmen. Darcy was bathed and dressed within twenty minutes and rejoined his guests in the garden.

"The carriage awaits us before the stables. Miss Elizabeth, may I now offer you a clean arm to escort you there." Darcy offered his arm and a brilliant smile to the young lady who owned his heart.

Elizabeth was surprised that he would attempt to tease her, and with an equally bright smile, willingly accepted his arm. He led Elizabeth in the same direction from which he had come only a short time earlier, with Mr. and Mrs. Gardiner following closely behind. Darcy handed Elizabeth into the open carriage before turning to assist Mrs. Gardner. He stepped back to allow Mr. Gardiner to enter first, but the gentleman waved him off.

"I believe with your height you would be more comfortable seated across from Elizabeth, Mr. Darcy," the gentleman said.

A pleased smile accompanied a reply of "thank you, sir." Darcy stepped up into the carriage and settled himself across from Elizabeth. He still wore the smile that caused Elizabeth to blush with both pleasure and confusion, for she had never again expected to receive such consideration from him after the way in which she had spoken to him during their last encounter in Hunsford.

Everyone quickly settled in the carriage. It moved past the front of the house and began its exploration of the park surrounding Pemberley. Darcy pointed out several of the scenic wonders of the estate and was gratified to see the delight in Elizabeth's expression at the natural beauty surrounding her. Through her eyes, Darcy saw his beloved home anew. He was also thrilled by her pleasure in his home, as for many months now he had pictured her there.

After about an hour, the carriage took a track that led towards the lake. Turning her head to take in more of the view, Elizabeth exclaimed, "How lovely!" In the shade of a large spreading oak sat a small iron table and chairs. She could see upon the table a pitcher of lemonade and several plates of other delicacies for the visitors to enjoy before continuing.

A footman moved forward to let down the steps and open the door. Mr. Gardiner stepped down first and turned to hand out his wife. Darcy stepped into the place Mr. Gardiner had vacated, then offered his hand to Elizabeth. Darcy was not surprised by the pleasurable feeling he experienced as he held her hand in his. However, he was pleased to note a look of delighted surprise on Elizabeth's face as his hand encompassed hers.

Darcy led the way to the table, assisting Elizabeth into a seat. Once everyone was comfortably settled, Darcy poured a refreshing glass of the cold drink for everyone before passing around the plates. There were strawberries and cream, biscuits, fruit tarts, and a sweet almond cake. Elizabeth teasingly asked, "Mr. Darcy, this was a delightful surprise. Do you treat all of the guests who tour your estate in such a grand fashion?"

"Indeed not, Miss Elizabeth. Though Pemberley is renowned for its hospitality, only the most special of visitors receive my personal attentions." Darcy gave her a warm smile and hoped she understood his meaning. He hoped she could see an improvement in his manners and behavior.

Seeing Elizabeth blush at the gentleman's words, Mrs. Gardiner nudged her husband.

"With the size of this lake and the number of streams we have observed, you must have good fishing in the area," Mr. Gardiner said.

Darcy tore his gaze from Elizabeth to answer her uncle's question. "There are some excellent fishing spots here at Pemberley. Do you enjoy fishing, Mr. Gardiner?"

"Very much so, Mr. Darcy, though I do not often get the chance to indulge my passion as much as I would like, residing in the city as I do."

"I would be happy to have you join me here one morning while you are in the area. My sister and some friends are due to arrive in the area tomorrow, so I would be unable to join you. Perhaps you would care to come the following morning?"

"I would be delighted, sir."

Darcy then turned to Elizabeth and spoke again. "Miss Elizabeth, there is one among the party tomorrow who would greatly like to make your acquaintance. Would you permit me to introduce my sister to you while you are in the area?"

A shy smile met his request. "I would very much like to meet Miss Darcy."

"Might we call on you tomorrow afternoon? You are staying at the inn in Lambton, I believe?"

## A Matter of Timing

Mrs. Gardiner nodded in response to Darcy's second question before replying, "We should be delighted to have you join us for tea. Would four o'clock suit you, Mr. Darcy?"

"That should be perfect, Mrs. Gardiner. Now, if everyone has finished their refreshments, perhaps we should resume our circuit of the park."

Darcy stood and assisted Elizabeth from her chair before offering his arm to lead her back to the carriage. The remainder of the drive passed very pleasantly for everyone in the party. Elizabeth began to relax and was able to join in the conversation more often. She even teased her host a time or two, bringing a smile to his face.

When they arrived back at the house, it was late afternoon. The Gardiner party needed to return to the inn to prepare for dinner at the home of one of Mrs. Gardiner's friends.

"It was a true pleasure to meet you, Mr. and Mrs. Gardiner. I am very glad you chose to visit Pemberley today, thereby giving me the opportunity to make your acquaintance and renew my association with Miss Elizabeth."

"The pleasure was truly ours, Mr. Darcy. You have a magnificent estate, and we received the best hospitality we have encountered during our travels." Mr. Gardiner took his wife's arm and moved to enter their waiting carriage.

Darcy turned to Elizabeth to take his leave of her, but she spoke before he had an opportunity.

"Mr. Darcy, when I first saw you this afternoon, I was mortified. I could not imagine what you must have thought, finding me here after our last encounter. Please allow me to apologize for my dreadful behavior in Hunsford. You did not deserve many of the rude remarks I directed towards you."

She looked as if she would say more, but Darcy interrupted her. "Miss Elizabeth, please do not apologize. Though I was at first insulted by your words, when that feeling wore off, I realized that much of what you said was the truth and well deserved. My parents taught me better, but for so long I used my haughty mannerisms to keep simpering debutantes and their matchmaking mothers away from me. Unfortunately, it changed from a mask to my real behavior. As I reflect back, I am appalled at my conduct in Hertfordshire as well as my thoughtlessly chosen words and misplaced anger at our last meeting. I pray that you can forgive me."

"Only if you will grant me forgiveness as well, sir."

"That is the easiest request I have ever received. Perhaps with our misconceptions corrected and our manners improved, we could start anew while you are in the area?"

"I gratefully agree."

Darcy held out his arm to Elizabeth and escorted her to the Gardiners' carriage, where he handed her up into the vehicle beside her aunt. Looking at his departing guests, Darcy said, "It was a pleasure to have you here today." He turned to look more closely at Elizabeth as he added, "I eagerly anticipate our next meeting."

---

Darcy watched until the Gardiner carriage was out of sight. Then, turning into the house, he called for Mrs. Reynolds.

"You wished to speak with me, Mr. Darcy?"

"Mrs. Reynolds, please tell me of the tour you gave to the group that just left. I hope you were most welcoming to them."

Worried the master was displeased with her for showing the library to visitors, she said, "I tried to impress them with Pemberley's grandeur as I do all visitors, sir. I am sorry if showing them the library displeases you. The young lady indicated a slight acquaintance and requested to see the room. They did not enter the library, sir, only observed it from the doorway. The young miss indicated she could not imagine a finer personal library. From the look on her face, it had enthralled her."

"What else did she say?" asked Darcy eagerly. "Did she make any particular remarks about the house?"

"Only that she thought it was perfect as it is. She seemed to appreciate the simple elegance of the furnishings and lack of ostentation."

Darcy smiled. It did not surprise him that Elizabeth was pleased with Pemberley; he had seen her distaste for the opulence of Rosings Park. One of the things he most admired about Elizabeth was her taste in gowns. Darcy much preferred the simplicity of her style to the frills and furbelows with which Miss Bingley bedecked herself. Elizabeth possessed the same classic elegance as his home.

Mrs. Reynolds was astonished to see the smile on her master's face. It had been some time since she had seen such an expression, and she wondered if the young lady was the cause of it.

"Tomorrow Mr. Bingley and his family will be arriving. They will be staying at least a fortnight. However, tomorrow afternoon I have made plans to have tea in Lambton, where I will introduce Georgiana to Miss Elizabeth. I will attempt to arrange things so that we may leave without the notice of our guests, but please see to them should they need something in our absence, and I would prefer they remain ignorant of our whereabouts."

"Certainly, Mr. Darcy. Do you expect today's visitors will be returning to Pemberley, sir?"

"I plan to have Georgiana issue an invitation tomorrow during tea. Mr. Gardiner has a love of fishing, and I have invited him to join the gentlemen. I wish for the ladies to spend the day with Georgiana and remain to dine with us in the evening. Please plan something special for the evening meal and seat Miss Elizabeth and Mr. Gardiner next to me, with Mrs.

Gardiner and Mr. Bingley next to Georgiana. Please place Miss Bingley at a distance from Miss Elizabeth. They met when Mr. Bingley resided in Hertfordshire and for some inexplicable reason Miss Bingley has taken Miss Bennet in dislike." The grin on her master's face told Mrs. Reynolds that he knew the exact cause of Miss Bingley's dislike.

Mrs. Reynolds bowed her head to hide the smile on her face. Her opinion of Miss Bennet improved if Miss Bingley disliked the young lady. "I will arrange everything as requested, Mr. Darcy, you need not worry."

Before dismissing Mrs. Reynolds, Darcy asked to have his steward sent to his study. For the remainder of the afternoon and evening, he worked with his steward on the problem that had required his early return to Pemberley.

When he finally retired for the night, Darcy was tired but extremely happy. In his mind's eye, he could see Elizabeth's face as he sat across from her during the tour of the park. Her face had glowed as she observed the grounds and sights of Pemberley. Then he recalled her generous acceptance of his apology, having seen the truthfulness of her words in her eyes. The relief he had felt at obtaining that forgiveness was overwhelming. Darcy had been surprised that she felt she owed him an apology. He felt he deserved most of what she had said to him in April, but if she felt the need of his forgiveness he was more than happy to give it to her.

Tomorrow could not come soon enough!

# INTRODUCTIONS

Since sunrise, Fitzwilliam Darcy had worked steadily on the large volume of correspondence that awaited him at Pemberley. Arriving home yesterday afternoon, he had been greatly shocked and thoroughly delighted to find Elizabeth Bennet enjoying the gardens of his home. At first, she had seemed as nervous as he, but they had passed a pleasant afternoon together, eventually regaining a level of comfort in being near each other. As the visitors were departing, Darcy and Elizabeth had each been able to offer the other a long overdue apology, after which they had agreed to begin anew. He wanted to have as much time as possible to spend with Elizabeth and her relations while they resided in Lambton. He could hardly wait to see her again, and even though it would be only a few hours, he was desperate to be in her company.

Darcy had just finished responding to the last of his business correspondence and had glanced up at the clock when a knock came at the door. "Enter."

"Mr. Darcy, two carriages have entered the park. They should be at the door in ten minutes."

"Thank you, Jeffers. I shall be there momentarily."

"Very good, sir," replied Pemberley's longtime butler.

Straightening into a neat stack the papers remaining on his desk, Darcy picked up his letters and exited the room. He turned and locked the door before pocketing the key. He knew Miss Bingley was prone to snooping and he had once observed her surreptitiously exiting his private study. Whenever she was in residence, Darcy kept several rooms locked—including his suite and the mistress' chambers.

He placed the letters on the table in the entryway and moved towards the front door, which a footman quickly opened. As he reached the top of the steps, the first carriage stopped before them. Bingley stepped out and handed down Georgiana, who rushed up the stairs and into her brother's arms.

"Hello, sweetling. How was the final stage of your journey?"

Georgiana rolled her eyes but did not need to answer, for at that moment Miss Bingley was handed down from the same carriage. Darcy cast a disgruntled yet questioning look at Charles Bingley. Darcy did not have an opportunity to determine how they had ended up in the same carriage before the lady in question determinedly marched up the stairs in his direction like an advancing army.

Darcy took a step back, placing himself on Georgiana's other side and folding his arms behind his back. In an expressionless voice, he said, "Good afternoon, Miss Bingley. Welcome to Pemberley."

Caroline Bingley was tall and willowy, to the point of being too thin, with angular features. Her hair was a dark red, and her eyes were an unremarkable, watery green. She moved to stand directly before Darcy, batting her eyelashes at him. "Thank you, Mr. Darcy, it is delightful to be at Pemberley again. It feels almost like coming home."

## A Matter of Timing

The horrified expression on Darcy's face might have been humorous under different circumstances, but everyone knew it was Caroline's greatest hope that she would soon call Pemberley home. Everyone except Caroline also knew it would never happen.

Ignoring Miss Bingley's words, Darcy turned to welcome Charles, the Hursts, and finally Mrs. Annesley, Georgiana's companion. He offered his arm to his sister and led the group inside.

Aside from the fact that each of the Bingley siblings had a reddish tint to their hair, their appearances were not at all similar. Charles' hair was a light copper color and his eyes were bright green. He was slightly above average in height and had an effervescent personality. Bingley was pleased with everyone and everything. It was his outgoing personality and lack of pretension that drew Darcy to him. Their personalities complemented each other. Mrs. Louisa Hurst was both shorter and plumper than her sister. Her hair was more brown than Miss Bingley's, though they shared the same eyes. Much like Kitty and Lydia Bennet, the younger sister was the more dominant of the two, and Caroline could always count on her sister's support. Gilbert Hurst had no remarkable aspects to his personality. He was moderately attractive, but his interests were limited to hunting, dogs, food, drink, and cards. No matter the time of day, he was often found slumped upon a sofa, softly snoring.

As soon as the newcomers had entered the house, Miss Bingley began to speak again. "I have always thought Pemberley the most beautiful and perfect of homes. How it will shine with a little updating and the right mistress."

Darcy did not mean to smile at the lady's words because he knew she meant herself. However, he could not help himself when he, again, thought of Elizabeth being in his home and what a wonderful mistress she would be. It was fortunate no one save for Georgiana saw the smile. She had a moment of panic thinking the smile meant William was considering Miss Bingley for a wife before recalling the opinion he had once expressed about the lady in question.

Caroline continued her monologue. "You are truly fortunate, Mr. Darcy. Not only do you have Pemberley to escape to for the warm summer months, for the remainder of the year you have a marvelous townhouse where you can enjoy all the pleasures of society. Your wife will surely enjoy that."

"There you are wrong, Miss Bingley. I prefer to spend as much of the year at Pemberley as possible. Once I take a wife, I anticipate that desire will only increase. I much prefer the country to life in town. I do not enjoy participating in society except for the theater, opera, and museums. As long as we have known one another, I am surprised you are unaware of this."

"But a gentleman such as yourself would certainly be willing to change for your wife, would you not?"

"People do not alter, Miss Bingley. I would not choose someone who wanted to change me. No, I would be much more careful in choosing someone whose interests and feelings about the matter are in line with my own." For a moment Caroline looked disconcerted, but as usual, she pushed aside that which she did not wish to accept.

Mrs. Reynolds, who had been quietly standing by, spoke at the pause in the conversation. "Mr. Darcy, luncheon will be ready in half an hour. Would you like me to show the guests to their suites?"

"Yes, thank you, Mrs. Reynolds. Georgie, might I speak with you a moment before you go upstairs?"

"Of course, William."

Darcy looked at his guests and said, "Shall we meet in the drawing room in half an hour?" So saying, he offered his arm to his sister and led her in the direction of his study. He waited before the door until the guests reached the top of the stairs and turned out of sight before he removed the key and unlocked the door. Darcy nodded at the footman stationed outside the study door as he closed it. Seating Georgiana on the sofa before the fireplace, he sat next to her. When Darcy looked into his sister's eyes, he was disconcerted to see the displeasure there. "Georgiana, is something wrong?"

"William, please tell me you are not considering Miss Bingley for a wife. I saw the way you smiled when she mentioned the right mistress for Pemberley!"

Darcy chuckled at his sister's words. "No, Georgiana. I am sorry if my smile concerned you. However, just yesterday Pemberley's perfect mistress was here with her relatives, touring the estate."

Georgiana's eyes widened in surprise. "Are you telling me you just met someone and have already decided to marry her?"

"No, it is not someone I just met. I have known Miss Elizabeth for almost a year."

"Miss Elizabeth?" Georgiana looked confused, as she could not place the name, but no explanation was forthcoming from her brother. Finally, she remembered where she had heard the name before. "Miss Elizabeth Bennet of Hertfordshire?"

"The very same."

"You say she was here yesterday? Is she still in the area?"

"She is. In fact, she is expecting us to join her and her relations for tea this afternoon."

"I have wished to meet her for such a long time. What is she doing here? Is she expecting to meet me? Do you think she will like me?"

Darcy could not help but laugh at his sister's rapid questions. When he calmed, he said, "She is in the area because she is traveling with her aunt and uncle. Yes, she is looking forward to meeting you, and I am sure she will like you. However, we must get away from the house without Miss Bingley's awareness. As you might imagine, Miss Bingley is not fond of Miss Bennet. While staying at Netherfield, I made a comment about Miss Bennet's fine eyes and ever since,

Miss Bingley has insulted and belittled Miss Elizabeth. I prefer for you to meet Miss Bennet for the first time without Miss Bingley's presence."

"When must we leave? I shall be sure to be ready. Shall I meet you at the stables?"

"Though it might be easier to meet at the stables, I shall not sneak about in my own home. I will have the carriage out front and ready to depart at quarter past three."

"I can hardly wait, but now I must hurry to freshen up, or I shall be late for lunch."

Luncheon was long and tedious. No matter what topic members of the group tried to introduce, Miss Bingley dominated the conversation with her effusive compliments about Pemberley and its next mistress. Darcy was relieved when the meal was over.

"I am sure you all wish to rest after such a long journey. I have some work I must finish if I am to have time to devote to visitors over the next few days. If you will excuse me." Darcy turned away from his guests but caught Georgiana's eye and winked at her as he headed for his study.

"Miss Darcy, will you not join us in the drawing room? It has been so long since we have had a chance to visit with you. Louisa and I have dearly missed your company."

"I am sorry, Miss Bingley, but I am feeling tired from the journey and must rest until tea time. I am sure we will have other opportunities to visit before your stay is over. I hope that you will both excuse me."

Caroline Bingley watched the young girl disappear up the stairs before turning to her sister. "Do you feel the need to rest, Louisa, or will you join me in my sitting room?"

"I do think I will rest as well. I will see you later, sister."

Annoyed that she could not spend time ingratiating herself with her hosts and furthering her goal for the joining of their families, Caroline swept up the grand staircase of Pemberley, making her way in high dudgeon to the sitting room attached to her bedchamber.

Caroline paced the room for a few minutes, making plans to ensure that Mr. Darcy would propose to her during this visit. She would wait no longer to achieve her goals. Finally, she summoned her maid and settled to rest until time for tea. After more than an hour, during which time sleep evaded her, she took to pacing her sitting room once again. It was as she passed the window that she noticed the Darcy carriage driving away from the house.

---

Georgiana had, indeed, tried to rest before they were to depart to Lambton, but she was too excited. She could hardly believe she was about to meet Elizabeth Bennet. Before last fall, her brother had never written to her of a young lady, and the things William wrote in his letters had piqued her curiosity. Wanting to prepare herself for the meeting, Georgiana found the letters her brother had sent her during his stay at Netherfield Park. She reread them all, searching for information about Miss Bennet. Georgiana found her brother's description of the young lady very intriguing.

Georgiana returned William's letters to their place and took a seat in the window embrasure. She took up the novel she had been reading, but could not concentrate on the words. Soon she was pacing the floor of her suite, waiting for the time to depart. Finally, the clock said thirteen minutes past the hour, so Georgiana grabbed her spencer and reticule and quietly opened the door. Seeing no one in the hall but the footman on duty at the entrance to the family wing, she quickly made her way to the main stairs. As she reached the bottom, William appeared and offered her his arm.

Before they reached the door, Bingley exited the billiard room. "To where are you two sneaking off?"

Georgiana and Darcy started at the sound and turned around to see Bingley regarding them with a curious grin. Bingley and Darcy had been friends since their time at Cambridge. Their differing personalities complemented each other.

Darcy gave him a quelling glare as he straightened to his full height. "We are not sneaking, but we must go into Lambton and we did not wish to disturb anyone who might be resting."

"As I am not in need of rest—just a break from my sister—might I accompany you?"

Darcy thought briefly before nodding his head. The butler passed the gentlemen their hats and walking sticks and the party exited the house and quickly boarded the carriage.

"So, what is this errand?"

"I wish to introduce Georgiana to a friend who is visiting in the area."

"And who might this friend be? Is it someone with whom I am acquainted?"

Darcy took a deep breath before replying. "It is Miss Elizabeth Bennet. She is traveling in the area with her relatives, Mr. and Mrs. Gardiner. I discovered them touring the estate when I returned yesterday. I asked Miss Elizabeth if I might introduce Georgiana to her while she was here, and she granted her permission. We are to take tea with them this afternoon."

"How delightful! I shall enjoy seeing her again."

"Perhaps you could wait a few moments. Allow me to introduce Georgiana and then inform Miss Bennet of your presence."

"I shall be happy to wait, but please give her my regards."

The carriage stopped before the inn and a footman let down the stairs. Darcy exited the coach and reached in to assist his sister. Her hand trembled as she placed it in her brother's. She looked up at him, a worried expression on her face.

"What if she does not like me?"

"I know Miss Elizabeth well, and I am sure she will like you. She expressed her delight in the opportunity to make your acquaintance." Darcy wrapped Georgiana's arm around his and patted her hand comfortingly.

The Darcys entered the inn and received a greeting from Mr. Burton. "Good day to you, Mr. Darcy. But who is this lovely young lady? She cannot be Miss Darcy, for she is much too grown up."

Georgiana smiled shyly at Mr. Burton as a lovely pink blush colored her cheeks. "It is nice to see you again, Mr. Burton."

"How can I help the Darcys today?"

"We are here to see Mr. and Mrs. Gardiner and their niece. Can you direct us to them?"

"Certainly, sir, please follow me." The innkeeper led them up the stairs to the third door on the left. He knocked firmly on the door, which opened. Mr. Burton announced, "Mr. and Miss Darcy to see you, sir." After the introduction, he returned downstairs.

"Mr. Darcy, welcome. We are pleased to see you today." Mr. Gardiner stepped back and waved the visitors into the sitting room of their suite. Elizabeth and Mrs. Gardiner were standing and awaiting introductions.

"Mr. and Mrs. Gardiner, Miss Bennet, allow me to present to you my sister, Miss Georgiana Darcy. Georgiana, this is Mr. and Mrs. Edward Gardiner and their niece, Miss Elizabeth Bennet."

They exchanged bows and curtsies, and Mrs. Gardiner invited her guests to sit. During the introductions, Elizabeth observed Miss Darcy. She was a lovely young woman, tall and slender, with hair a bit lighter than her brother's, though their eyes were the same deep blue. While the siblings bore a distinct resemblance, Miss Darcy's delicate features were in sharp contrast to her brother's stronger ones.

It was apparent to Elizabeth that Miss Darcy was very shy. To ease her companion, Elizabeth said, "Miss Darcy, we were fortunate enough to see your home yesterday. Pemberley is the most beautiful estate we have seen in our travels. You are quite lucky to live in such a lovely place. I was particularly pleased with the natural beauty of the grounds."

"Oh, yes!" said Georgiana, her tone shy and her voice quiet. "There is no place I would rather be than Pemberley. The grounds are lovely, and I try to ride my horse each morning to start my day."

"I do not ride, but I love to walk the paths around my home each morning. There is no better way to begin my day than communing with nature."

Georgiana looked surprised at Elizabeth's words. "You do not ride, Miss Elizabeth?"

"I am afraid not. My father had a team for working on the estate and his stallion. The only other horse was old Nellie. I could walk on my two legs much faster than she could go on four," said Elizabeth with a soft laugh.

Georgiana laughed as well. "If you are to be in the area very long, I am sure my brother would be happy to teach you to ride. He taught me many years ago and he says I am an excellent horsewoman."

"You are, indeed, an excellent rider, dear sister," commented Darcy.

A knock on the door announced a servant bringing tea. She deposited the tray on the table before Mrs. Gardiner, then departed. The conversation paused as Mrs. Gardiner served everyone.

As Miss Darcy took her first sip, Elizabeth said, "I understand you are very talented on the pianoforte. Who is your favorite composer?"

"I do love to play, but I imagine my brother has exaggerated my talents." A blush suffused Georgiana's face.

## A Matter of Timing

"It was not your brother who first told me of your talents; it was Miss Bingley who praised you so highly."

Georgiana's face wrinkled slightly in distaste before she composed herself. Realizing that Elizabeth had noted her expression, the young lady blushed profusely.

Elizabeth leaned closer and gently laid her hand over Georgiana's as she whispered, "Your secret is safe with me, Miss Darcy. You are fortunate to gain praise from Miss Bingley, as when she speaks about me it is only to belittle me. Some of her pronouncements are so silly, I can do nothing but laugh at them."

Georgiana relaxed and thanked Elizabeth, saying, "I cannot imagine what she could find to complain about. You are a wonderful person!" Again, her shyness consumed her at such an outspoken comment.

"How kind of you to say so, but let us return to the pleasant topic of music. Though I play very ill, I do love music. However, trying to choose a favorite composer would be like trying to choose a favorite book—nearly impossible."

"I am sure you underestimate your talent, Miss Bennet, for my brother told me that you play very well and have a lovely voice. Perhaps I will have the opportunity to hear you while you are in the neighborhood. Might you be willing to play a duet with me if the opportunity presents itself?"

"I would be delighted to do so, but please do not expect too much."

Having caught Bingley's name during the conversation between Georgiana and Elizabeth, Darcy said, "Miss Elizabeth, there is another visitor here who would like to renew his acquaintance with you. Mr. Bingley waits downstairs. Would you permit him to join us?"

Glancing at her aunt, who nodded, Elizabeth replied, "I would be pleased to see him again. Would you please invite him to join us?"

Darcy excused himself and went to the taproom to retrieve Bingley. As he reentered the room, he heard his sister laughing. Darcy was delighted to see the happy, relaxed expression on Georgiana's face. He had always felt that Elizabeth would be a good example for his sister.

When they joined the others, Darcy introduced Bingley to the Gardiners. Mr. and Mrs. Gardiner greeted the gentleman pleasantly enough, but both wondered how he could have hurt Jane as he did.

"Miss Elizabeth, how pleased I am to see you again. It has been far too long, not since the ball at Netherfield."

"It has been too long, Mr. Bingley. I hope that you are well?"

"I am, Miss Elizabeth. How is all your dear family?"

"They are well, Mr. Bingley."

"All of them?"

"Indeed, last I heard from them, all were doing well. Jane is at Longbourn. She is watching our Gardiner cousins as we travel."

"She is such a sweet woman; I am sure the children enjoy her company."

Mrs. Gardiner said, "They are very fond of Jane's gentle ways and they love the adventurous nature of Elizabeth, who plays exciting games with them."

Darcy smiled at Elizabeth when he heard this. He could imagine her holding their child in her arms, and the thought filled him with wonder and excitement.

As teatime drew to a close, Mr. Darcy invited Mr. Gardiner to join the gentlemen the next day for a morning of fishing.

"As we have no plans for the morrow, I would be delighted to join you, sir. I thank you for the invitation, Mr. Darcy. The opportunity to fish for the first time in a very long while will be the highlight of my trip," said Mr. Gardiner with a grin.

## A Matter of Timing

Darcy told him the time to arrive and then, looking at Georgiana, nodded discreetly. Georgiana looked at Mrs. Gardiner and issued an invitation of her own. "Mrs. Gardiner, I would be delighted if you and Miss Elizabeth would join us for breakfast and plan to stay for the day. I do not know if the men will join us for luncheon, but we would be delighted to have you stay for the evening meal as well. It will give us an opportunity to play that duet, Miss Elizabeth."

Mrs. Gardiner looked at her husband and niece. Seeing no disagreement, she said, "We would be delighted to join you. Thank you for the kind invitation, Miss Darcy." Everyone said their farewells and the visitors left. As soon as the door closed behind them, Mrs. Gardiner said, "We must prepare our wardrobes for tomorrow, Lizzy. We shall need to take a change of clothing if we are staying for the day." Grabbing her niece's hand, she pulled Elizabeth in the direction of her bedchamber.

---

It was a lively group that returned from Lambton with barely enough time to change for dinner. As Darcy descended from his chambers, Miss Bingley, who appeared to have been lying in wait for him, attached herself to his arm and practically dragged him into the drawing room. As his master entered said drawing room, the footman from the hall, as per instruction whenever Miss Bingley was in residence, took up his place inside the drawing room to prevent any risk of compromise. Miss Bingley cast a disgruntled eye at the footman as she took a seat on a small settee and patted the space beside her, giving the gentleman what she thought was a seductive smile. Darcy repressed a shudder and suddenly felt a kinship with the fox at a foxhunt. Miss Bingley's look was far more predatory than seductive and in no way inviting.

He tried to disguise his disgust at her forward behavior. Ignoring her invitation, Darcy moved to stand at the window overlooking the gardens. As he regained his composure, he pictured Elizabeth walking there. When Bingley and Georgiana joined the others already gathered, Darcy moved to sit with his sister, doing his best to ignore the disappointed glare that Miss Bingley gave him.

Dinner passed with more leading comments from Miss Bingley about the next mistress of Pemberley. Bingley attempted to change the subject each time his sister began on the topic, but to no avail; she simply spoke over him. Louisa Hurst was happy to support her sister in her endeavor to become the wife of Fitzwilliam Darcy. She would be glad to see Caroline married to anyone and out of her home. Caroline and Mr. Hurst did not get along well. Eventually, though, even Louisa was discouraging her sister's conversation. Greatly annoyed by Miss Bingley's sole topic of conversation, Darcy rolled his eyes several times and refrained from acknowledging any of the lady's remarks.

The more Miss Bingley spoke, the quieter Georgiana became. She spent most of the meal staring at her plate. Eventually, Darcy could no longer tolerate her behavior or conversation. In a cold voice, he spoke. "Miss Bingley, please desist from speaking about Pemberley's need for a mistress. I am aware of my duties and responsibilities and will make my choice when I find my perfect match. I find that the more I am pushed to do something, the less likely I am to do what others expect of me. I detest having my hand forced. It is a decided flaw in my character, but it is there nonetheless. Please do not speak again until you have found something new about which to converse."

Caroline stared at Darcy with her mouth agape, shocked at his rudeness. Did he really not see that she was his perfect match? Bingley glared at Caroline for upsetting their host. Louisa looked down, embarrassed for and by her sister, while Hurst grinned to see

## A Matter of Timing

Caroline spoken to thus. He could wish that Darcy had been more direct. Miss Bingley's face filled with color, but she refrained from speaking another word for the remainder of the meal.

Mrs. Hurst played for the group after dinner, and a card table appeared after the music stopped. Even at the card table, Miss Bingley did not regain the power of speech, but she cast frequent, speculative glances at her host throughout the evening. Darcy made a point of mentioning that the gentlemen would be fishing early in the morning, lasting perhaps through the midday meal.

At last the uncomfortable evening came to an end, and after Miss Bingley had departed to her bedchamber, several sighed in relief. Mrs. Hurst quickly followed her sister. When his wife was no longer in earshot, Hurst said, "Thank you, Darcy, for finally speaking up. I doubt it will stop her desire to be your wife, but perhaps it will still her tongue for a time longer."

"Darcy, I am so sorry for Caroline's behavior. I have tried to dissuade her from her thinking, but she refuses to believe me."

"I disliked the necessity of speaking rudely to your sister, but I could no longer tolerate her behavior. I hope you were not offended, Bingley. I hope you know it is not personal."

"Of course, Darcy. Well, I am for bed, good night. I shall see you tomorrow."

"I will come with you, Charles," said his brother-in-law.

When his guests had retired for the evening, Darcy took the time to speak with Mrs. Reynolds about the visitors they would receive the next day. He also stopped by to talk to Mrs. Annesley. "Please provide Miss Darcy with both support and encouragement tomorrow. Hopefully, as I will be out of the house, Miss Bingley will remain in her room until near midday. However, when she appears, Miss Bingley will be antagonistic to Miss Elizabeth and Mrs. Gardiner.

Miss Bingley believes Miss Elizabeth is a threat to her desire to be Mrs. Darcy."

Mrs. Annesley arched her brows in question.

"She would be correct, but nothing is yet settled," added Darcy with a blush.

When Darcy finally reached his bedchamber, he found sleep difficult. His thoughts were filled with Elizabeth and his anticipation of her visit the next day. When sleep finally claimed him, he drifted into slumber with a smile on his face.

# NEW FRIENDS AND OLD FOES

The visitors were afforded another perfect summer day on their second visit to Pemberley. Mr. and Miss Darcy cordially welcomed Elizabeth and the Gardiners. It was only a short time later when Mr. Darcy, Mr. Gardiner, Mr. Bingley, and Mr. Hurst departed for Darcy's favorite fishing spot on the estate. The gentlemen enjoyed a morning with the trout, with Darcy and Mr. Gardiner having the opportunity to become better acquainted. Mr. Gardiner entertained Darcy with stories of Elizabeth's childhood. Both men were successful in their catches, as was Mr. Hurst. Charles Bingley, with his usual exuberance and chattiness, did not catch anything and required rescuing after nearly falling into the stream during one of his casts.

Elizabeth, knowing that the 'superior sisters,' as she had dubbed Mr. Bingley's sisters during their stay in Hertfordshire, were also in residence, did not have high expectations for the morning spent without the gentlemen; she was not disappointed. Fortunately, the Bingley ladies were not early risers, allowing Miss Darcy, Elizabeth, Mrs. Gardiner, and Mrs. Annesley to enjoy breakfast and two hours of pleasant conversation before making their appearance. Elizabeth had been delighted by the opportunity to get to know Miss Darcy better. Mrs. Gardiner and Mrs. Annesley had observed with pleasure as Elizabeth's confidence and easy manners drew the shy Miss Darcy from her shell. Their relationship had progressed to the point that they were on a first-name basis. They were laughing like old friends when Miss Bingley and Mrs. Hurst entered the room, stopping short when they noticed the unwelcome additions to the party.

Caroline's lip curled into a sneer as she noted the friendliness between the two ladies. "Miss Eliza, perhaps you are not aware of it, but you are here far too early for proper visiting hours. Of course, coming from such a provincial village as Meryton, and with relations in trade, I imagine you could not be expected to know the rules of polite society." She looked at her sister and they tittered rudely.

The Bingley sisters were shocked when Georgiana spoke up. "The ladies are here at my invitation, Miss Bingley. They will be joining us for the entire day."

Caroline and Louisa looked aghast at Miss Darcy's pronouncement. "What?" screeched Caroline. Elizabeth looked down to hide her smile at Miss Bingley's obvious dismay.

"Indeed," continued Georgiana, innocently. "William and I are quite pleased with our new friends. I look forward to getting to know Elizabeth better.

"And, I, you, Georgiana," came Elizabeth's smiling reply.

Caroline fumed. She had never received an invitation to call Georgiana by her given name.

"Also, Mrs. Gardiner grew up in Lambton and has been telling me stories of her encounters with my parents," Georgiana continued.

"Miss Darcy, you are so young, I feel I must caution you," Caroline began in a condescending tone. "You must be careful with new acquaintances. With your status and connections, you will frequently be the

## A Matter of Timing

target of unscrupulous individuals who will say anything to get close to you. You must be very cautious when making new acquaintances." Miss Bingley fixed Mrs. Gardiner with a superior look.

Helen Gardiner had easily taken the measure of Caroline Bingley. "Indeed, Miss Darcy, you will meet all kinds of individuals, from all walks of life, who will attempt to manipulate you for their own purposes. However, I believe you are intelligent enough to know the difference, particularly with Mrs. Annesley to guide you." Mrs. Annesley exchanged a knowing glance with Mrs. Gardiner.

Georgiana's smile showed she was quite pleased with the compliment. Caroline Bingley had always intimidated her. Georgiana found the woman's constant compliments insincere and did not enjoy the way Caroline continually encouraged her to look down on all those around her. Georgiana was a kind and loving young lady, and she often found Caroline's officiousness intrusive. Mrs. Annesley and Mrs. Gardiner both had to lower their heads to prevent the obviously outraged Miss Bingley from observing their smiles.

The gentlemen returned to a room filled with tension. However, Darcy was pleased to note that Georgiana sat on a sofa beside Elizabeth and that Mrs. Gardiner and Mrs. Annesley flanked them. Across from her sat the superior sisters, both wearing decidedly aggrieved expressions. He was delighted to hear Georgiana's tinkling laugh mixed with the rich, warm sound of Elizabeth's melodious one.

Miss Bingley's nose grew further out of joint when she learned of the seating arrangement for the midday meal. Elizabeth sat next to Mr. Darcy, with Georgiana on her other side. Mr. and Mrs. Gardiner sat on Darcy's other side. Caroline found herself at the end of the table, as far from Darcy as possible. As only Charles sat between Caroline and Miss Darcy, Caroline frequently leaned forward, attempting to gain Georgiana's attention. Miss Bingley's frustration grew with this utterly futile endeavor, as Georgiana was totally absorbed in her conversation with Elizabeth and Mr. Darcy, though she occasionally turned to include Mr. Bingley.

By the end of the meal, Caroline was beyond angry—never a good thing, as, when in such a state, she frequently spoke without thinking. Caroline did not wait for assistance getting out of her chair. She jumped up, rushed to Darcy, and latched onto his arm before he could assist Elizabeth to rise.

"Mr. Darcy, you have been so busy since we arrived that we have hardly seen you. We require your attention for a bit this afternoon."

"Of course, Miss Bingley, I would not wish to be seen as a poor host," said Darcy as he attempted to disentangle himself from her grasping hands. Caroline Bingley continued clinging to him as she walked towards the drawing room. She dragged Darcy along, not noticing the distressed look he gave Elizabeth. Bingley helped both Georgiana and Elizabeth to rise from their chairs and, with a lady on each arm, he followed Darcy and his sister.

Arriving in the sitting room, Caroline pulled Darcy down beside her on the loveseat—sitting much too close for Darcy's comfort. It was fortunate that Miss Bingley released his arm, thereby allowing Darcy to stand for the entrance of the other ladies. Before Caroline could reattach herself to him, Darcy moved to stand before the fireplace, resting one arm along the mantle. From this position, he could easily stare at Elizabeth such that Miss Bingley could not observe him. Mrs. Hurst, nose in the air, dragged her husband forward so that they might precede the Gardiners from the room. Mrs. Gardiner looked at her husband and rolled her eyes, a slight smile gracing her face.

Miss Bingley immediately monopolized the conversation, speaking of events she had attended in London and of people whom the others would not have met. Darcy and Georgiana frequently tried to turn the conversation to more general topics, but with little success. Miss Bingley merely spoke over anyone who attempted to change the conversation. Eventually, she spoke of a ball that the new Earl of Westborough had held. Though Caroline had not been in attendance, she repeated the gossip from the papers as though she had been there.

"Was this the event held at the close of the season?" asked Mrs. Gardiner politely.

"Indeed it was. It was the premier event of the season," was Caroline's condescending reply.

"I do not recall seeing you at the event. Do you, Edward?" Mrs. Gardiner asked innocently.

"You were in attendance at the event of an earl?" asked Caroline incredulously.

"Indeed, we were. The earl and my husband were dear friends at school. The earl and countess always include us in their events, as do several of our other acquaintances."

Caroline's face turned an unattractive shade of green as she attempted to find a way to refute the Gardiners' claims.

However, Mrs. Gardiner was not quite finished. "You have roots in trade, Miss Bingley; you must be aware that the world is changing. Otherwise you would not find yourself so easily accepted within the ton." Caroline's face had gone from green to white to red. She was not pleased that Mrs. Gardiner had shown her up in this manner.

Caroline mumbled, "If you would please excuse me, I feel a headache coming on. I believe I shall retire until time for tea." She rose from her seat and practically ran from the room.

Darcy was delighted with the conversation. Mrs. Gardiner had handled Caroline Bingley's pretentions in a graceful and well-mannered fashion. Darcy had been impressed with the Gardiners from the moment he met them, but he was surprised to learn that they mingled with the ton. "I hope I shall have the pleasure of meeting you at events in the future, Mr. and Mrs. Gardiner."

Elizabeth was surprised at his words, but, again, they emphasized the fact that he had changed since last they met. Had he done this for her? It seemed Mr. Darcy had attended to all the things of which she had previously accused him.

"Would anyone care to join me for a turn about the gardens?" Though addressing his comment to the room, Darcy looked only at Elizabeth. All but Mr. and Mrs. Hurst joined the outing. As usual, Hurst was asleep on a sofa in the corner, and Mrs. Hurst felt it would be wise to check on her sister.

Darcy offered his arm to Elizabeth and led the group from the room. As Georgiana was on Mr. Bingley's arm, Mrs. Annesley trailed the group. After half an hour of walking, Mr. and Mrs. Gardiner said they would like to retire to rest until teatime. The others continued on, exiting the formal gardens and entering a vast expanse of bright green grass. At the far side of this area was a stone wall with a few steps. At the top of the steps sat a gazebo surrounded by lovely flowering trees, the mauve buds of which gave off a sweet scent that floated on the air. The group made its way to the shade that the gazebo offered.

When everyone had seated themselves, Bingley addressed Elizabeth. "How was Miss Bennet when you departed on your travels? I hope she was well." Elizabeth noted the interest and eagerness in his voice.

"I believe she was in good health, but her spirits were a bit low. To me, they seemed to have been that way for some time." Elizabeth watched him carefully as she continued. "I believe she was missing some of her friends who were no longer in the neighborhood." She observed Mr. Bingley's ears turn pink and a smile spread across his face, though it dimmed quickly. A look of confusion filled his eyes.

"Oh, oh," Bingley began to stammer. He clamped his jaw shut and took a deep breath. "I have missed the delightful friends I made there, as well, but my sisters did not seem to think anyone would miss our presence."

## A Matter of Timing

"Pleasant company and the companionship of friends are always missed, Mr. Bingley, some acquaintances more than others."

Darcy had the grace to flush with embarrassment during this conversation. He decided to make amends by contributing.

"I believe that to be very true, Bingley. I had the pleasure of seeing Miss Elizabeth while she visited her cousin Mr. Collins and his bride, the former Charlotte Lucas. I was at Rosings to attend to Lady Catherine's books." It was now Elizabeth's turn to blush in embarrassment. She had been so rude to him at Hunsford and her poor behavior still mortified her. "In fact, Miss Elizabeth made me aware of the fact that Miss Bennet had been in London all winter. I believe she even called upon your sisters. I am sorry I failed to mention it to you, and I am even more so for interfering at all. I was not close enough to Miss Bennet to see what you saw, and it was unpardonable for me to provide an unsolicited opinion."

Bingley was surprised at Darcy's words but much more surprised to learn that Jane had called at his home and that his sisters had not made him aware of that fact.

"You said nothing of your opinion until I asked you, so think nothing of it, Darcy. I know how busy you always are, and we have not seen much of each other since the holidays."

Darcy let out a soft sigh of relief. Though his haughty interference still bothered him, his feelings of guilt lessened at the look of appreciation and approval on Elizabeth's face. The foursome spent quite some time visiting as they enjoyed the pleasant atmosphere of the gardens.

---

If Elizabeth and the Gardiners had been impressed with the midday meal, the evening meal was an even more sumptuous event. The group had returned from the garden in time for afternoon tea. Though Miss Bingley joined the other guests, she was unusually silent. With a pained expression, she observed the relaxed interactions between her brother, the Darcys, and Eliza Bennet and her family. Caroline looked at her sister in annoyance, rolling her eyes, but surprisingly remained silent. She decided she would dress in her finest that night to highlight the differences between the unimportant country chit and herself. Surrounded by the splendor of Pemberley, Darcy could not fail to see how perfectly suited Caroline was to be his wife and the mistress of his homes.

Though careful to present herself at her best, Caroline hurried through her toilet. She dressed in a new gown of parrot green, with a daringly low décolletage and overly ornamented with furbelows. Though the color and style were of the latest fashion, because she was nouveau riche, Miss Bingley had a need to belong that made her believe more was better. Unfortunately, she failed to realize that fashionable did not always equate to becoming. The green of her gown made her skin appear sallow, and the décolletage did nothing to enhance her meager charms. Her plan was to arrive first in the drawing room, rather than make her usual dramatic entrance. This way she could command Darcy's attentions before the interloper appeared.

Caroline stood near the windows of the drawing room, out of sight of the doorway. When Darcy stepped into it, he did not notice her. He pulled out his pocket watch and checked the time. As the timepiece clicked closed, Darcy paced towards the fireplace and back again. He stepped into the hallway and glanced at the stairs, then hovered in the doorway.

"Do you plan to stand in the doorway all evening, Mr. Darcy?"

Darcy started, then turned slowly towards the sound of the voice that always put his nerves on edge.

## A Matter of Timing

"Good evening, Miss Bingley. How surprising to find you here so early."

Darcy remained in the doorway, looking down to adjust his cuffs in an attempt to avoid being alone with her. He surreptitiously watched for the reappearance of a footman to chaperone them. Darcy breathed a sigh of relief upon finally hearing footsteps in the hall.

Miss Bingley took a step towards him. "It appeared to be the only way I might find an opportunity for conversation with you, sir. Will you not join me, Mr. Darcy?" She lowered her eyes and fluttered her lashes as she gave him what she thought to be a seductive smile. Darcy wondered why he suddenly felt like something about to be caught in a spider's web.

Darcy folded his arms behind his back to prevent her from clutching them as she usually did. With his arms in this position, he was able to beckon to the footman without Miss Bingley's notice. The young man hastened to the doorway, standing where anyone within the room could see him. None of the staff members at either Darcy House or Pemberley wanted Caroline Bingley to become their next mistress. Consequently, all the staff took very seriously the duty of protecting their master from this grasping, manipulative woman. Caroline Bingley would make not only Mr. Darcy but the entire household unhappy.

When the footman was in place, Darcy moved farther into the room. Caroline sat on a small sofa, but he did not take the seat beside her that she patted invitingly. He moved to stand before the fireplace, where he could observe the entry to watch for Elizabeth's arrival. Miss Bingley forced herself to continue smiling in spite of the frustration she felt with his behavior.

Pasting a smile on her face, Caroline addressed her host. "I am sorry I was not able to join you earlier for your walk in the gardens. The grounds of

Pemberley are some of the grandest it has ever been my pleasure to visit."

Darcy acknowledged her words with a dip of his head but did not speak.

Caroline tried again. "You did not tell me how you came to have additional guests. I understood it was to be our usual small family party during this visit." She stared at him, awaiting his answer.

"As none of my relatives are present, with the exception of my sister, it cannot be a family party, Miss Bingley," said Darcy repressively. "I had thought it would be only your family but was pleased to encounter Miss Bennet and her relations as they toured the area. I was grateful for the opportunity to return some of the hospitality shown to me in Hertfordshire."

"Did you really feel it necessary to invite into your home those of a society so decidedly beneath our own to repay the meager hospitality—if it could even be called such—which we experienced last fall?"

"I believe we received the very best hospitality the neighborhood had to offer. Mrs. Bennet set a particularly excellent table, and it is incumbent that I offer my best in return." A gentle dignity filled his impassioned words.

"Oh, Mr. Darcy, how you do like to tease." Caroline tittered. "I am sure the residents of such an insignificant village would be completely overwhelmed by a full display of the hospitality that Pemberley has to offer. It was certainly not necessary to put yourself out in such a way."

"You may run your future home as you see fit, Miss Bingley, but Pemberley shall always offer its assistance and hospitality to all those who depend upon it and those the Darcy family chooses to host."

"What if your wife is not of the same opinion, sir? After all, the hospitality of your home falls under her purview."

"I cannot imagine choosing to marry anyone who would not graciously offer the hospitality for which Pemberley is renowned."

## A Matter of Timing

Caroline felt great affront at his words. "Mr. Darcy, I have visited Pemberley several times over the last few years. I am unaware of this reputation of hospitality to which you refer, as most of our visits pass very quietly."

"Your lack of awareness, Miss Bingley, does not mean it does not exist. My late mother was beloved by the tenants and villagers who depend upon Pemberley for much of their prosperity. Many of the traditions that Lady Anne began are still maintained, but they have lacked the thoughtful touch of a mistress. The woman I marry will wholeheartedly wish to continue with my mother's legacy and charitable works in the same caring and gracious manner."

"It will be necessary for you to choose carefully," came the sly voice of Miss Bingley. "Her background and education will need to be impeccable." Caroline preened and Darcy realized she was speaking of herself. Caroline believed she would be able to change his opinion about socializing with those of a lower social standing once they were married.

Seeing Darcy straighten and look in her direction, Caroline sat taller and turned to more fully face her host. She knew he would come to his senses if only he had the opportunity to be alone with her. Caroline saw his expression soften and a look of love come into his eyes, causing her to expect that a declaration would be immediately forthcoming. At his next words, Caroline's dreams crashed down around her.

"Good evening, Miss Elizabeth." Darcy moved to bow over her hand. "You look very lovely tonight." Light green vines and small white flowers adorned Elizabeth's pale yellow silk gown. Its simple elegance showed her good taste, and it becomingly clung to her voluptuous figure.

"Thank you, Mr. Darcy, and good evening to you, too." Elizabeth gave him an impish smile.

Before Darcy could lead Elizabeth to a seat, Georgiana and the Gardiners joined them. Bingley followed closely after the Gardiners, and the Hursts appeared but a short time later. The group had barely settled themselves for conversation when the butler announced dinner.

Darcy had ignored Caroline from the moment of Elizabeth Bennet's arrival in the room. After observing his expressions, Caroline realized that, throughout their conversation, he had likely been speaking of that nobody. Caroline needed a way to make sense of this, so she rationalized that Darcy was not the man she thought him to be if he could accept such a lowly individual as Elizabeth Bennet as his wife.

Caroline spoke little throughout the meal, confining her comments to her sister. As she ate, she continued to plan and rationalize. She did not need the Darcy name. Caroline was an attractive, properly educated, well-dowered young lady, and Darcy was a fool not to see it. She would show Darcy. When Caroline found her match, she would exclude the Darcys from her invitations, ensuring that Elizabeth Bennet never enjoyed her position as Mrs. Darcy—something which Caroline had worked to attain for more than three years.

The gentlemen did not separate from the ladies upon the conclusion of the meal. Everyone adjourned to the music room, where Georgiana, Elizabeth, and Mrs. Hurst entertained the company. The evening ended by ten, as the Gardiners had to return to the inn in Lambton. When Darcy requested that their carriage be prepared, he also ordered two armed outriders to accompany then.

Darcy and Georgiana escorted their guests to the door. Georgiana expressed the hope that she would see Elizabeth again before they departed the area and requested Elizabeth write to her after her return to Longbourn. While his sister spoke with Elizabeth, Darcy expressed similar hopes to the Gardiners. As Georgiana moved to farewell the Gardiners, Darcy gently touched Elizabeth's elbow, moving a few steps away from the others.

## A Matter of Timing

"Miss Elizabeth, I cannot tell you what a pleasure it was to have you join us here at Pemberley for the day. I hope you enjoyed yourself."

"Oh, yes, Mr. Darcy. As surprised as I find myself to be saying this, I must agree with Miss Bingley. Pemberley is quite the most magnificent estate of all those I have seen. You have a reason to be proud. You handle with fairness and compassion the multitude of responsibilities that rest upon your shoulders. You have raised a remarkable young woman. It has been a great pleasure to meet Miss Darcy, and I look forward to corresponding with her."

"I am certain she will become only more remarkable for knowing you."

Elizabeth could be in no doubt of his meaning, for his eyes spoke much more than his words.

"Come, Lizzy, we must depart," said Mr. Gardiner.

Darcy offered his arm to Elizabeth and moved in the direction of the door. Georgiana again said her farewells and stepped back. Darcy, with Elizabeth still on his arm, followed the Gardiners through the entry. He took the opportunity to hand Elizabeth into the carriage. Never breaking eye contact, he kissed her hand briefly before he stepped back, giving it one final squeeze before releasing it. Mr. Gardiner assisted his wife in and stepped up after her. He rapped on the roof with his walking stick and the carriage moved down Pemberley's drive. Darcy remained watching it until he could no longer see the carriage lights.

# UNDERSTANDING BEFORE DISASTER

THE AZURE SKY WAS BLINDINGLY BRIGHT and dusted lightly with fluffy white clouds. The sun shown brilliantly and birdsong floated on the light breeze that fluttered the curtains. He knew it was a bit early, but Darcy could wait no longer. He needed to see Elizabeth. Darcy had to know if she still despised him as she had in April. He believed that her opinion of him had changed—had improved—but he needed to be sure. After dressing carefully, Darcy descended the servants' stairs and made his way to the stables. As the stable hand saddled his horse, Darcy paced and tried to think of what he would say. Within moments he was on his way, and though he wished to gallop full out to arrive quickly, he kept the horse to a gentle canter.

As the Gardiners and Elizabeth prepared to depart for a visit with one of Mrs. Gardiner's childhood friends, the maid delivered two letters for Elizabeth. They were from Jane.

"There is still some time before we must leave, Lizzy, so your uncle and I will walk to the church and back while you read your letters," Mrs. Gardiner said.

"Thank you, Aunt Helen. I have wondered why Jane did not write sooner and am anxious to hear the news from home."

"We shall return shortly, Lizzy," said Mr. Gardiner as the couple exited the sitting room.

Elizabeth curled into a comfortable chair near the windows, briefly forgetting the letters in her hand as she relived the memories of the previous day at Pemberley.

Throughout the day, Elizabeth had received considerable attention from Mr. Darcy. He had been open and pleasant in each of their encounters. Mr. Darcy had encouraged her closeness with his sister and been solicitous to her needs. Elizabeth was grateful for the opportunity she had to apologize for her offensive behavior and touched by the way he had attended to her comments regarding his conduct. She had been pleased with the level of ease they had achieved by the end of the day. Elizabeth hoped there would, indeed, be another opportunity to visit with the Darcys before she returned home.

A knock at the door interrupted Elizabeth's thoughts. She called for the maid to enter and was surprised when Hannah announced Mr. Darcy. Placing her letters aside, Elizabeth rose to curtsey to her visitor.

"Good morning, Miss Elizabeth." Darcy's cheeks were red and his hair somewhat windblown due to his ride from Pemberley. Elizabeth's heart began to race and her breath caught in her throat. She had always considered Darcy to be a handsome man—even when she disliked him. This morning his rugged appearance caused her knees to feel weak.

Finally remembering how to breathe, Elizabeth replied. "Good morning, Mr. Darcy. I am surprised to see you so early this morning after your hosting duties yesterday. My family and I enjoyed the day immensely. I particularly enjoyed the opportunity to get better acquainted with Miss Darcy. She is a delightful young woman. She asked if we might write to each other when I return home. I was happy to comply, provided that meets with your approval. It was also a privilege to be permitted to see Pemberley and enjoy its hospitality."

Darcy could not believe his luck in finding Elizabeth alone. She wore a white muslin dress embroidered with cherries and trimmed with a red sash. It was very becoming and a favorite of his, even though he had seen her wear it many times. He thought the bright red cherries matched her luscious lips. Darcy noted the way her cheeks flushed as she stared at him when he entered. Her reaction made his heart beat faster and increased his determination. He had made a decision during his ride and intended to act upon it immediately. Darcy did not want to waste any more time. Elizabeth's day at Pemberley had proven to Darcy that she owned his heart and was the only woman who could ever fill his mother's role.

"I am glad you enjoyed your visit, and it was my pleasure to have the opportunity to host you. I did not dare to dream I would ever see you again, much less have the opportunity to show you the changes you inspired." A deep flush covered Elizabeth's face as she attempted to speak. Darcy gently placed a finger against her lips to prevent her from doing so. The touch was an intimate one, and Elizabeth again felt her heart race. Her breathing became rapid, and she needed to sit down before her knees buckled beneath her.

Elizabeth remembered her manners and waved Darcy to a seat. He took the chair opposite her and moved it closer. Leaning forward, he reached for one of her small, soft hands and held it between his large, warm ones. Elizabeth tingled from head to toe at his touch.

"Miss Elizabeth, I must beg your indulgence for a moment. I never expected to have the opportunity to see you again, but determined I would work to overcome the weaknesses in my character that you revealed to me. Since I have been so fortunate as to encounter you again here, I cannot waste this chance the Lord has given me. My feelings for you have not changed since the spring, except perhaps that I now love and admire you even more ardently. Your presence in my home has served to prove to me that you are the only woman I could imagine as my wife, the mother of my children, and the caretaker of those who depend upon Pemberley for their livelihood." Darcy still possessed Elizabeth's hand and unconsciously rubbed circles on the back of it as he spoke. Between the sensations his touch caused and the tender, loving expression in his eyes, Elizabeth was having a difficult time with coherent thought. "I know I was greatly mistaken in your feelings once before, but I hope that I now understand you better. After these last two days, it appears those sentiments may have changed; at least, I hope and pray they have."

Elizabeth could only nod; the hint of uncertainty and hesitation in his voice touched her greatly.

Darcy continued. "I find myself compelled to ask if there may be a chance for us in the future." He slipped to one knee, still grasping her hand. "Miss Elizabeth Bennet, will you do me the very great honor of becoming my wife? I love you most ardently, and I will strive every day to be a better man and continue to be worthy of your love and respect. Please let me add, if you need more time before committing, that I would be willing to accept a courtship first. I just could not survive should I lose you completely."

It brought tears to Elizabeth's eyes to see the once proud Mr. Darcy kneeling so humbly before her. She raised her hand and placed it over those that clasped her other one. With the tears still glistening, Elizabeth gave her answer. "Mr. Darcy, after reading your letter and gaining a better understanding of the situations you addressed, I found myself horrified by my behavior. I prayed for an opportunity to be allowed to apologize. Then I spent much time in reflection and came to realize that you were exactly the man who in talents and temperament would suit me, but I feared it was too late. As a gentleman, you may have permitted me to apologize, but I knew I could expect no more. I tried to adjust to the reality of my situation but doubted I would ever again meet a man who suited me so perfectly. You are the best of men, Mr. Darcy, and I can imagine nothing that would give me greater pleasure than to accept your hand. I am not worthy of this second chance to become your wife, but I shall spend my days trying to make you happy and proud of me." Taking a deep breath to calm herself, Elizabeth looked him directly in the eye. When she spoke, her voice was soft and steady and a lovely smile filled her face. "I love you as well."

Darcy's eyes never wavered from Elizabeth's. He saw the tears fill her eyes and felt a flicker of heartache, then a reigniting of the hope he had felt since the day before. In spite of her tears, Elizabeth gazed back at him with the love and devotion he had always wished to see in her expression. As she gave him the answer he longed to hear, the smile on his face widened until it revealed both of his dimples. When he heard her acceptance, his eyes, too, became misty. Darcy entwined his fingers with hers and squeezed gently. Then, when he heard her declaration of love, he could contain himself no longer. Darcy stood and pulled Elizabeth up with him. Placing his hand under her chin, he tilted it back until she met his eyes. He stared at her intently for a long moment, then slowly leaned his head down until his lips met hers. The kiss was brief and gentle, but it moved them both.

Darcy broke the kiss and pulled back so he could gaze into her eyes. Seeing a look of awakening passion, he wished to kiss her again. However, as they were unchaperoned, he did not desire to put her in an embarrassing situation should the Gardiners return. "Do you expect the Gardiners to arrive soon? I should like to speak to your uncle until I may travel to Hertfordshire to meet with your father."

"I do not believe they will be much longer. The Gardiners were to walk to the church and back to allow me to read my letters from Jane before going to visit with one of my aunt's friends."

Darcy lifted Elizabeth's hand to his lips, kissing the back softly. He turned it over and placed another kiss in her palm. "How fortunate for me to come upon you at such an opportune moment. Perhaps you would permit me to order tea and wait with you while you read?"

"That would be lovely, Mr. Darcy."

"Miss Elizabeth, with our betrothal, would you do me the favor of calling me Fitzwilliam or William, as my family does?"

"I would like that very much, Fitzwilliam."

Darcy felt a thrill of passion at the way she caressed his name when she replied. Before he could give in to temptation and kiss her again, Darcy moved to summon one of the inn's servants as Elizabeth returned to her chair and letters.

---

After closing the sitting room door, Darcy moved to gaze out the window, allowing Elizabeth a bit of privacy while she read her letters. He could hear the shuffle of the pages behind him.

"Oh, no! How could she do this?

Darcy turned from the window at Elizabeth's outburst. Her face was pale and her eyes wide with what appeared to be horror. "Good God! What is the matter?" He moved to kneel before her, taking her free hand in his.

"Oh, this is dreadful! Lydia has run away from Brighton. She believes she is going to Gretna Green with Mr. Wickham!"

At her words, Darcy released her hand and began to pace.

Bereft with the loss of his comforting touch, Elizabeth nonetheless continued. "Fortunately, Colonel Foster has put out that she is ill. He attempted to track the runaways but has found no evidence of them beyond London. At that point, he notified my family by express. Papa is ill, and Jane begs for Uncle's return to search for her." Elizabeth looked at the anger and disgust on Darcy's face as he paced, and her heart contracted painfully. Darcy had previously expressed his displeasure at the behavior of her younger sisters. Now, Lydia's thoughtless actions would bring disgrace on all those connected to her. Swallowing a sob, Elizabeth looked at the floor. "I release you from our engagement. I would not wish the scandal from Lydia's decision to touch you or Miss Darcy."

Darcy was immediately on his knees before Elizabeth's chair. He took both her hands in his and squeezed them. "No, Elizabeth. I will not allow you to end our engagement. I love you and my life would be meaningless without you. We will handle this together. I should have stopped Wickham sooner; this would never have happened."

"How could you possibly stop him without exposing and ruining your sister?"

"I am not sure yet, but there must be something." Darcy began pacing again. "I have been paying Wickham's debts for years; I imagine I have collected enough to put him in debtor's prison and keep him locked up for many years. If Colonel Foster managed to keep Lydia's disappearance quiet, we might be able to return her to Brighton without anyone being aware of the situation."

"What if Lydia refuses to leave him?" worried Elizabeth. "She can be incredibly stubborn and has often spoken of wishing to be the first sister to marry."

"Let us worry about that later. For now, we must find your aunt and uncle immediately and be on our way to London." Darcy stepped into the hallway again and called for another servant. When one appeared, he commanded, "Please fetch Mr. And Mrs. Gardiner immediately. They walked in the direction of the church."

"Certainly, sir," said the maid before rushing away to fulfill her task.

Darcy was still pacing and thinking when, a short time later, a knock sounded at the door. Elizabeth rushed to open it, expecting it to be the Gardiners. She found Hannah with the refreshments Darcy had ordered. Elizabeth held the door for her to enter and remained there, watching the maid put the tray on a table near the window before quickly exiting the room.

Elizabeth closed the door securely and moved to pour them each a cup of tea. In spite of the situation, Darcy took enjoyment in watching her perform this simple task. She handed him a cup, and he took a sip. Elizabeth had prepared it exactly as he liked without needing to ask him his preferences. He gave her a smile as he took another sip and set the cup on the table before returning to his pacing. Elizabeth sat sipping her tea and watching him. She could almost determine his thoughts as she observed the expressions that crossed his face.

Darcy was still pacing and Elizabeth still silently observing when the Gardiners rushed into the room. They hurried to Elizabeth's side, asking what had occurred. Darcy's comforting presence allowed her to calmly explain the content of Jane's letters.

Mr. Gardiner turned to Darcy. "It was kind of you to remain with Elizabeth until our return. I am sorry that this family emergency shall force us to leave before we intended. I shall miss the opportunity to fish one more time before returning to the city." Darcy noted the rueful expression on his face as well as the disappointment in his eyes.

"Mr. Gardiner, I believe we must make some plans before we depart. I have —"

"We, Mr. Darcy?"

"Yes, as I was about to say, I have known Wickham since childhood. I have knowledge of some of his friends and favorite places in London and have something that may be useful in dealing with him. I also have an interest in protecting the Bennet family's reputation, as Miss Elizabeth accepted my offer of marriage barely half an hour ago."

Darcy's words could not have surprised Mr. Gardiner more. He looked first at his wife, who merely shrugged, then at his niece. Elizabeth's face showed her happiness even through the concern she felt for Lydia. Her eyes blazed with love as she stared at Darcy. Mr. Gardiner's gaze returned to his wife, who had also seen the look on Elizabeth's face. This time she gave him a slight smile and a nod.

"Our congratulations to you both," was Mr. Gardiner's exuberant reply as he reached out to shake hands with Darcy.

"Thank you, sir. I remained to speak to you about this, but Miss Lydia's problem must take precedence. I understand the need for urgency, but I would like to propose that we depart first thing in the morning. There are a few things I must attend to, and if I might secure a ride with you in your carriage, I can have Georgiana follow in mine. We shall have plenty of time to make our plans as we travel."

"Perhaps we should leave today so that I may deliver Elizabeth to her family at Longbourn?"

"No!" Darcy and Elizabeth cried at almost the same moment before turning to look at one another in surprise.

"Forgive my outburst, sir, but I believe that Miss Elizabeth may be of some use in recovering Miss Lydia."

"Indeed, Uncle, I insist you allow me to help. I have some knowledge of Mr. Wickham's habits of which Lydia is unaware. I may be in a better position to speak with her than you or Mr. Darcy."

Mr. Gardiner glanced at his wife, seeking her opinion without words. "All right, then. Perhaps we should order additional refreshments and work out our plans for the morning before we both begin to make preparations for departure."

Darcy nodded and seated himself at the table. Elizabeth sat beside him and gave him a grateful look for valuing her opinion and assistance. Darcy placed his hand over hers briefly, caressing it before releasing it.

Elizabeth poured tea for her relations. Once the servants had delivered the order items and departed, the conversation turned to travel plans. Darcy spoke of the preparations he needed to make and agreed to meet them at the inn at six in the morning. After a pleasant luncheon, Darcy took his leave of the Gardiners, who permitted him a moment alone with Elizabeth.

"Elizabeth, I hope you will take pity on me and agree to a short engagement. Knowing that you have finally accepted my hand makes parting from you far more difficult than I anticipated."

Darcy held and caressed her hands as he spoke, and Elizabeth briefly wondered if he even realized what he did. "I feel bereft at the thought of your leaving and do not know how I will manage until I see you again."

Thrilled with her words, Darcy wished to remain, though he knew it to be impossible. There was much that needed his attention for him to leave early in the morning. Darcy leaned in and sweetly kissed Elizabeth's forehead before departing. Elizabeth rushed to the window and observed Darcy mount his horse, then hurry in the direction of Pemberley.

She let out a sigh and moved to her bedchamber to begin packing her trunk.

# MAKING ARRANGEMENTS

When Darcy stepped through the doors of Pemberley, the butler greeted him with a worried look.

"Is everything well, Jeffers? Is Georgiana all right?" Darcy asked.

Respectfully keeping his eyes averted, the man replied, "I believe Mr. and Miss Bingley have had a disagreement, sir. Mr. Bingley is in the billiard room, I believe. Miss Darcy is currently in the library, as it is a place Miss Bingley rarely frequents. I believe Mrs. Annesley is with her. Miss Bingley is currently in the gardens, but if she saw you return, I am sure she will arrive here shortly."

"Thank you for the warning, Jeffers, and for watching over Georgiana in my absence. Would you please escort Miss Darcy to my study and wait with her until I arrive there? I must speak to both Mr. Bingley and my sister."

"Certainly, sir." Jeffers moved towards the library as quickly as his arthritic knee would carry him. Darcy watched the old family retainer until he was out of sight, a small smile on his face.

Darcy moved quickly to find Bingley. As he opened the door to the billiard room, he heard the crack of the balls. Bingley was bent over to take another shot. "Perhaps you should take out your frustration on something that will not break," chuckled Darcy.

Bingley straightened and looked at his friend. "Would you care to fence?"

"In your present state of mind, I would fear for my continued well-being." Darcy gave his friend a wry grin. "Would you care to tell me what is bothering you?" Darcy sat on the edge of the billiards table and picked up the cue ball, tossing it from hand to hand as he waited for Bingley to speak.

"I had a row with Caroline. I confronted her about her knowledge of Miss Bennet's presence in town. She gave so many excuses, even going so far as to say she had told me, and I did not seem to care or that I must have forgotten. Caroline claims I can do better than a poor girl from an insignificant county. She says it is my duty as head of the family to advance us as far in society as possible and that Jane cannot help to do so. I reminded her that Jane, as a gentleman's daughter, is already above us socially. I asked if my happiness was meaningless in the finding of a wife. Caroline said if I would just forget Jane, in no time at all I would become enamored of someone more suitable. At that point, I stormed from the room with her harping still ringing in my ears. I was afraid I might shake her or worse. I needed some separation from her."

"I believe I may be able to help with that. I have something I wish to discuss with you. Would you join me in my study?"

"Certainly." Bingley lay down his cue and followed Darcy from the room. When Darcy opened the door to the study, he found Georgiana already waiting there.

"Brother, how was your visit with Miss Elizabeth? Did you make plans for her to visit again?"

Darcy smiled broadly at his sister and best friend. "My visit began very well. I will ask that you say nothing to anyone else at present, but Miss Elizabeth Bennet has agreed to be my wife."

Georgiana threw herself at her brother, wrapping her arms around his neck as she squealed in pleasure. "Oh, William! I am so happy for you and for me!"

Darcy chuckled as he took hold of Georgiana's upper arms, pushing her back so he could see her face. "What about my engagement makes you happy for yourself?"

"I am gaining the most wonderful sister I could ever imagine, of course!" All three of the study's occupants laughed. "Have you set a date yet? Will we go to London to be closer to her?"

Darcy held up his hands, his palms facing Georgiana as though to ward off her questions. "No, there is no date, and we will not be able to set one until we deal with a troubling situation facing Elizabeth's family."

"What has happened, Darcy? Is Miss Bennet well?"

"That is what I wished to talk about with you both. I know this will be difficult for you to hear, Georgiana, but I believe you have a right to know." Darcy told his companions about the content of the letter and his plans to go to London in the morning with the Gardiners and Elizabeth.

"Poor Miss Lydia," came the soft voice of a pale Georgiana.

"Let me come with you, Darcy. I would be happy to be of assistance to Miss Bennet and her family."

"I believe I have a way you can help both the Bennets and me. I was hoping that you would accompany Georgiana and Mrs. Annesley to London in my carriage. Then you can pick up your vehicle in town to proceed to Netherfield. I am sure Miss Bennet would appreciate your presence since Miss Elizabeth will accompany the group to London rather than return to Longbourn to assist Miss Bennet. If you send your sisters and Hurst on from here to visit your relations as planned, it will give you the separation you mentioned you desired."

"I would be happy to do that. When would you like us to arrive?"

"I would recommend you leave in three days. With any luck, Mr. Gardiner and I will have located the runaway Miss Bennet by that time and handled things to protect her. I hope whenever I conclude my business you will welcome Georgiana and me to visit at Netherfield. I must, of course, obtain Mr. Bennet's approval of our engagement and I would not wish to be far from Elizabeth for any length of time." The expression of happiness on Darcy's face when he spoke of Elizabeth made both his companions smile.

"Of course, you would be welcome to stay at Netherfield for as long as you like. I shall write to the housekeeper immediately to have the house prepared."

Darcy smiled at his friend's enthusiasm. "Georgiana, I am sorry to leave you to play hostess alone. I hope you understand why I must go."

"Of course, William, you need not worry about anything. I believe we should tell the others that an emergency requires you to leave for London and that you may have to stay for some time. As a result, we must cut their visit short, as I will be joining you in Town."

"That is an excellent idea, Miss Darcy," said Bingley. "We shall not mention, however, that I will be escorting you to London. I shall hand Caroline into the coach and have the coachman depart immediately. Once it is moving, she shall not be able to make a fuss about going with me to London."

Darcy fought to contain his grin at the pleased, mischievous expression his friend wore. "Well then, if you two will excuse me, I must send an express to Colonel Forster, as well as meet with my steward and send out notes about our travel. I will include information for your travel dates as well. I will see the two of you at dinner." Just before his companions reached the study door, Darcy called out, "Georgie, will you ask my valet to pack for a fortnight's stay? He can pack the rest to come with you when you travel."

"Of course. William, will you please tell Miss Elizabeth that I will pray for her family and that I look forward to seeing her in London?"

"I will, Georgie."

Darcy was already busy scratching out letters before the others had left the room. When he had finished the express, he rang for Jeffers.

"I must have this sent express immediately. There will be several others that must go the same way as soon as I have them finished. I wish my messenger to take the others. He can await me at Darcy House, as I will likely have further need of him. As I prepare the other letters, have the messenger make ready to depart. Also, please ask the steward to join me here in half an hour."

"I shall attend to it immediately, Mr. Darcy," replied Jeffers as he accepted the first letter.

As the butler departed, Darcy quickly reached for another sheet of paper. He was pressing his signet ring in the wax of the last letter when the steward knocked on the door.

"Come," called Darcy.

The door opened and Jeffers entered with Mr. Moore. Darcy handed the letters to his butler.

"Is there anything else I can assist you with, sir?" Jeffers asked.

"No, that will—actually, yes. Jeffers, I am away at first light. Please let Henry know to have a vehicle prepared to transport me and my luggage to the inn in Lambton. I will be journeying from there with friends. Also, let him know that Miss Georgiana, Mrs. Annesley, and Mr. Bingley will be traveling to London in the traveling coach in three days' time. I have already made arrangements for them to stay in our usual inns. I am trusting him to ensure they make the journey safely. I am uncertain when I will be returning but will notify you when my plans are firm."

"Yes, sir. Everything will be in readiness, and we shall ensure the comfort of Miss Georgiana and your visitors until they depart. Safe travels, Mr. Darcy."

Jeffers cast a brief glance back at his master, already shuffling through papers on his desk as he spoke to the steward; he exited the study, closing the door quietly after him.

---

Darcy diligently worked all afternoon to ensure all was in readiness for his unexpected absence from the estate. He had not seen Miss Bingley all day and was not sure what to expect. She had addressed very few remarks to him since their conversation before dinner the previous evening.

The others had just seated themselves when Darcy rushed through the dining room door.

"Well, there you are, Mr. Darcy. In spite of the fact we are sharing a residence, I have not seen my host all day." Miss Bingley eyed him, speculating on where he had been.

"I am afraid it was necessary. After a morning ride, I received information regarding an emergency that requires my immediate presence in London. I will be leaving in the morning and do not know when I will return. I am afraid it will demand your visit be cut short. I wish for Georgiana to join me in London in a few days.

Caroline looked extremely displeased. In spite of her anger of the previous evening, she had hoped to make one last attempt to gain his attention or to cause a compromise. Caroline could not lose what could be her last opportunity to gain the position she desired. She would see what she could accomplish this evening.

"Oh, that is too bad. I had so looked forward to this visit. First you were forced to entertain those who can barely claim an acquaintance with you, and now

## A Matter of Timing

you must be away to London. It has been so long since we could enjoy the company of our closest friends in peace." Caroline cast a pouty look in his direction as she fluttered her lashes. "Perhaps your business will end more quickly than you expect and we can meet here again after our visit to our family in the north."

Darcy had to turn away and stop himself from rolling his eyes. He knew that she was begging for another invitation to Pemberley, but he did not know if he would allow that after the way she had treated Elizabeth. He would never allow in his home anyone who would not treat his wife with all the respect she deserved—and that included Aunt Catherine.

"I may not be back until just before the holidays, Miss Bingley, so I am afraid that will not be possible."

"The holidays! That would be the perfect thing. We have not seen Pemberley in the winter."

"As I said, that would not be possible; I will be hosting family for Christmas this year."

Caroline, who was finally seated next to Darcy at the table, looked down to hide her annoyance. She had long desired to meet Darcy's aunt and uncle, the Earl and Countess of Matlock. An acquaintance with them would do much for her social standing. It would also bring her into company with the viscount. She hoped that if she could not gain Darcy's attention, she might have an opportunity to attract the attention of his titled cousin.

"Then we will see you in town for the little season, sir. Perhaps you will then have time for your closest friends."

Charles directed a question to Georgiana to prevent Caroline from saying anything further. The remainder of the meal passed pleasantly enough. Caroline attempted to monopolize Darcy's attention but was unsuccessful. Following the meal, the gentlemen did not separate from the ladies, instead going to the music room. Georgiana entertained them with several pieces, at the close of which Darcy rose.

"If you will excuse me, I must retire, as I have an early start in the morning. Again, I am sorry for the disruption of your visit and I wish you all safe travels. Georgie, I will see you in London soon. Good night, all."

"Please come say good-bye in the morning, William," Georgiana said.

He raised a brow at her in question, and she gave him an almost imperceptible nod in return.

"If you wish it, of course I shall." With a bow to those present, Darcy quit the room. After preparing for the night, he settled before the fire with a small glass of brandy. As he completed the necessary business before for the trip, he had managed to keep thoughts of Elizabeth at bay, but now that he was at leisure, she filled his mind. Thinking of their time together earlier in the day, he recalled every word and look that had passed between them. While riding out that morning, he had hoped she was not totally opposed to a relationship with him any longer. Though he had always dreamed of receiving her love, he had not expected the overwhelming sensation that had filled him with her declarations. Darcy thought his heart would burst from his chest. Then he had kissed her. Darcy had kissed her in his dreams many times, but that could not hold a candle to the actual softness of her lips or her sweet taste. Her skin had been softer than silk, and she had enveloped him in the sweet scent of lilac that always filled his senses when he was near her. He hoped that sleep would come easily and morning quickly, for he could not wait to see her again. In spite of the fact that they traveled on an urgent matter, he greatly looked forward to the days he would spend in the carriage in close company with his beloved Elizabeth.

With thoughts of his betrothed and their future, Darcy must have dozed off in the chair before the fire, for a curious sound woke him. He heard a gentle scratching at his chamber door. Darcy moved to the door and called softly, "Who is there?"

## A Matter of Timing

"It is Fields, sir," replied one of the Pemberley footmen. I am sorry to disturb you, sir, but felt you might wish to know. Miss Bingley attempted to enter the family wing. She did not see me originally, but as she tried to pass, I called her name and asked if she needed directions to the guest wing. Miss Bingley pretended to startle and then looked around as though confused as to where she was. Miss Bingley said she often walked in her sleep and claimed it must have been happening again. However, I previously observed her looking stealthily around as she proceeded from the guest wing towards the one housing the family, sir."

"Thank you, Fields, you have done well. I was afraid she might attempt something, as I am leaving in the morning. I appreciate your diligence in protecting my privacy."

"If you will forgive me for saying so, sir, it is a pleasure to prevent Miss Bingley from succeeding. Most of the staff does not believe Miss Bingley would make Pemberley a happy home should she become the mistress."

"I could not agree more, Fields. Good night, and thank you again."

"Good night, Mr. Darcy."

Darcy closed his chamber door and climbed into the massive poster bed, where dreams of Elizabeth soon overtook him.

# The Quest Begins

Darcy was up before the dawn, but he felt extremely well rested. He readied himself quickly and exited his room, silently acknowledging the footman on duty in the hallway. Darcy made his way quietly to his sister's room. He knocked softly and opened the door, slipping inside. He called, "Georgie," as he took a seat on the edge of her bed.

Georgiana rolled over and opened her eyes.

"I came to say good-bye as you requested."

Georgiana sat up in the bed, sleepily pushing the hair from her face. She leaned forward, hugging tightly to Darcy as she whispered, "Please be careful, brother, when you are dealing with Wickham; do not let him hurt you or Elizabeth. Do not forget to tell Elizabeth how happy I am that she will become my sister."

"I will not forget," he promised. Darcy pulled away from Georgiana and kissed her forehead before tucking the covers back around her.

"I will see you at the townhouse in less than a se'nnight, William." Georgiana had returned to her slumbers almost before she finished speaking.

Darcy kissed her forehead one last time and hurried to the carriage.

He arrived at the inn just as the sun crested the horizon. When Darcy entered, the landlord greeted him. "Good morning, Mr. Darcy. All is as you requested. The Gardiners and Miss Bennet just entered the private dining room, and the meal will arrive momentarily."

Darcy thanked him and walked down the hall. He knocked briefly, then entered. His eyes immediately sought Elizabeth's as he greeted those present.

"Good morning, Mr. and Mrs. Gardiner. Good morning, Elizabeth."

"Good morning, Mr. Darcy," said Mrs. Gardiner.

"Morning, Darcy," Mr. Gardiner was heard to say.

"Good morning, William." The warm smile and loving look Elizabeth bestowed on him filled him with joy.

Before he could say more, someone knocked at the door. Elizabeth opened it to reveal the innkeeper's wife and a servant carrying the breakfast that Darcy had ordered.

"Thank you, Mrs. Burton. Will you be able to have the baskets ready for us by the requested time?"

"Certainly, sir. Everything will be as you wished."

As the group dined, Elizabeth asked, "How did Georgiana take the news?"

"I am glad you asked, for she entrusted me with a message for you."

"Oh, and what was that?"

"She made me promise to tell you how thrilled she is to be gaining such a wonderful sister."

Elizabeth smiled in pleasure before replying. "I am delighted to be gaining another sister, particularly one as sweet as Georgiana! So, she was not upset about your departure?"

## A Matter of Timing

"Georgie took the information very well. She said you and your family would be in her prayers and begged that I be careful in my dealings with Wickham and not allow him to hurt either you or myself."

"I most heartily agree with her sentiments," Elizabeth concurred.

---

Less than an hour later, everyone was settled in the Gardiners' carriage and heading for London. Elizabeth and Mrs. Gardiner sat on the forward-facing seat, with Darcy and Mr. Gardiner across from them. No one spoke for a time as they watched the miles slip past. They traveled for almost two hours in silence. Darcy and Elizabeth stared at each other the entire way, oblivious to the reaction of her relations, who turned to the windows to hide their smiles or covered a laugh with a cough.

Eventually, Mr. Gardiner broke the silence. "What will we do first upon arrival in town, Mr. Darcy?"

"I sent several expresses yesterday. The first was to Colonel Forster to confirm what had happened and how he had reacted to it, what he had said. I also asked him to buy up Wickham's debts for me. The second was to arrange our lodgings along the way. The final one was to an investigator I have used in the past. It is my hope that by the time we arrive he will have discovered the location of Mrs. Younge. He was also to dispatch someone to Meryton, to buy up Wickham's debts there."

"Who is Mrs. Younge?" asked Mrs. Gardiner.

Darcy looked at Elizabeth in question, only to see her shake her head. "You gave me that information under duress, and I would never betray such a confidence," came her quiet reply.

Darcy looked at Mr. and Mrs. Gardiner. "Mrs. Younge was my sister's former companion." Darcy took a deep breath. "Mr. and Mrs. Gardiner, I must ask you to keep what I am about to tell you in the strictest of confidence."

"Of course, Mr. Darcy," replied Mr. Gardiner, while Mrs. Gardiner nodded her assent.

"A year ago, my sister was removed from school and placed with a companion. Her companion, Mrs. Younge, suggested they spend some time in Ramsgate, where Georgiana would be able to continue her drawing lessons with a master while enjoying lovely scenes to sketch. After careful consideration, I agreed and made all the arrangements for their stay. I escorted them to the house and stayed for a week before it was necessary for me to return to London to attend to an important matter of business. I finished my business several days sooner than expected and returned to Ramsgate several days ahead of schedule as a surprise. I arrived to find Mrs. Younge and Wickham with my sister, discussing plans for a departure the next morning.

"When Georgiana saw me, she ran to tell me about her 'wonderful' news. They were going to Gretna Green the next day. Georgiana said she and Wickham were in love. They had planned to get married and surprise me when they arrived at Pemberley. I misled Wickham, allowing him to believe that Georgiana's dowry was forfeit if she eloped. When Wickham heard that, he complained about the time he had wasted trying to seduce her and disparaged Georgiana, telling her that he could not imagine being stuck with such a tiresome young lady for life without her fortune to allow him to indulge his pleasures.

"Georgiana was heartbroken. Though I would have liked to have chased after Wickham and run him through, attending to Georgiana's hurt and disillusionment was more important. I should have exposed his depraved character when he arrived in Meryton, but I did not know how to do so without damaging Georgiana's reputation. She was not yet sixteen at the time of the attempted elopement and has such a generous heart. She remembered Wickham from her childhood, when he and I were friends. He was always personable, with a talent for charming others. I had not seen fit to warn her about the changes in his behavior, as they were not a subject one usually discusses with a gently bred young lady.

"I nearly lost my sister to this scoundrel, and because I failed to act, Miss Lydia and her sisters could suffer ruination because of the same reprobate. I will do anything within my power to make this right, as the fault is mine."

Mr. and Mrs. Gardiner listened in stunned silence. "Oh, Mr. Darcy, I believe you are too hard on yourself. You must let go of the anger you hold in this or it shall overwhelm you," was Mrs. Gardiner's soft comment when Darcy finished speaking.

"You must learn some of my philosophy, Mr. Darcy."

"And, what is that, Miss Elizabeth?" He gave her a cheeky grin as he waited for her reply.

"Remember the past only as it gives you pleasure."

"I shall try to do just that, but it will not prevent me from taking the responsibility to clean up this current mess Wickham has created, just as I have done all his life."

"Being responsible for the actions of another is a heavy burden to place upon yourself, Mr. Darcy. Being of a similar age as Wickham could not have made the situation any easier."

Darcy nodded his agreement. "All my life, I have seen Wickham charm his way out of trouble, never having a care as to how his reprehensible behavior affected others. We were friends as children, and he was my father's godson. I was disgusted by his behavior but felt I had no choice but to clean up after him."

"Allow me to pose a thought for consideration, Mr. Darcy," Mr. Gardiner said. Darcy nodded, so Mr. Gardiner continued. "When you become a parent, you will realize that children learn best when they experience the consequences of their actions. We do all we can to protect them. However, when they choose to go against what they have learned, children—and adults—will continue making the same poor choice again and again if they never experience the results of their poor choice and actions."

Darcy considered the man's words for a few minutes before speaking. "Do you mean that if I had informed my father of Wickham's behaviors, his words and those of Wickham's father would have carried more weight with him?"

"William, I am sure you have observed my attempts to correct my sisters."

He nodded.

"You have also seen that it has no effect on them because my words are not backed up by my parents. I am too close to their age for them to believe that I could know better than they."

"I can see your point and can only wish I had learned this sooner. Perhaps my sister would not have suffered if I had told my father or even Wickham's father of his wild behavior at school."

Mr. Gardiner nodded his understanding.

"If our plan is successful, Wickham will suffer the consequences on this occasion. Unfortunately for him, those consequences could be quite severe. He has run away from his militia unit without permission in a time of war. The repercussions of his actions could cost him his life."

Elizabeth and Mrs. Gardiner gasped at Darcy's words as Mr. Gardiner nodded in agreement.

"In spite of the awful things Mr. Wickham has done, I do not know how I would live with myself were our actions to cause his death. Is there nothing we can do?" Elizabeth asked.

"I do not believe anything I might say could sway the army, but I will ask my cousin, Colonel Fitzwilliam, to request transportation rather than death if that would be acceptable to you." Darcy looked at the women as he spoke.

"Thank you, William. That would be acceptable." Mrs. Gardiner nodded in agreement with Elizabeth's sentiments.

"Then I shall explain our request to Fitzwilliam, but please understand that the military will act as they see fit."

The carriage and its occupants were on the road from dawn until sundown. As the miles slipped by, they talked about the best way to handle the situation once they found the couple. Elizabeth had a suggestion that they reviewed and debated from all sides, ultimately finding it to be an excellent idea. They made plans for the couple to marry as well as plans for Lydia should she not wish to continue with Wickham. They discussed every possible situation and outcome, planning for as many of them as they could.

After two long days of travel, the tired group finally arrived in Gracechurch Street. Darcy declined an invitation to come in, promising that he would send a note if the report from his investigator had arrived. After helping Elizabeth from the carriage, Darcy placed a lingering kiss on the back of her hand. He turned it over and placed another gentle kiss on her palm before re-entering the carriage and heading for Darcy House.

Just before the family retired for the night, a note came from Darcy.

*Mr. Gardiner,*

*I have had word from the investigator. He has found Mrs. Younge's address. I will visit there early tomorrow morning. It may take a visit or two before she provides the information we need. I will come straight to Gracechurch Street immediately after meeting with her.*

LINDA C. THOMPSON

## *Darcy*

The next morning a hired carriage pulled up before the boarding house at No. 12 Edward Street. The neighborhood had once been prosperous, but the years had not been kind to it. Mrs. Younge's boarding house was one of the nicer buildings on the block, but it was in need of some repair. Darcy convinced the driver it would be worth his time to wait and then deliver Darcy to his next destination.

Darcy rapped firmly at the front door. A pale, underfed maid with lank blonde hair eventually opened it. "Can I 'elp ye, sir?"

"I am here to see Mrs. Younge about a room." Darcy's voice was firm but kind.

The maid opened the door wider and showed Darcy into a small, neat parlor. He stood with his back to the room, gazing out the bay window that looked over the busy street as he waited for the mistress' arrival.

"I understand you are looking for accommodations," came the voice of Mrs. Younge as she bustled through the door. "I do have a few rooms available. How long do you plan to stay?"

Darcy turned slowly from the window and watched the color drain from the woman's face. He did not immediately speak but gazed in an intimidating manner at the woman before him.

"M—M—Mr. D—Darcy! Wh—wh—what are you doing here?"

"As I told your maid, I am looking for a room—the room where I can find Mr. Wickham and his young companion."

"What do you want with Wickham? You are no friend of his!"

"Mrs. Younge, when I hired you, I thought you to be an intelligent woman. However, the fact that you have not yet seen through Wickham's behavior makes me question my original opinion. I am in a hurry. I will offer you twenty pounds to provide me with this information immediately. If you force me to wait for the information I need, I will reduce the amount by two pounds each time I must return. It is your choice how much you earn for providing the information I desire."

Darcy stared steadily at the woman. He could easily discern her thoughts as she mulled over the matter.

"What do you want with Wickham?" she asked suspiciously.

"He has convinced an innocent young girl to run away with him. Being a friend of her family and well acquainted with Wickham, I offered my assistance in helping to recover her."

"You will not hurt Wickham, will you?"

"That will depend entirely on Wickham. I have no intention of harming him. I merely wish to recover the girl for her family."

Mrs. Younge considered a few moments longer. "I will provide you with the address for twenty-five pounds," she declared boldly.

"I have given you my terms, Mrs. Younge. If I must come back tomorrow for the information, the most you will receive is eighteen pounds. However, if you give me what I desire today, I will add two pounds provided you do not inform Wickham that I am looking for him. I will provide the two additional pounds after I have met with Wickham."

Mrs. Younge was tempted to argue, as she felt her treatment at Mr. Darcy's hands to have been excessively harsh. However, the money would go a long way towards putting food on the table and perhaps even allow her a new dress. "Agreed."

Darcy pulled out a small bag containing the promised payment. Mrs. Younge put out her hand to collect it, but Darcy pulled it back, raising an eyebrow at her. The woman moved across the room to a small desk. Taking a sheet of paper from the drawer, she dipped her quill in ink and quickly jotted down the address of the inn where Wickham was staying. Darcy handed her the bag as he took the paper she held out to him.

As Darcy exited the room, he paused in the doorway. "Remember, the additional funds are yours only if you do not inform Wickham or anyone else that I am looking for him." Darcy gave the woman a nod of his head and was gone.

Mrs. Younge stayed rooted to the spot until she heard the street door close. Then she collapsed in a chair, shaking the bag in her hand to hear the jingle of the coins.

---

Darcy arrived at the Gardiners' home just before the midday meal. Elizabeth greeted him happily. She could tell by the look on his face that he had good news.

"What did you learn?"

"I have the address we need; we can go this afternoon to see your sister."

"Oh, William, that is good news!"

He turned to greet Elizabeth's aunt and uncle. "Good day, Mr. and Mrs. Gardiner."

"Good day, Mr. Darcy. Did I hear you say you had the information we needed?" asked Mr. Gardiner

"Yes, Mrs. Younge was unusually cooperative."

"How much did her cooperation cost?" asked Elizabeth, a frown creasing her forehead.

"A mere pittance. By the way, Mrs. Gardiner, I hope you will forgive me, but I invited my cousin, Colonel Fitzwilliam, to meet me here. He will accompany us this afternoon."

"We will be delighted to meet him, Mr. Darcy. Do you know when he will arrive?"

"I expect him any time now."

"Then, if you will excuse me, I will speak with the housekeeper about setting another place for luncheon."

She had hardly completed her sentence when there was a knock at the door. A few moments later, Mrs. Browning, the Gardiner's housekeeper, showed Colonel Fitzwilliam into the room.

"Richard, thank you for coming. Allow me to introduce you to our hosts, Mr. and Mrs. Edward Gardiner."

"Mr. and Mrs. Gardiner, it is a pleasure to meet you. Thank you for receiving me."

"I believe you remember their niece and my betrothed, Miss Elizabeth Bennet."

The broad grin on Darcy's face was a shock to his cousin. "It is a pleasure to see you again, Miss Elizabeth. Did I hear my cousin correctly when he introduced you as his betrothed?"

"Indeed you did, sir."

Richard clapped his cousin on the back. "Congratulation, Darcy, Miss Elizabeth. I wish you both every happiness!"

"I know there is an important meeting that must take place this afternoon. Please excuse me while I speak with my housekeeper. Our meal should be ready very shortly," Mrs. Gardiner said.

Mr. Gardiner invited the gentlemen to take a seat as they awaited the call to lunch. While they waited, Darcy filled Richard in on the situation with Wickham and Elizabeth's youngest sister. He also related the scenario they had devised on their trip from Pemberley.

Richard smiled appreciatively. "Excellent plan, Miss Elizabeth. You would make a brilliant strategist."

"Thank you, Colonel," said Elizabeth with a cheeky grin. Darcy reached over and squeezed the hand that rested between them on the sofa.

Mrs. Gardiner appeared at the door and announced that luncheon was ready.

## Unexpected Results

As another hired hack took the colonel, Darcy, Elizabeth, and Mr. Gardiner to the address that Mrs. Younge had provided, they reviewed the plan once more.

"You know, Darcy, should Miss Lydia not wish to marry Wickham, we have within our power two options for ending his reign of mischief."

"To what are you referring, Richard?"

"You hold all of Wickham's many debts, do you not?"

A grin appeared on Darcy's face. "I do, indeed. What is the other option you feel we have?"

"Wickham is away from his post without permission during war time. The army will transfer him to the front, or they could decide to hang him."

The others in the carriage were unsettled at hearing the colonel reiterate that death could be a possibility for Wickham. Though a part of Elizabeth thought Wickham deserving of an incredibly harsh punishment, she could not imagine being the cause of someone's death, even someone as contemptible as Wickham.

"William," Elizabeth began, "I do not think I could resign myself to . . . "

"I understand, Elizabeth. I could not do such a thing to someone I once called a friend."

"I will make a recommendation for transportation or debtor's prison, then," said Richard matter-of-factly. "However, the final decision will be up to the court martial panel.

Elizabeth turned to gaze out the window. Darcy, who sat across from her, could see her eyes widen as they took in the worsening conditions while the carriage approached the neighborhood where Lydia and Wickham were staying.

"Elizabeth, I must ask that you stay close to my side from the moment we step out of the carriage. When you are not beside me, you must stay close to your uncle or Richard."

"Certainly, William. I wonder how Lydia is handling her surroundings," she mused.

The carriage stopped before the address Mrs. Younge had provided. The rundown building seemed to lean upon its neighbor, as though it were too tired to stand up straight any longer.

"I will go in and arrange for the private parlor," said Mr. Gardiner. "I will check to see if Wickham is in the taproom. If I do not see him, I will ask for the room number."

The others remained seated in the carriage until Mr. Gardiner reappeared in the doorway. Darcy opened the carriage and stepped down, handing Elizabeth down next. The colonel stepped down behind her. Flanking Elizabeth, the trio moved into the tavern. Mr. Gardiner pointed out the private room for their use, and the colonel disappeared inside and closed the door. Darcy walked up the stairs, followed by Elizabeth on Mr. Gardiner's arm.

Darcy knocked on the door of the room that Wickham and Lydia occupied. They heard some scuffling within the room; then a disheveled Wickham opened the door.

"Darcy, old friend! What are you doing here? I see you brought company, the lovely Miss Elizabeth, and do I know you, sir?" It was obvious that Wickham was somewhat intoxicated, though it was only the middle of the afternoon.

Darcy moved to block Wickham's view of Elizabeth. "I am sure you know why I am here. As a friend of the Bennet family and with my knowledge of your rather questionable habits, they asked for my assistance." Darcy's unreadable mask was firmly in place, his look and voice both dispassionate. "I have reserved a private room downstairs so that we might talk privately. While we are talking, Miss Elizabeth would like to speak with her sister."

"I do not think I wish to speak to you, Darcy. I should prefer to stay with Lydia."

Lydia's voice came from a corner of the room, not visible from the door. "It is all right, George. I am happy to speak to my sister. Oh, Lizzy, did you come for my wedding?"

Wickham cast Lydia an aggrieved look.

"Make yourself presentable, Wickham. We shall leave the ladies to this room for their talk."

Wickham turned away angrily, grabbed the coat that rested over the back of a chair, shrugged it over his shoulders, and followed Darcy from the room. Elizabeth could hear Wickham stomping down the stairs like a petulant child. Mr. Gardiner gave Elizabeth an encouraging smile as he closed the door, remaining outside while the two sisters spoke.

Elizabeth looked around the room in disgust. Empty liquor bottles, mugs, and glasses littered the table. Clothes lay about the room. The windows were grimy, allowing little sunlight to penetrate the shadows. The linens were threadbare and dingy, and the room smelled stale. Wrinkling her nose, Elizabeth looked for the least offensive place to sit. She decided to take a seat at one of the straight-back chairs next to the small table in the room. "How do you like your accommodations, Lydia?"

"They are not very pleasant" Lydia replied, "but Wickham said it should not be long before we can move to better accommodations."

"How long have you been here?"

"We left Brighton early Sunday morning. It has been very dull stuck in this room all day every day. What day is it now?"

"It is Thursday. You have been here for a week and a half. Does it not bother you that you have lived in this hovel with a man to whom you are not married?"

"As we will be married soon, it does not matter that we are already living together," replied Lydia airily.

"What would happen to you if something were to happen to Mr. Wickham?"

"How would something happen to Wickham?"

"Does he stay here in the room with you all the time?"

"Well, no, he goes out each evening."

"Then what would happen if he were set upon by footpads and wounded or killed?"

Lydia's eyes widened.

"What would happen if he abandoned you? Do you have the funds to get back to Brighton or Longbourn?"

Lydia's eyes grew wider as she stared slack-jawed at her sister.

"You probably would not be able to come back to Longbourn because you ran away with a man and are not yet married. Papa would have to disown you to protect the rest of his daughters. Otherwise, we would all share your shame. Did you think about that when you ran away with Mr. Wickham?"

Though the words her sister spoke bothered Lydia, she was too immature to accept any responsibility for her actions. "Oh, la, Lizzy. Nothing has happened to Wickham, and soon we will be wed. I, the youngest, shall be the first of my sisters to marry."

"And just what will you live on when you are married?"

"On Wickham's pay, of course."

"Where will you live? Shall you share his room in the officers' barracks? Do you know how to cook your meals, or wash your clothes, or mend his uniform? You will not have any servants on the pay of a militia lieutenant."

Again, Lydia's eyes widened in disbelief. "I am sure Papa will assist us," she said imperiously.

"You know very well that Papa needs all his funds to care for our family without adding another mouth to feed. He may be willing to continue your allowance, but even with that and Wickham's pay, you would not be able to afford anything better than your current accommodations. You grew up the daughter of a gentleman. Is this how you see yourself living for the remainder of your days? On such a small salary, there would be no extra money for ribbons, new bonnets, or new gowns."

"I am sure my dear Wickham will receive frequent promotions, and with each one, he will earn more."

"Actually, Lydia, he deserted his position with the militia in a time of war. They can send him to France, or they could hang him," was Elizabeth's sharp response.

"No!" she cried. "Lizzy, you must not let them hurt my Wickham."

"Lydia, he is a grown man who signed commitment papers with the militia. He knew the risks of running away. And while you have been here in this room day and night, he has been out drinking, gambling, and likely worse."

"He says he is gambling only to increase our funds."

"Believe that if you wish, but you know what I say is true. Lydia, you now must face up to the consequences of your actions."

"I do not know what you mean," she said dismissively.

"I mean you must make a difficult decision. You must decide whether you wish to marry Wickham or return home." As Lydia opened her mouth to speak, Elizabeth held up her hand to stop her. "You will be able to again live at Longbourn only if you are still innocent."

Lydia's face blushed bright red.

"If you are no longer pure, you will have to be married off to someone whom Papa can pay to take you."

Here Lydia's face turned pale.

"Have you and Wickham anticipated your vows?"

Lydia shook her head sheepishly. "Wickham wanted to, but I said not until we were married."

Inwardly, Elizabeth sighed with relief, but she continued relentlessly. "If you choose to marry your Wickham, you will have to live on far less than Papa's annual income. You will not have servants, nor will you have pretty dresses for going out. Are you prepared to cook and clean? When you have your first child, you will have even less on which to live. You will also have to follow him from post to post with nowhere to call home. Also, Lydia, I am engaged to Mr. Darcy. You would never receive an invitation to Pemberley or Darcy House. Wickham has behaved in an infamous manner to Mr. Darcy."

"No, it is all Mr. Darcy's fault! He should not have denied Wickham the living his father left him. That is why he is poor now," Lydia shouted angrily.

"No, Lydia, that is another of Wickham's lies. He told Darcy he did not want to be a clergyman and asked for money instead."

Lydia shook her head in denial.

## A Matter of Timing

"He has the agreement Wickham signed renouncing his claim to the living and receiving four thousand pounds in exchange."

Lydia's eyes widened. "That is a fortune!"

"It was," Elizabeth agreed, "but he has wasted it all." Elizabeth stared at Lydia, giving her time to comprehend all the things she told her. After several minutes, Elizabeth said, "What is your decision, Lydia? Do you wish to marry Wickham or to return home?"

Elizabeth knew the moment her sister made her decision, and she shook her head in disappointment even before she heard her answer.

At the thought of going home in disgrace, Lydia's stubbornness returned in full force. "I will not be separated from my dear Wickham."

"Very well, let us go down and tell the gentlemen of your decision." Elizabeth moved to the door of the room and opened it to find Mr. Gardiner patiently waiting and watching over them. She saw the expectant look in his eyes and gave her head an imperceptible shake. Mr. Gardiner's eyes narrowed in anger and his shoulders drooped a little.

---

When the trio arrived outside the private room where the gentlemen waited, Mr. Gardiner looked at the girls. "Please remain here while I check to see if you may enter at this time," he said.

Elizabeth and a mutinous Lydia nodded.

Mr. Gardiner rapped on the door once and entered, leaving the door open several inches behind him. "Well, gentlemen, how go the negotiations?" asked Mr. Gardiner tersely.

"So far, Wickham has only made ridiculous demands," said Darcy, irritation evident in his voice.

"I believe, Darcy, you should let me handle the situation," came the colonel's voice, his hand resting on the hilt of his sword.

"So, Wickham, you have yet to tell me why you chose to bring Miss Lydia along when you left Brighton."

"I needed to get away from several pressing debts. Lydia had the spending money from her father. Bringing her gave me the traveling funds I needed. The girl is desperate for attention, so it was easy enough to convince her. I thought with the promise of marriage I would get to enjoy her charms as well, but she became priggish and said not until we were married," was Wickham's irritated reply.

"What is your fascination with such young women, Wickham?" came Richard's sarcastic voice. "Do your paltry charms not work on more mature women?"

At the slur, Wickham snarled, but with a glance at Darcy he managed to rein in his anger. "My charms are sufficient to any challenge. It must rankle Darcy to know that Miss Elizabeth cared for me first, and it was so easy to manipulate her dislike of you. It was apparent from our first meeting in Meryton that you were attracted to her. It would have been a total triumph if I could have seduced her. Though, I must admit, she was far more captivating than any other woman I have ever met."

"Miss Elizabeth has nothing to do with why we are here, Wickham. You will cease to mention her name." Darcy's terse words were no deterrent, but when he saw the look in Darcy's eyes, Wickham restrained himself from speaking about her further. "Though no woman deserves to be so ill-used, why did you feel it necessary to choose a gentleman's daughter for your little adventure?"

"She may be a gentleman's daughter, but she is no lady. Lydia is a little tease. She flirts with every man in sight and is not above sharing her kisses with many of them. Being denied her charms was no great hardship, as there is always someone I can charm into my bed. However, she had better change her ways or she will find herself with someone less considerate than I am."

"How dare you, sir!"

Elizabeth worried at the anger she heard in her uncle's voice.

Darcy gave the man a stern look and spoke quickly. "Did you have any intention of marrying her?" he asked in a disinterested tone.

"Of course not! She is an annoying creature with no fortune, though I might consider it if you plan to make it worth my while, Darcy."

"I think we should find out if Miss Lydia wishes such a worthless cad for a husband. Just to be clear, are you saying you will not marry her without being paid to do so, in spite of the promises you made her?"

"I will not be tied to the likes of Lydia Bennet without significant compensation. I would not take less than fifteen thousand pounds. That is a bargain, Darcy. It is only half of what I would have received if I had succeeded in my attempted elopement with Geor—"

"You will not speak her name," growled Colonel Fitzwilliam as he sprang from his chair to tower over Wickham, his hand again resting on the hilt of his sword.

Darcy fought hard to not react to Wickham' reference to his sister. When he felt in control of himself, he said, "If her family is forced to pay for someone to wed her, I am sure they could find someone much better suited than you, and for far less."

"No one in their right mind would marry the little flirt. Lydia cannot stop talking about the most inane nonsense. I can barely stand to be in the room with her for more than five minutes. Why do you think I am intoxicated in the middle of the day?"

At that, the door to the room flew wide open, crashing against the wall. The men all turned to stare.

Elizabeth and Lydia waited in the hallway just outside the private room. With the door left slightly ajar, they could hear the conversation among the gentlemen. Elizabeth put a finger to her lips, indicating they should listen quietly. She kept her eyes on Lydia's face as they heard Mr. Gardiner ask, "Well, gentlemen, how go the negotiations?"

Lydia started at the word. *What are they negotiating?* she wondered. Lydia missed the next few comments as she wondered about the negotiations. Then she heard Mr. Darcy ask why Wickham had chosen her. Her face went white at Wickham's reply.

At the mention of Elizabeth's name, Lydia saw her sister's face flush at his words. Lydia could not help but wonder if Wickham had cared more for Elizabeth than for her.

On the heel of these disturbing thoughts, Lydia heard what Wickham truly thought of her. Her face again went white at the disparaging things he said about her. Her embarrassment quickly turned to anger. Before Elizabeth could stop her, Lydia's arm shot out and pushed the door farther open.

---

Wickham's eyes widened in surprise and dismay. If Lydia had heard his words, his chance of gaining funds from Darcy to marry her would no longer exist. Recovering quickly, Wickham stood, saying, "Lydia, my dear, I believe we shall be able to marry soon, as Darcy has decided to provide what he has so long denied me." He gave her his usual charming smile as he advanced to greet her.

Wickham reached for her hand, but she jerked it back, raising it instead. She swung it with all her might, smacking Wickham across his cheek. He staggered back with the force of the impact.

## A Matter of Timing

"I hate you!" she cried as she advanced on him with her fists raised. The young girl beat upon his chest and attempted to scratch his face with her nails.

Mr. Gardiner and Richard pulled the girl away and Wickham collapsed in a chair. He lifted his hand to his cheek, where blood appeared. Lydia's uncle enfolded the girl in his arms as her tears fell.

"Well, Wickham," said Darcy with evident amusement, "it would appear your charms have failed you in this instance." Darcy turned to the girl. "Miss Lydia," he asked in a soft voice, "do you still wish to marry Mr. Wickham?"

"No! I hate him and never want to see him again!" The words came out a bit muffled, as she had pressed her face into her uncle's chest as she cried.

Darcy turned to Wickham. "It would seem you now find yourself in an awkward situation. I hold all your debts; if I were to call them in, could you pay them?"

"You know I could not," came Wickham's disgruntled reply.

"Then I could have you thrown in debtor's prison."

Wickham's face paled at the words.

"However, the military's claim on you may supersede my wishes."

"What are you talking about, Darcy?"

It was Colonel Fitzwilliam who answered. "You are away from your post without permission during a time of war, Wickham."

Wickham looked at the colonel without understanding.

"The army can flog you for this, or send you to the front to face the French. Though, coward that you are, you would probably desert again. However, it is more likely that they will hang you when they consider the way you have mistreated a gentleman's daughter."

Wickham's face drained of all color. Falling to his knees, he began begging and stammering. "D-D-Darcy, you must protect me. We were childhood friends—almost brothers. Your father loved me; he would not wish harm to come to me."

Darcy looked down at the man kneeling before him. "You will not play on my sensibilities by speaking of my father. You know very well if he had seen the real you, he would have washed his hands of you long ago, and you would have received nothing in his will. Father gave you an education that you did not value. I gave you a small fortune that you squandered on drink, cards, and women. You have wasted every advantage given you. I will not waste any more time or money on you." Darcy turned his back on the man. Elizabeth moved to his side and slipped her arm through his, giving it a comforting and supportive squeeze.

Wickham looked around. Mr. Gardiner still held Lydia as she sobbed. Elizabeth spoke softly to Darcy, who seemed to have forgotten his presence. Wickham knew he would receive no sympathy from anyone in the room. He looked towards the door and wondered if he could make it to the busy streets, where he could disappear. The thought had no sooner crossed his mind than the Colonel moved in front of the room's only exit.

"Do not even attempt it," came the deep, menacing voice of the colonel. "Mr. Gardiner, would you step into the taproom and summon the soldiers."

"Soldiers, no—no soldiers," Wickham cried. "I would rather go to debtor's prison."

"You signed commitment papers with the militia, Wickham. Essentially, you belong to them until your time of service is up."

"But they will hang me!" he cried, terror evident on his face.

"Perhaps you should have thought of that before you ran away from your post," said the colonel in a voice full of contempt.

Mr. Gardiner settled Lydia in a chair in the corner before exiting the room. Elizabeth knew she should comfort her sister, but she was still too angry with her to do so. Instead, she remained with her betrothed, speaking quietly, though Darcy shifted the two of them to conceal Lydia from view.

Within minutes, the door opened again, and Colonel Forster and several of the largest soldiers from his unit entered the room. Seeing Wickham cowering on the floor, the soldiers looked at him with disgust.

"My thanks, Mr. Darcy, for tracking down this miscreant." Repressed anger was evident in Colonel Forster's voice. "He shall be placed in irons and returned to Brighton. His court martial shall occur within the week."

"Colonel Forster, did you bring the list of Wickham's debts from Brighton?"

"I have it here, Mr. Darcy," said the officer as he removed a sheaf of papers from his jacket.

"Thank you, sir," said Darcy as he accepted the papers. "I will ensure these are repaid. Colonel, I do not know if there is anything you could do, but many of those present would not be comfortable causing another man's death."

"I will relay your comments to those at the court martial, but Wickham's misdeeds are many, and I cannot guarantee the outcome."

"We understand, Colonel Forster. I ask that you write to me at Netherfield, Mr. Bingley's estate near Meryton, with the results of the trial."

"Certainly, Mr. Darcy," the colonel said. He then turned to Wickham. "Stand up, Wickham," he ordered.

Wickham was slow to rise, so two of the soldiers yanked him to his feet. A third soldier grabbed Wickham's arms, while another clapped the irons on him. With a soldier holding each arm and the other two walking ahead of and behind him, Wickham left the room.

Elizabeth did not miss the sigh of relief that escaped William. "It is over," he murmured.

She squeezed his arm again and whispered, "Remember the past only as it gives you pleasure."

He gazed down into her softly smiling face. "Let us forget the past for a time and look forward to our future. I love you, Elizabeth."

"I love you too, my William. Shall we go home?"

"I am home, so long as I am with you."

Darcy's words touched her like a caress as he offered his arm to Elizabeth. Mr. Gardiner assisted a very subdued Lydia, and Colonel Fitzwilliam followed as they exited the inn and boarded the still-waiting hack.

The return trip to the Gardiners' passed in silence. The carriage had barely come to a stop when Mrs. Gardiner appeared in the open front door. Mr. Gardiner stepped down and handed out Lydia, who ran up the stairs and threw herself into her aunt's arms. Mr. Gardiner mounted the stairs and shared a look with his wife over his niece's head.

"Come, Lydia, let us get you settled," said Mrs. Gardiner gently as she led the girl up the stairs. By the time she returned to the sitting room, the others were all settled and a tea tray had arrived. Mrs. Gardiner sat down and poured tea for everyone as they related the events at the inn.

"She heard everything he said about her?" asked Mrs. Gardiner. "That would explain her subdued manner. Well, let us hope it will bring about a positive change in her behavior. There is one thing that surprised me though, Mr. Darcy. How did you know Colonel Forster would be there?"

"In my express to the man, I suggested he meet us in London, bringing Lydia's belongings and some assistance," Darcy humbly remarked. "The gentlemen all rode on horseback, with the recovering Lydia in the carriage. The colonel dropped the men at the city barracks, explaining he would escort Miss Lydia to her uncle's."

Elizabeth shook her head and gave a small chuckle. "You truly do think of everything, Mr. Darcy."

## A Matter of Timing

"I try, Miss Elizabeth," he replied with a grin. "We were all lucky the way things turned out. No one in Brighton is aware Miss Lydia was gone before 'returning' to her family with the colonel yesterday. As long as they managed to contain the information within the walls of Longbourn, no one will ever know of her indiscretion."

"Yes, I shall be sending an express to Longbourn later today to let them know of Lydia's recovery. I shall be sure to tell them to speak only of her having been ill and out of company for some time," remarked Mr. Gardiner.

"That sounds perfect, sir. Please be sure to notify them that Colonel Forster has returned her to you and that I will convey the young ladies to Longbourn in a few days' time."

"Mr. Darcy, Colonel," said Mrs. Gardiner, "we would be happy to have you remain to dine with us."

"Our thanks, Mrs. Gardiner, but I know that Georgiana is waiting for word on the outcome. She has been quite concerned for Miss Lydia. Perhaps you all would join us tomorrow evening for dinner at Darcy House. Perhaps also tomorrow we can determine which day would be best to return to Longbourn. I do not wish to wait too long, as I must speak with Mr. Bennet on an important matter." Darcy's smile showed his dimples as he looked at his beloved Elizabeth. They made plans for the next day and the gentlemen departed.

Elizabeth sat down to write to Jane. She wanted to let her know that Lydia had been found and was now in residence at the Gardiners' home. She also asked for further information about her father's accident and illness.

# A LONDON INTERLUDE

Preparing for dinner at Darcy House, Elizabeth donned her finest gown, a sea-green silk. Mrs. Gardiner sent her maid to assist Elizabeth with her hair. The maid piled it high, creating a mass of curls at the crown of her head, with several ringlets left to fall over one shoulder. Tucked among the curls were white rosebuds. A single pearl on a chain drew the eye to Elizabeth's décolletage, and small pearl drops dangled from her delicate lobes. A white shawl woven with silver and gold threads completed her outfit.

"You look very lovely tonight, my dear," said Mr. Gardiner as she entered the sitting room where her relatives waited. Lydia was not present, as they felt it necessary to continue with the subterfuge regarding her ill health. She had been unusually silent since her recovery. Elizabeth frequently heard crying coming from her sister's room. She had tried to speak to her earlier in the day, but Lydia was not yet ready to talk. Elizabeth promised herself she would try again after they returned from Darcy House.

As the carriage drove through the London streets, Elizabeth quietly watched the changing neighborhoods. In spite of its nearness to the business district, the homes in the Gracechurch Street area of Cheapside were surprisingly spacious, with pleasant yards at the rear of each property. As they approached Darcy House in Mayfair, the houses became significantly different. Here the homes were much larger, many of them quite ornate. Darcy House was on Park Lane, overlooking Hyde Park. Elizabeth was delighted with the thought that such a beautiful location would be her future home.

The townhouse before which the carriage stopped was one of the largest on the street, though somewhat modest in appearance, for it lacked the ostentation of many of the nearby mansions. The front of the house contained several windows on each floor, and many of them glowed brightly from the light of the candles within. Mr. Gardiner stepped down and reached in to hand out his wife. Before Mrs. Gardiner's feet had touched the sidewalk, the door of Darcy House opened and their host was moving down the stairs. Mr. and Mrs. Gardiner moved aside and Mr. Darcy reached into the carriage to hand out Miss Elizabeth. Placing Elizabeth's hand on his arm, he welcomed his guests before he and Elizabeth led the others into the house and up the stairs to the drawing room, where Georgiana waited.

"Lizzy!" Georgiana cried as her friend entered the room on Fitzwilliam's arm. "I am so glad to see you again. I am particularly pleased to offer my congratulations on your engagement. I am so delighted you will be my sister!"

"Thank you very much, Georgiana. I am happy to gain another sister, especially one as sweet as you."

As the guests moved fully into the room, Elizabeth saw that Colonel Fitzwilliam was also present. While the Gardiners continued in discussion with Miss Darcy, Elizabeth moved across the room to greet the colonel.

"Good evening, Miss Elizabeth. How lovely to see you!"

## A Matter of Timing

"Good evening, Colonel Fitzwilliam. Please allow me to thank you again for your assistance in recovering my sister."

"I was delighted to be included in the drama, especially as it allowed us to find a permanent resolution to an unending problem." A satisfied grin accompanied the colonel's words.

"I just hope the end will come quickly, without Wickham having much opportunity to speak." Worry was evident in Elizabeth's tone.

Darcy wrapped Elizabeth's arm around his and covered the hand resting there. "All will be well, Elizabeth."

"Indeed, Miss Elizabeth, because he deserted in time of war, nothing but his desertion and debts will be raised at the trial."

"That is good to know, but I am afraid that will not stop Wickham from attempting to gain his revenge."

"It is likely they will ask him only whether he had permission from his commanding officer to leave Brighton."

"Let us hope that is the case," replied Elizabeth. "Let us pray his smooth tongue remains still."

At that moment, the butler, Simmons, entered and announced dinner. Darcy, with Elizabeth still on his arm, led the others to the dining room. He seated Elizabeth on his right and Mrs. Gardiner on his left. Georgiana sat opposite Darcy, and Mr. Gardiner and Richard flanked her. With such congenial company, pleasant conversation flowed throughout the several courses of the meal. There was a brief separation of the sexes following supper.

"Mr. Darcy, I must congratulate you on your incredible forethought and planning in arranging the recovery of Lydia. Your attention to detail and ability to organize and carry out a plan that protected Lydia's reputation was a remarkable sight. Our family will be eternally grateful."

"It is my family as well, Mr. Gardiner, since Elizabeth has accepted my proposal of marriage."

"Mrs. Gardiner and I are delighted to welcome you to the family. I feel sure that you and Elizabeth will be very happy together."

"I know we will, sir."

They talked a bit longer before rejoining the ladies.

Meanwhile, in the music room, Georgiana spoke to her soon-to-be-sister. "Lizzy, when must you return to Longbourn?"

"As we are pretending that Lydia is ill, I imagine we must wait a few days before we travel."

"I was wondering if you would like to accompany me to my dressmaker tomorrow. I thought perhaps I could assist you in picking out your wedding gown or some items for your trousseau."

"I would enjoy shopping with you, Georgiana, but as we have not yet received my father's permission, I do not know if that would be appropriate."

"Lizzy," began Mrs. Gardiner, "I believe it would be acceptable to start this process. Have you given any thought to how soon you wish to marry?"

"Due to unexpected circumstances, Mr. Darcy and I have not had an opportunity to discuss the matter. I would hope to marry in a few weeks—perhaps as soon as the banns can be called."

"I would agree with that wholeheartedly," said Mr. Darcy, who entered the room in time to hear Elizabeth's words. I am even willing to obtain a special license. We need not wait for the reading of the banns."

"Mama will most likely be unhappy with only three weeks to plan. She will certainly desire an extravagant wedding and wedding breakfast since you are a man worth ten thousand a year. However, I am hopeful we can convince her that we do not wish to delay."

"Shall we set a definite date, Miss Elizabeth?"

## A Matter of Timing

"I would be very happy to do so, Mr. Darcy. Aunt, Uncle, do you think we will be able to travel by Wednesday?"

Mr. Gardiner thought for a moment. "I do not see why not. Are you available to travel to Meryton that day, Mr. Darcy?"

"I will make myself available whenever necessary. Georgiana, do you wish to accompany me or would you prefer to wait until we set a wedding date?"

"I would be delighted to travel with you, William. Do you think Mr. Bingley will be able to host us at Netherfield?"

"An express can be sent in the morning letting him know we will arrive on Wednesday. Now, did I hear mention of some shopping tomorrow?"

"Georgiana offered to introduce me to her modiste and perhaps begin shopping for my wedding gown and trousseau. I was hesitant because we have not received my father's approval of our engagement."

"Are you concerned about obtaining your father's permission?" A frown creased Darcy's forehead.

"No, but he is not yet aware of my changed feelings for you. He is aware only of the dislike I held for you last autumn," was Elizabeth's sheepish reply.

Though he smiled confidently at Elizabeth, Darcy wondered if Mr. Bennet would give his approval of the betrothal. Consequently, he asked, "Miss Elizabeth, when is your birthday?"

"My birthday is September third, Mr. Darcy."

"Then I believe September sixth would be an excellent date for a wedding. Does that meet with your approval, Miss Elizabeth?"

"That sounds like a perfect day, Mr. Darcy."

Darcy's smile showed his pleasure, for now nothing could stand in the way of their wedding.

"With the wedding so soon, shall we shop tomorrow?" Georgiana asked again.

Elizabeth looked at her aunt, who nodded her agreement.

"Yes, we shall," Elizabeth replied with a smile.

Both Elizabeth and Georgiana entertained the group on the pianoforte. Then they made arrangements for Georgiana to pick up the ladies at ten o'clock in the morning for their shopping adventure. With many expressions of thanks and a discussion about an outing to the theater three days hence, the evening broke up.

---

The next morning, the Darcy carriage arrived promptly and the ladies were off to Bond Street. The carriage pulled up in front of a shop with several gowns in the window. The sign above the door read "Madame LaRue, Modiste". A footman let down the steps and assisted the ladies from the carriage. A bell above the door tinkled as they entered the shop.

The proprietress glanced up to discover who her first client of the day would be. She offered a welcome in a heavily accented voice. "Bonjour, Mademoiselle Darcy. 'ow lovely to see you today. Did we 'ave an appointment?"

"Good morning, Madame LaRue. We did not, but I wished to introduce you to a dear friend who is looking for a wedding gown and some other items for her trousseau." Georgiana extended her arm in the direction of the other ladies. "Miss Elizabeth, Mrs. Gardiner, this is Madame LaRue. Madame, this is my friend, Miss Elizabeth Bennet, and her aunt, Mrs. Gardiner."

"I am 'appy to meet any friends of Mademoiselle Darcy. How can I 'elp you ladies?"

"My niece will be marrying in just over a month. We would like to have you make her wedding gown, and at least three other dresses. More will be needed, but we realize with short notice that they may have to wait."

"Please follow me, ladies, to a room where we can measure Miss Bennet."

Madame LaRue nodded in the direction of a group of workers as she led the trio into the largest of her private rooms. Two assistants immediately appeared to help with the measurements. A short time later, a third carried in a tea tray. As the assistants measured Elizabeth, Madame LaRue asked, "'Oo is your betrothed, Miss Bennet?"

Elizabeth glanced in the mirror and looked at her aunt and Georgiana. "He is a member of the ton, but I am afraid I cannot say who at this time because he has not yet had a chance to obtain my father's permission. Once it is received, we plan to arrange for the banns to be called and to marry shortly after their completion."

Madame looked speculatively between Miss Bennet and Miss Darcy but said nothing further.

When the assistants had finished measuring Elizabeth, another appeared with a book of patterns and several ladies' magazines. They spent an hour looking through the patterns and discussing which would best suit Elizabeth. Once they had decided on the dresses, three stock boys entered the room carrying bolts of fabric.

Elizabeth looked at all the material and at the patterns she had chosen. "This ivory silk is so beautiful. I would like to have the wedding gown made from it."

"I think this amber silk with the thin green stripes would be lovely with your coloring, Lizzy," added Georgiana.

"What is your opinion, Aunt?"

"I agree with both selections. What about the day dresses, Lizzy?"

Elizabeth selected a royal blue sprigged muslin and arranged to have small yellow and white flowers embroidered on it and a dark purple wool for the day dresses.

Madame LaRue called for an assistant to bring a selection of trims from which Elizabeth could choose adornments for her dresses. After Elizabeth had made all her choices, the modiste cut a sample of each fabric for the ladies to take with them so they could purchase the necessary accessories. While arranging to have the gowns sent to Gracechurch Street, Mrs. Gardiner ordered several sets of silk undergarments to accompany Elizabeth's new gowns.

Upon leaving the dress shop, the ladies stopped at a tea shop located in the next block. Over tea and scones, they discussed the other shops they would need to visit before returning home.

"Do you mean that after two hours with the modiste, there is still more shopping to be done?" said Elizabeth in mock distress.

"I know how you dislike shopping, Elizabeth. We will try to make it as painless as possible," replied her aunt with a smile.

"Fear not, Aunt, I am enjoying this shopping expedition far more than I usually do. I believe it was the bickering of my youngest sisters over who got which fabric or my attempts to prevent Mama from drowning my gowns in lace that caused my previous aversion to the activity. With congenial company and excellent suggestions, not to mention the attention we received from the modiste and her staff, I find that under such circumstances, I could enjoy shopping more often than in the past. It has also been rather pleasant making these choices as I imagine Mr. Darcy's reaction to seeing them." All three of the ladies laughed softly at Elizabeth's words.

"I can assure you that William will admire your choices, but I imagine he would find you lovely even if you were wearing sackcloth," said Georgiana with a smile, causing the others to laugh again.

They left the shop in high good humor and headed for a store that specialized in accessories. Georgiana purchased a shawl for Elizabeth as well as several sets of adorned hairpins. As an additional gift for her niece, Mrs. Gardiner bought Elizabeth a lovely beaded reticule and fan to accompany her evening gown. The next stop was the cobbler and boot maker, where Elizabeth ordered two pairs of slippers for her wedding dress and evening gown, as well as a pair of kid boots for her day dresses.

As they entered the Gardiner residence, they could hear the deep sound of male laughter coming from the vicinity of Mr. Gardiner's study. Mrs. Gardiner moved down the hallway to the door of her husband's office. "How nice to find you home early, Edward. Mr. Darcy, this is a pleasant surprise. Can you join us for dinner this evening?"

"We would be delighted to stay, Mrs. Gardiner. How was your day of shopping?"

"It was a success, but I will let Lizzy tell you about it. Would you gentlemen care to join us in the parlor? I shall order tea."

Darcy was on his feet in an instant, causing Mr. Gardiner to laugh as he replied, "We would be delighted to join you, my dear."

Darcy excused himself and stepped past Mrs. Gardiner, then hurried down the hall. Mr. and Mrs. Gardiner exchanged a smile. Mrs. Gardiner remained by the door, waiting for her husband. As he joined her, they shared a quick kiss before walking arm in arm to the sitting room.

After a conversation about the shopping excursion, the group discussed the trip to the theater on Monday evening. On Tuesday, Elizabeth would walk in Hyde Park with Darcy and Georgiana. Then, on Wednesday, they would return to Longbourn.

---

On the morning of the theater outing, Elizabeth again attempted to speak with Lydia. However, as she had previously done, Lydia turned her sister away, saying she was not ready to talk with anyone.

Discouraged, Elizabeth strode to the parlor to speak to her aunt.

"I am concerned for Lydia, Aunt Helen. She is still refusing to speak to me about what happened. I do not know if she is embarrassed or heartbroken. Surely, she must be very confused about the way in which things ended with Wickham. Has she by any chance spoken with you?"

"I understand your concern, Lizzy. I have tried talking with her as well, but the only things I could get out of her were a request for a copy of Fordyce's *Sermons* and a book about proper behavior for young women."

Elizabeth's face showed her surprise. "Well, I will leave her be for one more day, but I will insist she speak to me before we return home on Wednesday."

"I will join you in your endeavor," said Mrs. Gardiner.

Later that morning, a letter arrived from Jane.

*Dear Lizzy,*

*I am relieved to know that Lydia is recovered and safe. I have informed the family of this news. First, Mama was prostrate with relief, but a short time later wished to share the good news with all the neighbors. I was forced to remind her that no one knew of her situation and that it must remain so to protect the reputation of all her daughters as well as the family.*

*As to Father's illness. He had been out riding the estate on the morning before Colonel Forster's arrival when a sudden storm broke. Apparently, the lightning and thunder spooked his horse, and he was thrown. We assumed he had taken shelter with a tenant, but we discovered this was not the case when his horse returned riderless.*

*Due to the weather, we could not make an immediate search for him. It was late afternoon before he was found and brought to the house. Papa was soaking wet and seemed a bit disoriented. A thorough examination did not find any bumps or broken bones, so Mr. Jones assumed Papa would be well when he got over his cold.*

*Papa quickly developed a fever and was delirious for more than a day. Once his fever broke, he seemed much improved, though a bit weak. His usual sense of humor appears lacking, but I can only assume it is caused by his general ill health or from a headache.*

*I look forward to your return, dear sister.*

*Love,*

*Jane*

---

After arranging the theater outing, Mrs. Gardiner had taken Elizabeth to her modiste to obtain a new dress. In her window, the seamstress had a lovely blossom-colored silk gown with a cream-colored lace trim. Another customer had ordered the dress but decided she did not like the finished gown.

Fortunately, only a few alterations were necessary to make the dress fit Elizabeth.

Descending the stairs, Elizabeth could hear Darcy's deep voice. She entered the sitting room, noting that Georgiana and the colonel were also present.

The gentlemen stood at her entrance.

"Oh, Lizzy, what a lovely dress," cried Georgiana.

"Indeed, you are a vision, Miss Elizabeth," added the colonel.

Darcy stepped forward and took her hand, bowing over it as he kissed the back. "You look very beautiful tonight, Elizabeth." His eyes spoke far more than the few words he said.

Mr. and Mrs. Gardiner were thrilled. Darcy was the perfect match for their niece. They looked forward to watching the couple throughout the years as they faced parenthood and life's challenges. "I believe we should depart," said Mr. Gardiner, "or we shall miss the opening act."

Darcy's largest carriage was quite comfortable for the six of them. The ride to the theater passed quickly, with interesting conversation.

The crowds at the theater were light, as many of the ton were still at their country estates and would not return for another month or two. Darcy stepped down and handed Elizabeth out of the carriage, tucking her hand into the crook of his arm. Mr. Gardiner followed, assisting his wife. Finally, the colonel exited to assist Georgiana. The couples followed as Darcy led the way into the building and up the stairs to his box. Though they received many surprised looks, no one had the opportunity to speak with the new arrivals. Many wondered about the fashionable young lady on the arm of London's most eligible bachelor. Speculating glances followed the fashionable older couple who trailed in Darcy's wake. By the time they reached the Darcy box, word had spread throughout the theater about Darcy's presence with an unknown beauty.

## A Matter of Timing

The performance that evening was a production of Shakespeare's *Much Ado About Nothing*. Elizabeth was delighted at the opportunity to see one of her favorite plays performed on the stage. Soon the lights dimmed, and Darcy hesitantly reached out and grasped Elizabeth's hand, entwining their fingers. The first act seemed to end much too quickly. Darcy released Elizabeth's hand just as the lights returned.

"Would anyone care to walk during intermission or may I fetch refreshments for you?" Darcy asked.

"I believe I would prefer to stay here for the present," said Mrs. Gardiner.

"As would I," seconded Georgiana.

Elizabeth, who had been glancing about the theater since the lights came back on, agreed with the other ladies. "I, too, would wish to remain for the present."

Georgiana spoke with Mrs. Gardiner, while Mr. Gardiner and the colonel began a discussion on the progress of the war. With everyone else thus occupied, Darcy and Elizabeth had a moment of relative privacy. "William, there seems to be a great deal of interest in your box. Is it always like this when you are in public?"

"It is as I have said before. I am often the target of unwanted interest. However, tonight I think the beautiful woman at my side is the cause of the interest," said Darcy as he lifted Elizabeth's hand to his mouth and placed a lingering kiss on the back of it. A loud murmur ran around the crowded theater as the audience members observed Darcy's action.

A short time later, the lights dimmed again and the second act was underway. As soon as it was dark, not waiting for William to initiate the contact, Elizabeth moved her hand towards Darcy's, and again their fingers entwined. Darcy was quite pleased with the fact that Elizabeth did not hesitate to return her hand to his. He also enjoyed watching her excitement at the play unfolding before her.

When the second intermission occurred, Elizabeth and the three gentlemen decided to leave the box and seek out refreshments. They had barely left the box before a couple who could claim only a slight acquaintance with Darcy accosted the group. They sought an introduction (or, as Elizabeth whispered, gossip). Darcy made the introductions but deflected most of the intrusive questions, giving only a minimal amount of information.

The group was barely able to take a few steps before being stopped again. Mr. Gardiner excused himself to retrieve glasses of lemonade for the ladies still in the Darcy box. Richard remained at Darcy's side to help him deal with the inquisitive society members who made claims on his time and attention.

After several minutes, Richard Fitzwilliam could tell that Darcy's patience was wearing thin. Stepping in to end the current conversation, Richard said, "Please excuse us, Lady Symington. If we do not retrieve our refreshments, we will miss the beginning of the final act."

Darcy nodded to the woman as Richard spoke, then began moving away with Elizabeth. He retrieved three glasses of wine and handed one to Richard as the colonel rejoined them.

"Thank you for securing our release, Richard. If the interruptions had continued, I am afraid I might have said something I would later regret."

"I am well aware of that, cousin," said the colonel with a grin. "I suggest we make for our box quickly before the hordes again descend upon you."

"You are showing unusual wisdom, dear cousin." So saying, Darcy led Elizabeth back to their box. He kept his eyes straight ahead and pretended not to hear those who called out to him. Elizabeth restrained the smile that she felt threatened to break out across her face. Having observed Darcy this evening, she now understood his behavior at the Meryton assembly. No one would enjoy the constant barrage of attention that Darcy had endured this evening. Elizabeth smiled to hear Darcy release a relieved sigh when they finally gained the privacy of his box.

---

Elizabeth slept late the morning after the theater. After breaking her fast with her aunt, the two of them ascended the stairs to Lydia's room. After knocking on the door, they waited, but no answer came. Mrs. Gardiner tried again. "Lydia, you must let us in. We need to talk before you return home tomorrow."

At first, no sound came from within the room, and Lizzy became concerned. Just as she raised her hand to knock again, the key turned in the lock. The door opened slightly. Mrs. Gardiner pushed it open farther to see a despondent Lydia returning to a chair near the window. It was the fifth day since Lydia's recovery. Dark circles rimmed her eyes, which no longer held a spark for life in them, and her face appeared thinner.

Elizabeth's heart broke at the sight of her youngest sister. "Oh, Lydia! Oh, my poor dear sister. You should have let us in sooner. Are you well? Have you been eating and sleeping?"

"I am well enough, Lizzy, do not fuss. I do not deserve your concern."

"I cannot help my concern; you are my baby sister."

"I am sorry I did not listen to you and Jane, Lizzy. You tried to tell me about proper behavior, but I ignored you because your words disagreed with Mama's. How could Mama have been so wrong? Why would she tell me to behave in a manner that would make men think I was loose?"

"Mama is concerned for her future and the future of her daughters if they are unmarried. She did not come from the same society she entered; perhaps she is telling you the same thing her mother told her."

"Papa is a gentleman. Would he not have realized her teachings were incorrect?"

"You know how fond Papa is of his library, and he rarely accompanies us to events. Perhaps he was not aware of what was occurring." Elizabeth offered this to soothe her sister, knowing their father preferred to laugh at the behavior of his youngest daughters rather than correct them.

"But you and Jane behave better. Neither of you followed her instructions for attracting a man."

"From a younger age, Jane and I were fortunate enough to have the example of Aunt Gardiner. Though her father was in trade, her mother was the daughter of a gentleman and was raised to be a gentlewoman, as was Aunt."

"He said I was no lady, but a flirt and a tease. He said I was stupid and annoying. I did all the things Mama told me to do to catch a husband, but he did not truly want me. I do not know what to think or what I should do differently next time."

Thus far, Mrs. Gardiner had remained quiet. "What of the things you read, Lydia? Did you learn anything from your reading?"

"Yes. Much of the information agrees with the things Mary says and with the behavior I have observed in Jane and Lizzy."

"What do you think you should do?" asked Mrs. Gardiner.

Lydia hesitated. The things her mother permitted her to do made life fun and exciting. Then she remembered Wickham's words. They had not been pleasant to hear. "I must behave more like Elizabeth and Jane." She turned to her sister. "Would you please help me?"

"Of course I would, Lydia," said Elizabeth as she embraced her young sister. Lydia felt like crying, but she had no more tears left. "Would you like to come with me today to walk in Hyde Park with the Darcys? I think you could use some fresh air and sunshine to help your outlook."

Lydia gave her sister a gentle smile, but she seemed hesitant. Looking at the ground, she quietly asked, "Are you sure they would not mind? Mr. Darcy must think poorly of me."

"Not at all. Mr. Darcy feels guilty that he did not make our neighbors in Meryton aware of Wickham's less-than-honorable behavior before he caused the trouble he did and made off with you."

"But no one liked Mr. Darcy before. They would never have believed him." Lydia had the grace to blush at her less-than-kind remarks, remembering how she had felt upon hearing Wickham's hurtful words.

"Yes, Mr. Darcy's shyness made him appear aloof and unfriendly. And though Wickham spoke so politely and charmingly to everyone, everything he said was a lie."

"Are you really engaged to Mr. Darcy?"

"I am, except for obtaining Papa's approval. Mr. Darcy will return us to Longbourn tomorrow and then speak to Papa."

"He must care for you a great deal to go out of his way to help me," said Lydia.

"Mr. Darcy and I have not had the smoothest of relationships, but we have come to care for each other very much."

"I am happy for you, Lizzy."

"Thank you, Lydia. I am very happy as well!" The two sisters laughed and hugged one last time. Lydia set about to improve her appearance and prepare for their outing.

Elizabeth and Aunt Gardiner descended the stairs to await Lydia. "She will be well, Lizzy. Do not worry. I believe this experience has been good for her. And as Kitty follows Lydia's behaviors, this should also bring about a change in her. If you can lighten Mary's somberness, there will be hope for her, too!"

A short time later, the Darcy carriage arrived. It took the girls to Darcy House, where they met the Darcys before beginning their walk in Hyde Park. Lydia and Georgiana walked ahead of Darcy and Elizabeth. Georgiana's natural shyness and Lydia's recent embarrassment made their conversation stilted. Instead of looking about with her usual eagerness, Lydia kept her head down, making eye contact with Miss Darcy only when directly addressed.

Elizabeth shook her head in resignation as a small sigh escaped.

"Are you well Elizabeth?"

"I am fine, William. I always wished to see Lydia behave with more decorum, but I do not like to see her joy for life extinguished."

"How is Miss Lydia feeling?"

"I was anxious about her," said Elizabeth, "but after our discussion earlier today, I hope she will be well. Aunt says she will be better than ever with her new understanding of proper behavior." Elizabeth related to William the conversation she had with her youngest sister.

"I am sure she will regain her joy, but perhaps her new understanding will temper it," offered Darcy reassuringly.

"That is what Aunt said as well. She also pointed out that because Kitty follows Lydia in everything, another of my sisters should soon be behaving more appropriately." A small smile accompanied her words. Darcy patted her hand comfortingly.

After a very pleasant afternoon in the park, the Darcys remained for one last dinner with the Gardiners. The siblings had become very fond of the Gardiner family. Before departing for the evening, they made arrangements for the return to Longbourn the next day. Mr. Gardiner would join them in his carriage so he could bring his children back to town.

# A SURPRISING HOMECOMING

THE NEXT MORNING, AT PRECISELY nine, the Darcy carriage pulled up to the curb behind another carriage already parked before the Gardiners' home in Cheapside. The butler welcomed Darcy and Georgiana and ushered the guests into the parlor. After exchanging quick greetings with the newcomers, Elizabeth and Lydia departed to gather their bonnets and reticules.

While waiting for them to return, Darcy said, "Mr. and Mrs. Gardiner, I must thank you so much for bringing Elizabeth to Pemberley. You gave me an opportunity I did not think I would ever have. The chance to meet again and to apologize and make amends for my poor behavior allowed us to begin anew. I was fortunate to receive Elizabeth's forgiveness and to discover that she had learned that some of her concerns about me stemmed from misinformation and misunderstandings. I will be forever grateful to you both. Your actions have given me a future brighter than I could have imagined. Please know that you are welcome to visit us at Pemberley whenever possible. We will also look forward to visiting with you whenever we are in London."

"There is no need to thank us, Mr. Darcy. We enjoyed visiting your lovely estate and the kind hospitality you extended to us. Mr. Gardiner and I are delighted for the both of you. You are well-matched, and we wish you both a long and happy life together," came Mrs. Gardiner's earnest reply.

"Whom are you wishing such joy, dear aunt?" came Elizabeth's teasing voice.

"Why, my favorite niece and the exceptional gentleman she will be marrying."

After hugging Mrs. Gardiner and thanking her for all she had done for them, Darcy led Elizabeth, Georgiana, and Lydia to his coach and assisted them into the vehicle. Mr. Gardiner stepped into his carriage. Then the two carriages began their journey to Hertfordshire.

---

The carriage reached the main road out of London. Darcy and Elizabeth sat next to each other and across from Georgiana, Lydia, and Mrs. Annesley. A quiet conversation was ongoing between the younger girls, while Georgiana's companion watched the changing scenery through which they passed.

Leaning quietly towards his betrothed, Darcy said, "How do you think your parents will respond to our desire to marry so soon?"

Elizabeth thought for a moment before replying. "I cannot imagine Papa denying me anything that would truly make me happy."

"As he claims you are his favorite, I, too, would hope he had no objections, but what if he does? I did not make a very good impression upon the residents of Meryton when I visited last fall. If your father has heard of my unkind words about you at the assembly, he may not be inclined to grant me permission to marry you. Have you ever spoken of my first proposal?"

## A Matter of Timing

"Only Jane is aware of that misstep, so we must hope for the best. However, as I will be of age very soon, we will keep to our plans. If my father refuses us his permission, you will arrive at Longbourn on my birthday, and I will be prepared to leave with you. We can either marry from Netherfield if Mr. Bingley will allow it or go on to town and marry from Darcy House."

A relieved expression appeared on Darcy's face at Elizabeth's words. "From which home would you prefer to marry? If your father says no, I will make all the necessary arrangements so that we can marry on September sixth."

Again, Elizabeth paused to think before answering. "It might be easier to marry from Netherfield, as my mother and sisters would then be able to attend. However, it might be better to marry from London so that my father's absence would not cause gossip. If we are not in Meryton, we can claim he is in ill health and could not attend, but that he did not wish to delay the wedding."

"You make excellent points for both locations, my dear Elizabeth. Unfortunately, it does not answer my question," said Darcy with a small chuckle.

Their conversation moved on to plans for a wedding trip, the little season, and the holidays, continuing until they stopped to change horses and enjoy some refreshments midway through their journey. Before returning to their carriages, Darcy stopped to speak with Mr. Gardiner and briefly explain what he and Elizabeth had discussed. Darcy also asked if the gentleman would be willing to speak for him in the event Mr. Bennet were to refuse Darcy's request to marry Elizabeth. Mr. Gardiner was only too happy to give his agreement.

The second half of their trip passed pleasantly. Elizabeth's head rested on Darcy's shoulder as she closed her eyes and listened to his sonorous voice reading to her from a book of Shakespeare's sonnets. As she listened, she heard a few of the words that Georgiana and Lydia exchanged. She heard Mr.

Wickham's name mentioned and hoped that Lydia could keep Georgiana's delicate secret.

Finally, the two carriages turned in at the drive of Longbourn and pulled to a stop before the front entrance. Mr. Gardiner and Mr. Darcy were the first to disembark. As Darcy handed out Elizabeth and Georgiana, Mr. Gardiner stepped up to offer his assistance to Lydia and Mrs. Annesley. As they approached the door, it opened before anyone could knock. Mrs. Hill stood there, waiting to welcome the newcomers.

"Oh, Miss Lizzy, it's so good to 'ave you 'ome again. Mr. Gardiner, it's nice to see you, sir," said the housekeeper warmly. Looking at Lydia, her tone changed to one of disapproval. "Welcome 'ome, Miss Lydia. I hope you are feeling better." With her new awareness, Lydia realized the housekeeper's tone when greeting Lydia was not as warm as it had been for her sister and uncle. Understanding Mrs. Hill was probably aware of the truth of her situation as well as the story of her illness, the young girl could understand the difference in Mrs. Hill's tone. However, Lydia could not help but wonder if it had always been thus, as she recognized that her behavior towards the servants in her home was usually troublesome or dismissive. It was yet another fault upon which she would need to improve, thought the young girl with a sigh.

"Mrs. Hill, I believe you will remember Mr. Darcy from his visits last fall. Allow me to introduce his sister, Miss Georgiana Darcy, and her companion, Mrs. Annesley. Ladies, this is our housekeeper, Mrs. Hill.

The group had barely finished removing their outerwear when they heard Mrs. Bennet's voice screeching out her youngest daughter's name. She arrived in the hallway, followed by the remaining girls and Mr. Bingley.

"Oh, my dear Lydia, you are returned to us. Are you well? Did that dreadful man hurt you?"

## A Matter of Timing

Blushing a deep red, Lydia said, "Of what are you speaking, Mama? My illness is gone."

Mrs. Bennet became flustered and blushed as well when she realized several others were in the entryway with Lydia.

"Yes, yes, to be sure." She spoke even more loudly in her confusion.

"Good afternoon, Fanny," said Mr. Gardiner.

"Good afternoon, brother. I am so glad you have come. It has been trying to my nerves to have the children in the house during this difficult time. When will you be leaving with them?" she asked in a voice filled with testiness.

"I do hope you will allow them to remain one more night, as it is too late for us to return this afternoon. Are the children in the nursery?"

"Yes, Uncle. Mama has required that they remain there over the last week or so unless they are out of doors," responded Mary.

Upon hearing these words, Mr. Gardiner registered his disapproval on his face. "Well, if you will excuse me, I shall go up to see them. Helen and I have missed them greatly while we were away."

The gentleman moved towards the staircase, and everyone could hear the sound of his footsteps retreating.

Noting that her father had not joined the rest of his family to welcome the new arrivals, Elizabeth turned to Jane and asked, "How is Papa? Has he recovered from his illness?"

With a beaming smile, Jane answered. "He is much improved. In fact, he is in his book room at present."

Wondering at the smile on her sister's face, Elizabeth asked, "Jane do you have some news to share with me?" A suspicious grin and arched brow accompanied her question.

"Oh, Lizzy. I am so happy! Mr. Bingley returned several days ago and called upon me immediately. He said he was unaware of my being in town during the winter and he apologized for not calling on me. Charles, er, Mr. Bingley begged my forgiveness and told me I was never far from his thoughts. He has visited every day, and this morning he asked Papa for permission to marry me. We are engaged, Lizzy!"

Throwing her arms about Jane, Elizabeth cried, "I am so happy for you, Jane. You deserve to be loved and have a wonderful life!"

Darcy and Georgiana, who were standing close to Elizabeth and had heard the conversation, both offered their congratulations. As Darcy turned to greet Bingley, Elizabeth introduced Georgiana to her dearest sister.

"It is a pleasure to meet you, Miss Darcy," said Jane politely.

"I am pleased to meet you as well, Miss Bennet. I have heard so much about you from Lizzy."

Mrs. Bennet, who had been nattering on at Lydia as they stood in the hallway, was finally recalled to her duties as hostess and invited everyone into the parlor. Before introducing her mother to Georgiana, Elizabeth was able to remind Mrs. Bennet that the Darcys had kindly conveyed her and Lydia home. Mrs. Bennet was effusive in her welcome of Miss Darcy and her compliments about the young lady's expensive attire. She then turned and offered Mr. Darcy a cold, haughty welcome.

Embarrassed by her mother's behavior, Elizabeth left Darcy and Georgiana talking to Jane and Bingley, excusing herself to greet her father. She knocked on the door of the bookroom and entered upon her father's call of "Come."

"Hello, Papa, how are you feeling?"

With an indifferent expression on his face, Mr. Bennet looked up at his favorite daughter. "Lizzy, what has taken you so long to return? I expected you upon the receipt of Jane's letter."

"It was felt I might have more influence then my uncle or Mr. Darcy in getting Lydia to return with us."

## A Matter of Timing

"What does Mr. Darcy have to do with this matter?"

"Mr. Darcy was visiting when I received Jane's letters. Because of his past dealings with Mr. Wickham, I told him what had happened. He immediately offered his assistance in recovering Lydia.

"Humph," was the only response from her father.

"Will you not join us in the parlor? Uncle Gardiner has arrived, and I should like to introduce you to my friend, Miss Darcy."

"I do not wish to be bothered right know. I shall see the visitors at teatime if they are still here," said Mr. Bennet, turning his attention back to his book.

With a look of disappointment on her face, Elizabeth left the room to discover Darcy waiting for her in the hallway.

Noticing her look, Darcy asked, "Is everything alright?"

"I am not sure. Jane tells me that Papa's cold is gone, but he seems extremely out of sorts. Instead of sharing his humor about recent events, he dismissed me and refused to join us until time for tea."

Darcy discreetly took her hands and gave them a squeeze. "Perhaps he is not as recovered as he has led everyone to think. Or maybe he is just tired. Jane did say this was his first day out of bed."

"I think it might be best if you do not speak to Papa until the morning, when he will be in better spirits."

As she looked into Darcy's eyes, Elizabeth knew he was disappointed. Still, he merely smiled and agreed that it might be for the best. He offered her his arm and escorted her back into the parlor, where they joined Bingley and Jane in conversation. Darcy was pleased to see that Georgiana was quietly discussing music with Miss Mary Bennet. As a result, he looked to Elizabeth. At her nod, they shared their news with the couple, saying they only awaited the obtaining of Mr. Bennet's permission on the morrow.

Mr. Gardiner rejoined the group just before the tea things arrived. Mr. Bennet never made an appearance. At the conclusion of tea, Mr. Bingley and the Darcys departed for Netherfield Park.

After dinner, Elizabeth's father asked her to join him in his study. "Now, Lizzy, I wish you to tell me everything that happened in the recovery of your sister. I can only assume by her return to our home that she has not given herself to Wickham."

"No, Papa. Mr. Wickham apparently pressed her to anticipate their vows, but Lydia had sense enough to refuse."

"Well, I suppose we must be grateful for the little things."

"Papa, how can you say that? Mr. Wickham is a practiced seducer. It is no wonder a girl like Lydia, who has had little training in proper behavior, would not be able to resist such a man. He even deceived me when first we met." Elizabeth went on to tell her father about the plans to recover Lydia. She spoke of the way Mr. Darcy had taken charge, contacting Colonel Forster about a story to keep the disappearance quiet. He also sent his investigator to locate some of Wickham's former acquaintances. Elizabeth also informed him of her idea for returning Lydia home as well as the plans they had made should Lydia refuse to leave Wickham. She told of how they had found her on their first full day in London and how Colonel Forster had taken Wickham into custody."

"What will become of Wickham? How can we be sure he will not speak about Lydia and the elopement?

"Colonel Fitzwilliam—"

"Who is Colonel Fitzwilliam?" interrupted Mr. Bennet.

"He is Mr. Darcy's cousin and someone of whom Wickham is afraid. He helped in Lydia's recovery."

"Good grief! Is there anyone in London who does not know what took place?"

## A Matter of Timing

"Whatever do you mean, Papa? We have kept this situation as quiet as possible, and we were very fortunate to have had the help of Mr. Darcy and the colonel. I doubt Uncle Gardiner would have been able to locate Lydia otherwise. He is the first to admit he would not have come up with such a successful plan to retrieve her."

"Humph."

Elizabeth looked at her father in confusion, unable to understand his attitude. Then she continued with her explanation. "As I was about to say, Colonel Fitzwilliam informed us that Mr. Wickham would face military discipline. The colonel said there are many possible outcomes, one of which is flogging before going to France to serve with the Regulars. A second outcome is dismissal from the militia, in which case Mr. Wickham will immediately find himself in debtor's prison. Mr. Darcy has been paying the debts on which Mr. Wickham ran out since their days at university. Thirdly, Mr. Wickham might hang for desertion. In fact, we expect word soon regarding what has happened to him. Mr. Darcy's attorney, with all the outstanding debts, will be at Wickham's trial. No matter the outcome, he will not escape punishment of some kind."

"How does any of this prevent him from speaking about Lydia and the elopement?"

Colonel Fitzwilliam said the only questions asked would be about Mr. Wickham's being away from his post without permission. Also, the military will not wish the public to learn about his poor treatment of a gentleman's daughter. Such information will make it more difficult for them to find locations willing to house the militia units."

Elizabeth waited for her father to speak again, but he said nothing, so she continued.

"After returning to Aunt Gardiner's, Lydia was terribly hurt and confused. She heard the unkind things Wickham had said of her and she does not understand why Mama would have her act in such a way if that were to be the outcome. She is much subdued and will need care and affection in the coming weeks."

"Yes, well, you may go now, Lizzy."

Unable to understand her father's attitude and not used to being dismissed so coldly, Elizabeth stared at him. "Papa, are you sure you are completely recovered from your illness? You seem to have lost your usual sense of humor. Perhaps you should retire for the night and get some additional rest." Elizabeth's expression clearly showed her concern for her beloved father.

"Do not fuss. You know how I dislike it," grumbled Mr. Bennet.

His second eldest daughter merely stared at him before quietly leaving the room.

# AN UNEXPECTED OCCURRENCE

Breakfast was prepared for eight that morning, as Mr. Gardiner wished to be on the road as early as possible. Only Mr. Bennet, Elizabeth, and Jane were present to see the Gardiners off on their return trip to London. The children had to hug and kiss Elizabeth and Jane several times before they could settle enough to depart. As Jane assisted them into the carriage, Elizabeth spoke with her uncle.

"I cannot thank you enough for taking me on this trip with you. My presence in Derbyshire allowed me to make amends with Mr. Darcy and for us to reach an understanding after a series of events that seemed destined to cause confusion and dissent between us. If I searched the world over, I could not have found a more wonderful husband or someone better suited to me."

"You know it was our pleasure to have you with us, Lizzy. Traveling with you is always an exciting adventure, as your enthusiasm is contagious. Helen and I are both very happy for you and Mr. Darcy. I hope we shall be invited to Pemberley again when we can stay longer." Mr. Gardiner laughed at his words, as did Elizabeth.

"I am sure you will be, Uncle Edward. Do you think you could get away for Christmas?"

"We will see, Lizzy, we will see."

Mr. Gardiner kissed Elizabeth and joined his children in the carriage, stopping only long enough to thank Jane and kiss her as well. The children called their farewells as the vehicle moved forward. The sisters remained on the porch, waving until the carriage was out of sight.

---

After breaking their fast, Elizabeth and Jane returned to their room to continue discussing the events that had occurred during their separation. When they had retired the previous evening, Jane had told Elizabeth all that had happened since the arrival of Colonel Forster's letter. She spoke of their father's illness and the fits of nerves to which her mother had been subjected. She also praised both of her younger sisters for helping with the care of their parents.

Then she spoke of Mr. Bingley's return and all that had passed between them.

"Oh, Lizzy, he went down on his knees before a bench in the garden and proposed on his third day back. He apologized yet again for not seeing me while I was in London and begged my forgiveness before promising he would cherish me for all the days of our life together if only I would give him a second chance and agree to marry him! When I said yes, he kissed my hands and my palms. The sensations this created are beyond description. I felt as though thousands of butterflies were tickling my insides. Then Charles pulled me up into his arms and gently kissed my lips." Jane's expression was blissful. "It was so romantic! Everything a girl could want a proposal to be!"

## A Matter of Timing

Elizabeth could not help but laugh at the dreamy look on her sister's face. "I am truly happy for you, Jane. I know how heartbroken you were when he left and I am delighted that things have worked out so perfectly for you!"

Today it was Elizabeth's turn. She gave Jane a detailed account of their travels up to their arrival at Lambton. She spoke of agreeing to see Pemberley because Mr. Darcy was away, only to have him return two days earlier than planned. Elizabeth talked about his kindness to her and the Gardiners and his unexpected request to introduce her to Miss Darcy. Then she told Jane about tea at the inn and Mr. Bingley joining them. Elizabeth went on to describe the house and grounds and spoke of the day they had spent at the magnificent estate.

Elizabeth could not help but relay the ridiculous words of Miss Bingley and told Jane of the row which had occurred when Mr. Bingley confronted his sister about not informing him that Jane had been in town during the winter. (On the way to Longbourn, Mr. Darcy had quietly told her of the event, including Miss Bingley's attempt to enter the family wing the night before they departed for London.)

Then Elizabeth went on to speak of the engagement and her reading of Jane's letters. She talked in detail about Lydia's recovery and of Lydia's feelings following her return to the Gardiners'.

"I will speak to Mary and Kitty. We will do all we can to help Lydia recover," said the eldest Miss Bennet.

When they had shared all the happenings that had occurred during their separation, the sisters sat in the window seat and watched for the arrival of their beaus. Upon hearing the carriage wheels coming up the drive, Elizabeth and Jane checked their appearances and descended the stairs to greet their guests.

The occupants of Netherfield arrived at Longbourn the next morning as early as politeness would allow. They opened the front door and stepped outside to await the gentlemen's exit from the carriage. Darcy stepped down first and smiled at Elizabeth while reaching back to help his sister from the carriage. Following Georgiana was Bingley, who rushed to the side of his angel. He offered her his arm, and they moved in the direction of the gardens. With a lady on each arm, Darcy followed.

"How is your father feeling this morning, Elizabeth?" Darcy asked his betrothed.

"I am really not sure. Papa's behavior is very different from what it was before I went away. His sense of humor seems to have vanished. I questioned whether we should have Mr. Jones return to check on him, but Jane assures me his symptoms have all disappeared."

"Do you think I should speak with him today or wait a bit longer?"

"If we wish to have the banns read this Sunday, I believe you will have to talk to him today. Why do we not return inside, and I will take you to see him. Georgiana, would you mind waiting with Mary for a bit? I shall join you soon."

"Of course not, Lizzy. I am as eager for your father's approval as the two of you are. After all, when you and William marry I will gain a wonderful sister. I have wanted a sister for a very long time!" The three of them laughed as they turned back towards the front of the house.

---

Darcy turned back to face his beloved's father and took the seat Mr. Bennet indicated. "Good morning, Mr. Bennet. I hope you are well, sir."

Mr. Bennet said nothing, only continued to study the face of the young man before him. Darcy returned the scrutiny, trying to determine what the gentleman was thinking.

## A Matter of Timing

Finally, Mr. Bennet spoke. "What was it you wished to discuss with me, Mr. Darcy?" The words were devoid of emotion as the older gentleman continued to stare at the younger man.

"Mr. Bennet, I was very fortunate to meet Miss Elizabeth and Mr. and Mrs. Gardiner when they toured my estate several weeks ago. Our reunion was extremely pleasant, and over the course of the three days we were in company, Miss Elizabeth and I came to understand that we each had feelings for the other. I asked Miss Elizabeth to be my wife, and she agreed. I have come to ask for your permission to wed and for your blessing," said Darcy humbly.

Mr. Bennet spoke not a word but continued his unrelenting stare at Darcy. Several minutes passed before Mr. Bennet deigned to answer. "Why on earth would I grant you permission to marry my favorite daughter? Even before making her acquaintance, you grievously insulted my daughter in full hearing of many of the attendees at the assembly."

"Miss Elizabeth and I have worked through that, sir. I had a great deal on my mind that evening and was not in a proper mood to attend an assembly. I am also uncomfortable in large crowds where I do not know many people. I did not even look at Miss Elizabeth before replying. I merely wished to discourage Bingley from his efforts to make me dance."

"You seem to have an excuse for everything, do you not?" A sneer showed on Mr. Bennet's face, and his tone was spiteful. "How, then, can you explain that you visited in this community for almost two months, but when a dangerous rake and thief joined the neighborhood, you did not see fit to protect the community? Many of the merchants lost large sums of money when Mr. Wickham ran out without paying his bills. He also managed to abuse several of the merchants' daughters as well as one of my own. But did you see fit to warn anyone of his true nature?" Mr. Bennet did not pause long enough for Darcy to answer.

"No, you did not! Instead, you allowed everyone to believe his charm showed his real personality."

"Mr. Bennet, I am aware that I failed to make his behavior generally known, though I had a good reason for not doing so. I am also conscious that my natural reserve did not endear me to the neighborhood. However, I did relate to Miss Elizabeth the truth of my history with Mr. Wickham, believing it would be best coming from a respected member of the community rather than from myself."

"Why did you choose my daughter for this? Why not myself or Sir William Lucas?"

"I spoke with Miss Elizabeth because it came to my attention that Mr. Wickham had shown an interest in your family, and I did not wish your daughters to be at risk. Miss Elizabeth said she spoke with you about it before Miss Lydia departed for Brighton." Darcy regretted the words as soon as he said them, for it could appear as though he were criticizing Mr. Bennet.

At Darcy's words, annoyance and guilt flashed across the older man's face. Mr. Bennet recalled Elizabeth begging him to not allow Lydia to go to Brighton. She was concerned about just such an event happening.

"It was inappropriate for you to speak of Wickham's dissolute behavior with a young lady. How was she to relate it to those who would be able to deal with a man of Wickham's ilk?"

"I can only say that Miss Elizabeth demanded to know why I had treated Mr. Wickham with such contempt. I felt it necessary to defend myself against his slander. Miss Elizabeth assured me that she would share what she had learned regarding his habits."

"Irrespective of the Wickham situation, I will not give you permission to marry my daughter. Now, please leave me to my book."

Darcy looked at the older gentleman across from him. "Are you denying Elizabeth her chance at love and happiness?"

"I am protecting my daughter from a cold relationship in which she will not be respected and valued for the treasure she is."

"There you are wrong. I have loved Elizabeth almost from our first meeting. We have had our ups and downs, and it has brought us to a deep and abiding love. I respect her intelligence and delight in her witty conversation. I love her! She is as necessary to me as breathing, and I would defend her with my life if need be."

"Rich men like you do not know how to love. You know only how to own. Elizabeth would be miserable in such circumstances. Now, I asked you to leave. Do so, or I shall call Mr. Hill to escort you out of my house. Do not return!"

The door burst open and Elizabeth entered the room, closing the door behind her. "Papa, how can you say such cruel things to Mr. Darcy? He has apologized for his part in the situation, and he is responsible for rescuing Lydia. I love him, Papa, and it is my greatest wish to be his wife as soon as possible."

Mr. Bennet jumped up, placing his hands on his desk and leaning towards Elizabeth. His face was an unhealthy shade of red as he bellowed, "Are you out of your senses, Lizzy? This man is not worthy of you."

In the face of her father's anger, Elizabeth's response was calm and controlled. "He is the best man I know, Papa. All of us, especially me, were wrong in our opinions of both Mr. Darcy and Mr. Wickham."

Mr. Bennet opened his mouth as if to speak again, but his face suddenly drained of all color as he grabbed his head in his hands and fell to the floor. Elizabeth and Darcy rushed to his side. Darcy shouted for help as Lizzy cradled her father's head in her lap. She stroked his forehead as Darcy chaffed his hands, first one and then the other.

The study door crashed open to reveal Jane and Bingley, who spoke at almost the same moment.

"Lizzy, whatever is the matter?"

"What happened, Darcy?"

"Jane, send for Mr. Jones immediately," Elizabeth said. "We were speaking to Papa when he just collapsed."

"Bingley, send an express to Dr. Munroe and ask him to bring Dr. Lennox, the surgeon, with him. Tell him the patient possibly sustained a head injury that did not show any external signs." Both Jane and Bingley rushed from the room to attend to their assigned duties.

Elizabeth looked at Darcy in confusion. "How could you possibly know that?"

"Are we not both great readers?" Darcy smiled, trying to calm Elizabeth and ease the tension. "A tenant sustained an injury similar to your father's, and this happened. After speaking with the doctor, I read up on head injuries to learn more."

"What can be done for Papa?"

"The doctor will speak to Mr. Jones and learn exactly where the small bump on your father's head occurred. Instead of the injury swelling to the outside, which is most common, it may have swelled on the inside. If this is the case, the surgeon will likely drill in your father's skull and drain the blood or fluid that is building up. It probably created pressure on your father's brain and caused him to lose consciousness. Once the pressure is relieved, he should begin to recover."

"I am sorry for the way Papa spoke to you." Elizabeth's words were a mere whisper, and she would not meet his eyes.

Darcy released Mr. Bennet's hand and placed a finger under Elizabeth's chin, raising it so that he could see her eyes. "There is nothing for which to be sorry. It was more than likely that the pressure to his brain caused his ill humor and harsh words. What do you wish to do about having the banns read?"

"Will Papa recover in time for us to marry on September sixth?"

"I am not sure. However, it is early enough that the doctors should arrive by tonight. We can wait to make a decision until we have spoken to him. In the meantime, we should move your father off the floor. We could place him on the sofa here and then move him to his bed if Mr. Jones grants permission to do so."

"I will fetch Mr. Hill to help you."

Elizabeth made a hasty exit and returned a short time later with the long-time family retainer. Darcy looked the man over. Mr. Hill was as tall and thin as his wife was short and plump. "Mr. Hill, if you will take Mr. Bennet's feet, I will lift his shoulders. We will move him only as far as the sofa there." Darcy pointed to the designated piece of furniture. Elizabeth stood out of the way but hovered nearby. She removed the blanket from the back of the sofa and clutched it to her chest.

With a grunt, the gentlemen lifted Mr. Bennet from the floor and carried him the short distance, gently setting him down. Mr. Hill began removing his master's boots, while Darcy untied his neckcloth and loosened the top of his shirt to allow Mr. Bennet to breathe easier. Elizabeth had just finished placing the cover over him when Mr. Jones knocked at the door. While it was open, she could hear her mother moaning and crying in the background.

Mr. Jones insisted that Elizabeth leave while he examined her father. Though hesitant to do so, she agreed when Darcy promised to tell her everything that took place. Elizabeth made her way to the parlor, where the others were waiting. The younger girls, even Georgiana, showed signs of tears in their eyes. Mrs. Bennet continued her wailing, which did not help the situation. Elizabeth whispered something to Bingley, who nodded in agreement and departed the sitting room to attend to her request.

"Jane, allow me to help you get Mama to her room. It would be best for everyone if she quietly rested until we know more about Papa's condition," Elizabeth said. She and Jane each took one of their mother's arms.

"Oh, what is to become of us?" wailed Mrs. Bennet. "I know that your father will die and Mr. Collins will throw us to the hedgerows."

Elizabeth had no patience with her mother when she behaved like this. However, the ever calm and kind Jane patted her mother's hand. "Do not fret so, Mama, or you will make yourself unwell. I am sure Papa will be fine. Mr. Darcy sent for his personal physicians from town to attend to Father."

As soon as they reached her mother's room, Elizabeth departed, leaving Jane to care for Mrs. Bennet. Elizabeth returned downstairs and sought out Mrs. Hill. "I believe we could all use some tea and refreshments if you please, Mrs. Hill."

"Of course, Miss Lizzy. Cook has been making biscuits this morning. As soon as the water is ready, I will bring everything to the drawing room."

"Thank you, Mrs. Hill. It is reassuring that we can always count on your help in a crisis."

Elizabeth returned to the parlor. She stopped in the doorway and surveyed the young ladies. Just before entering the room, Jane descended the stairs.

"How is Mama?" Elizabeth asked.

"I gave her something for her nerves. She was sleeping when I left," replied Jane.

"I requested that Mr. Bingley send for Mrs. Annesley. I believe she will be a big help in finding something for the girls to do while we wait for news of Father. I have also asked Mrs. Hill for refreshments. Shall we visit with our sisters until then?"

"That sounds like a good idea." The two eldest Bennet daughters pasted smiles on their faces as they prepared to enter the parlor and alleviate some of the stress their younger sisters faced.

Before they could move, the door to the study opened.

"You join our sisters and guest," Elizabeth said to Jane. "I will learn what I can about Father's condition." With a nod, Jane entered the parlor and Elizabeth moved towards her father's study.

## A Matter of Timing

William reached out his hand to Elizabeth as she approached. "How is my father, Mr. Jones? What can I do for him?"

Mr. Jones responded to Elizabeth's inquiry in a quiet tone. For now, your father is as comfortable as we can make him. I believe Mr. Darcy to be correct about his condition and am glad that he has already sent for his doctor and surgeon."

"So, you believe there is swelling on father's brain?"

"I do," replied the apothecary. "While you wait for the physicians to arrive, someone should sit with your father at all times. If there are any changes in his breathing, color, or heart rate, send for me. I must see little Robby Smith, who fell from a hayloft and broke his arm, but I will return to check on Mr. Bennet as soon as I finish there. Provided there are no other emergencies, I will remain with your father until the physicians arrive."

"I thank you, Mr. Jones. Is it safe to move Father to his bed?"

"I believe so. When moving and changing him into his nightclothes, try to jostle Mr. Bennet as little as possible. I would also recommend that you use an invalid feeder to give him broth and tea. It is important that he retain his strength in preparation for the operation."

"Mr. Hill has gone to get two of the stable hands. The more of us involved in moving him, the better able we will be to keep him as still as possible." Darcy gave Elizabeth's hand a squeeze as he explained things to her. "All will be well, my love, do not worry." He added a reassuring smile to his words.

Elizabeth smiled in return. "Thank you, William. I do not know that I would have managed had you not been here."

"I will remain with your father for the time being if you will watch over Georgiana for me."

"Of course, William. I hope you do not mind, but I had Mr. Bingley send the carriage to retrieve Mrs.

141

Annesley. I believe she will be a tremendous help with my sisters and Georgiana during this trying time."

"That was an excellent idea, Elizabeth."

At that moment, Mr. Hill entered the room, followed by two others. Elizabeth stood in the hallway and watched as they lifted her father and carried him from the room. She held her breath as the group ascended the stairs. Elizabeth was relieved to see that her father's body did, indeed, remain quite still as they traversed the staircase.

---

As the group turned towards Mr. Bennet's room once they had reached the top of the stairs, Elizabeth moved to join the others in the parlor. When she arrived at the door, Mrs. Hill was exiting the room after having delivered the tea things. Hearing a knock at the front door, Elizabeth paused while waiting for Mrs. Hill to answer it. She was very relieved to see Mrs. Annesley arriving. Pausing in the doorway, Elizabeth waited to speak to the new arrival before entering the room.

"Might I speak with you a moment, Mrs. Annesley?"

The woman nodded and followed Elizabeth into the empty dining room.

"Thank you so much for coming. During a meeting with Mr. Darcy and myself, my father fell into an unconscious state. The occurrence seems to have deeply unsettled Miss Darcy and my sisters. I am hoping you can be of assistance in keeping them calm and occupied as we await the arrival of Mr. Darcy's physician and a surgeon from town."

"I will be happy to help, Miss Elizabeth."

Looking around to ensure no one was close enough to overhear her next words, Elizabeth continued. "I know you are aware of what occurred with Miss Darcy in Ramsgate. I would like you to know that the reason for our rush to town was because the same miscreant made off with my youngest sister, Lydia. With Mr. Darcy's help, we were able to recover her with relative speed and secrecy." Elizabeth explained to Mrs. Annesley how they had protected her sister's reputation. "Unfortunately, Lydia is very distraught about what occurred." Elizabeth paused and looked Mrs. Annesley directly in the eye. "I hope you will not judge me too harshly for my next words and that I can count on your discretion. Lydia's primary distress arises from the fact that she had done everything my mother instructed her to do to gain a husband. However, she overheard Mr. Wickham's real opinion of her and her behavior, and it has left her devastated. She cannot understand why my mother would have her behave in such a fashion if it led gentlemen to such an opinion of her.

"Before marrying my father, my mother was the daughter of the local attorney. And though I love Mama, she is of weak understanding and is very concerned for our futures, as well as her own. You see, there is an entailment on Longbourn away from the female line. We will all be homeless upon the death of my father. Though my elder sister is engaged to Mr. Bingley, when Mother's nerves come upon her, she does not seem capable of rational thought. We have sedated her to keep her calm until we know more about Father's condition.

"Mrs. Annesley, I am hoping you will be able to use my sister's situation to help my younger sisters learn to think about more than officers and dancing, to learn and grow from Lydia's experience. All three of my younger sisters could use improvement in their manners and their understanding. Would you be willing to take this matter upon yourself, to help them during this rather trying time?"

"As you will soon be Mrs. Darcy, I am more than happy to assist you. I did notice Miss Lydia's downcast spirits during our journey. Though I did not spend much time with your other sisters, I would guess that Miss Kitty is a follower and that Miss Mary is of a serious nature."

"You are very observant, Mrs. Annesley, and correct in both your assumptions."

"Do you think they might be interested in a group reading assignment and discussion to keep their minds occupied?"

"Lydia and Kitty rarely read anything more than the latest fashion magazines when they make their way to our neighborhood. Mary's taste in literature leans towards religious and moralistic texts."

"I will bear that in mind as I decide on our literary selection." Mrs. Annesley gave Elizabeth an encouraging smile. I believe I know of a few pieces that will work for our purposes. Some would make good comparisons to your sister's situation."

"Might I suggest you use my father's study for your endeavors? There is a small table, a large supply of books, and several seats. It would also be quieter and allow you to keep their attention with greater ease. Now, will you please join us?"

"A cup of tea would be lovely, Miss Elizabeth."

The two ladies crossed the hall and joined the others. Jane poured tea for them, and Elizabeth took a moment to explain to everyone what Mr. Jones had said about their father's condition.

When everyone had completed their refreshments, Elizabeth turned to Mr. Bingley. "Sir, would you be so kind as to carry a cup of tea up to Mr. Darcy? He said he would remain with my father until Mr. Jones can return. I must speak with my sisters and Miss Darcy for a moment in private."

"Certainly, Miss Elizabeth. I shall take this tray to the kitchen and ask Mrs. Hill to prepare a fresh pot for Darcy. I will join him for a time until I am needed elsewhere."

"Thank you, Charles," Jane replied with a blush. "I will fetch you soon, and perhaps we could take a walk in the garden."

## A Matter of Timing

Bingley rose and bowed to the ladies. He kissed Jane's hand, saying, "I will look forward to our walk." He exited the room, closing the door behind him.

# TALES OF WICKHAM

When the door closed behind Bingley, Elizabeth turned to look at her sisters. "There is an important issue we must discuss. I have included Miss Darcy and Mrs. Annesley for a particular reason, one that I believe will benefit all my sisters."

The expressions on the faces reflected back at Elizabeth ranged from confused to embarrassed.

"I know this will be difficult in many ways, but it is important we talk about it. Lydia, I would like you and Georgiana to come and sit here on the sofa with me. The rest of you may choose any seat, but you may wish to draw it close to us so that we may speak in quiet tones."

Elizabeth sat on one end of the sofa, placing Lydia between herself and Georgiana.

"Lydia, I feel it is crucial for you to share with your sisters what happened with Mr. Wickham and what you learned from the experience."

Lydia's face paled, but Elizabeth took her sister's hand and nodded at her encouragingly. On her other side, Georgiana did the same. She leaned in and whispered something in Lydia's ear.

"I am not sure you should say anything. Kitty and Mama are not good at keeping secrets and Mary will judge you harshly," Lydia whispered back.

"When William and Lizzy marry, we are to become family. If I cannot trust my new sisters, whom can I trust?"

"If you feel you must, I will not stop you, but perhaps you should not give too many details."

Fortunately, they spoke quietly enough that only Elizabeth could hear them. Georgiana turned to look at her new friends. Her face flushed and her hands trembled, so this time Lydia gave Georgiana's hand an encouraging squeeze.

Taking a deep breath, Georgiana began to speak. "I do hope that you will not be too hard on Lydia, for she is not the only one Mr. Wickham has deceived. He managed to fool my father into believing that he was as good a man as his father, but it was all pretense. Last summer, shortly before my brother arrived at Netherfield, Mr. Wickham, with the help of my former companion, tried to convince me that he loved me. I thought he and William were still friends, and George had been kind to me when I was a child. Mr. Wickham pushed me to elope with him. When I raised concerns, he said all the right words and had a reasonable response to everything. Fortunately, before he required an answer, William arrived for a surprise visit. I confessed everything to him, and when Wickham came to visit that afternoon, William confronted him. He told Mr. Wickham that according to my father's will I would not receive my dowry if I eloped. Wickham was angry with me and said he had wasted time and money for nothing. I was worth taking only because I had a large dowry. He spoke many words of love, but he did not mean any of them." Tears glistened in Georgiana's eyes as she completed her tale. Georgiana could not look at her future sisters, as she waited for the words of condemnation she expected to hear.

## A Matter of Timing

Jane, Mary, and Kitty sat spellbound as they listened. Jane's eyes also held tears as she thought of the hurt and heartbreak Miss Darcy must have felt at hearing Mr. Wickham's words. "Oh, Miss Darcy, how dreadful for you!"

Mary was astounded. How could Mr. Wickham deceive a young woman as intelligent and proper as Miss Darcy? Perhaps it was not strange that someone like Lydia, who lacked appropriate guidance, could act as she had. "It would appear Mr. Wickham was a practiced deceiver. It seems no young woman would be safe from him."

Kitty wondered what she would have done if a handsome young officer had spoken to her of love. Would she have fallen prey to a Mr. Wickham? "What an awful man! No wonder he was so quick to change his affections from you, Lizzy, to Mary King when she inherited her ten thousand pounds."

"That is a good observation, Kitty, for Mr. Wickham managed to fool even me. Everything he said about the living was a lie as well. He told Mr. Darcy he did not wish to be a cleric and demanded money to study the law. Mr. Wickham received over four thousand pounds and lost it all through drinking, gaming, and, well, other means, in less than two years."

A gasp escaped all the sisters.

Turning to Lydia, Elizabeth said, "I think it is time you tell our sisters of your experience."

Nodding, Lydia recounted for her sisters everything that had happened from the moment she left Brighton until they had found her and Mr. Wickham.

"Oh, Lydia," cried Kitty. "I am so sorry. I would never have thought that Mr. Wickham could have been so mean!"

With earnest intensity, Lydia turned to look at Kitty. "Kitty, we must change our ways. What Jane and Lizzy have tried to tell us is correct. We must act more like them and listen less to Mama."

Mrs. Annesley decided it was time for her to intervene. "I am sure your mother did not intend for you to experience such treatment, Miss Lydia. You must remember that she was not born a gentlewoman and could not be expected to know all that is proper in dealing with society. She is also concerned for your welfare should something happen to Mr. Bennet. She thought you would be protected by marriage as she was when she married your father."

"That is true, sisters," added Jane in her usual caring manner. "You cannot doubt that Mama loves each of you."

Mrs. Annesley continued. "I would be happy to have Miss Mary, Miss Kitty, and Miss Lydia join Miss Georgiana and myself for lessons over the course of our stay here. I believe I could help each of you learn what is necessary to be a proper young lady and to know how to handle the various situations you will encounter as you enter society. Would you like to join us? I am sure Mr. Darcy would send his carriage to pick you up, and we could have the lessons in the Netherfield library."

Mary felt somewhat indignant at her inclusion with her unruly younger sisters. "Why do you feel that I should participate, Mrs. Annesley?" she asked in a slightly aggrieved tone.

"I am aware you dislike social situations, Miss Mary, but it is a requirement for the daughter of a gentleman. I could help you learn to be more comfortable in such settings, to speak about issues of general interest, and to display your talents and yourself to best advantage."

Mary considered her answer and realized that if Miss Darcy still took instruction in proper behavior, Mrs. Annesley's offer would perhaps benefit her. "I thank you for including me, Mrs. Annesley, and will be happy to participate."

Before further discussion could take place, Mrs. Hill announced that luncheon was ready. Mrs. Bennet was still sleeping, and Mr. Hill offered to sit with Mr.

Bennet so the gentlemen could join the ladies for the meal.

After everyone had their cup, Elizabeth asked, "How is my father, William?"

"I am sorry to tell you there is no change. However, Mr. Jones did not expect any improvement until he sees the doctor and surgeon."

Mrs. Annesley sat in Mrs. Bennet's place at the table, with the young ladies on either side of her. After observing their behavior for several minutes, Mrs. Annesley began instructing them on proper table manners, conversation partners, and topics as well as the volume one should use indoors. It was one of the quietest meals Elizabeth and Jane had ever observed at the Bennets' table.

The couples sat across from one another at the other end of the table. They spoke about their engagements and wedding plans. "I do not know if we should be making plans, William. What if Father's opinion does not change after they have dealt with this head injury?"

"You know that I shall accede to whatever you wish regarding this matter, my dear. Your father has never denied you in the past, has he?"

"No, William, he has always been concerned for my happiness and well-being."

"In his absence, we could obtain permission from your uncle or your mother. Or I could simply purchase a special license, and we can marry as planned."

"What do you think, Jane?"

"I expect that Papa will give his approval for you to wed, Lizzy, especially if he knows your feelings on the matter. They will not read the banns for two more days. When Papa awakens, you may still have an opportunity to gain his permission before Sunday."

"I hope that will be the case."

"Darcy, it sounds as though you and Miss Elizabeth have already set a date."

"We did, Bingley. We plan to marry on September sixth, which is just three days after Miss Elizabeth gains her majority."

"Jane, what would you think of sharing that date with your sister and Darcy?"

Both sisters spoke at the same time. "That is a fantastic idea!"

"With your father's health and your mother's nerves," Darcy paused with a smile, "do you think you mother can prepare an event by that time? Might her activities interfere with your father's recovery?"

"I could always offer her the use of Netherfield and its staff for the wedding breakfast. She would need to be there to plan, leaving Longbourn quiet and peaceful for your father." Bingley's smile was infectious, as the sisters could imagine their mother's delight at such a prospect. They continue to discuss the matter for some time.

Just before the meal ended, Mrs. Annesley directed a question to Mr. Darcy. "Sir, Miss Elizabeth asked if I would be willing to include her younger sisters in Miss Darcy's lessons while in the area. I believe it would help keep them from worrying about their father's condition, and they have expressed an interest in participating. Would it be acceptable if we took your carriage to Netherfield for the afternoon to begin? I will ensure we return in time for the ladies to change for dinner."

Darcy smiled broadly at Elizabeth, showing his pleasure with the plan. "I believe that would be an excellent idea, Mrs. Annesley. Perhaps you could have Fletcher and Mr. Bingley's valet pack items for us so that we, too, might change for dinner."

"Certainly, sir. Young ladies, why do you not take a moment to refresh yourselves and gather your bonnets and gloves. Then we shall journey to Netherfield."

Georgiana, Mary, Kitty, and Lydia left the dining room amidst a murmur of conversation and the rustle of skirts. Elizabeth went to the kitchens to request that Mr. Darcy's carriage be made ready. Darcy was preparing to return to Mr. Bennet's room when a knock came at the front door. Mrs. Hill admitted Mr. Jones, who immediately asked about Mr. Bennet. "I will sit with him for a while. My housekeeper knows where I am should an emergency arise. Before mounting the stairs, Mr. Jones offered, "I hope the physician and surgeon will arrive before dinner. I do not like leaving him in this condition for much longer." The crease in his brow and look of worry created a feeling of dread in the pit of Elizabeth's stomach.

---

The two engaged couples decided to walk in the gardens. They strolled arm in arm some distance apart to enjoy a little private conversation.

"William, what shall we do if Father does not recover? We will be forced to wait at least six months to marry."

"Because of your concerns about your father's behavior, I wrote to my solicitor last evening and requested that he obtain special licenses for us as well as for Bingley and Miss Bennet. I included a letter to the Bishop of London, who was a good friend of my father's. I explained the situation with your father's precarious health and said that we wished to marry quickly should the need arise."

"That was good thinking, though I hope it will not be necessary. Perhaps if all goes well, we can go to London to shop for a few days next week. There is not time for me to obtain much of a trousseau, but I will have at least my wedding dress and the three new gowns already ordered. I doubt Jane has even had time to do that much. Now with the doctors' fees, I do not know if I will be able to afford more than the three dresses."

"I intend to pay for the physician and surgeon for your father, as I am the one who called for them. I am also happy to purchase your entire trousseau. I am sure Bingley feels the same about Jane's."

"I just would not wish that to become known. I am confident there will be many who will think me no more than a fortune hunter for marrying so far above my current circle. If they knew that you purchased my trousseau, they would be sure of it."

"We can have all the bills sent to your uncle, and I can arrange matters with him. No one need know."

"That is very kind of you, William, but it distresses me that I bring so little to this marriage."

"You bring that which is most important to me, and that is you. I have more than enough money and more connections than I would like, but you, my Lizzy, are priceless. It has taken us a while to get to this point. You deserve all that any other society bride would have and more because you are irreplaceable."

Elizabeth leaned her head on his shoulder. "I love you, too, William. You are the best man I know and the most perfect husband I could ever imagine." He placed a quick kiss on her temple as he hugged her arm more tightly to his side.

As teatime neared, the couples returned to the parlor and continued discussing plans for their wedding and wedding breakfast. Darcy informed them of the requests for special licenses in case the worst were to happen. It was not long after they had each received their tea cups that they heard Mrs. Bennet's voice calling for Mrs. Hill.

"Please, excuse me," said Jane. "I had best check on Mama." Jane bustled out of the room. Soon they heard her footsteps on the stairs. As Mrs. Bennet's door opened, everyone in the house could hear her wails.

"Mama, please be calm. You shall make yourself ill if you continue in this way. If you are unwell, how shall you ever plan our weddings? Mr. Bingley and I have decided to have a joint marriage with Lizzy and Mr. Darcy on September sixth."

"Whatever are you talking about, Jane? Lizzy and Mr. Darcy?"

"Yes, Mama. Mr. Darcy was trying to obtain Father's permission this morning when he fell ill."

"Oh, this is all that awful man's fault," Mrs. Bennet screeched.

"Shh, Mama, or he will hear you. Mr. Darcy has been everything kind since father fell ill. He sent for his personal physician and surgeon, and sent for special licenses so that we might marry in a hurry if Papa's prognosis is not good."

Mrs. Bennet's eyes grew wide at the mention of special licenses. "Oh, Jane, dear, you will be the first young lady in the area to marry by special license. I suppose I will have to thank him for that, but he is just so disagreeable."

"That is most unkind of you, Mama. Mr. Darcy is a bit shy and does not put himself forward in company."

"Do not be ridiculous, Jane. Men are never shy. Lydia said Mr. Darcy saved her, but how can that be if she returned home unmarried? Marriage is the only thing that can save her reputation."

"Mama, you know that is not true. Mr. Darcy worked with Colonel Forster to protect Lydia's reputation. No one but us knows she ran away. Everyone believes she was ill. You must remember never to speak of it to anyone, or you will be responsible for the ruin of all your daughters."

"But I do not have any daughters married, and Lydia so wished to be the first. I am sure it is Mr. Darcy's fault that Wickham did not marry Lydia. If only Darcy had given Wickham the living, then Wickham could have afforded to marry my sweet daughter."

"That is not true, either, Mama. He did what Lydia wished and helped save her reputation at the same time." Jane repeated Lydia's tale to her mother. "You should know, Mama, that Mr. Wickham's harsh words have left Lydia very confused about your instructions."

"Nonsense, Jane. I told her everything I did to catch your father. It worked for me, so I cannot see why it did not work for Lydia. I am sure you must have the information wrong."

Jane tried to hide the disgust she felt at knowing her mother had behaved in such a fashion to entrap their father. She shook her head sadly. "Perhaps, Mama, but I would suggest that you discuss the matter with Lydia. You should also be aware that Miss Darcy's companion has taken Mary, Kitty, and Lydia under her wing and is instructing them in comportment and other subjects to help them improve themselves and to keep them from worrying over Father."

"My goodness, my daughters are the first in the area to have a companion. I cannot wait to tell my sister and Lady Lucas."

"Hill will be up with your tea in a moment, Mama. Will you be joining us for dinner or shall you take a tray in your room?"

"I do not believe I am well enough to come downstairs just yet. Please let Mrs. Hill know to bring me a tray."

Mrs. Hill entered with Mrs. Bennet's tea things, allowing Jane an opportunity to escape and return to her betrothed.

When Jane reentered the parlor, she could see the look of embarrassment on her sister's face. Obviously, her mother's words had carried to the others. Jane caught Elizabeth's eye and rolled hers as she shrugged her shoulders.

"Mr. Darcy, I apologize for my mother's words. She is even less cautious in her speech when her nerves beset her."

"Do not worry, Miss Bennet. I know that I did not leave a good impression upon the residents of Meryton during my visit last fall. I shall endeavor to change her opinion of me in the coming days.

# THE DOCTORS' DIAGNOSIS

The residents and guests of Longbourn were just finishing their meal when Mr. Darcy's physician and surgeon arrived. Mrs. Hill led the gentlemen to the dining room and announced them.

"Dr. Munroe, Dr. Lennox. Thank you for coming so quickly." Darcy extended his hand to shake with both gentlemen. As they exchanged introductions, Mrs. Annesley gathered the younger girls and ushered them from the room.

"It is always a pleasure to see you, Mr. Darcy. How can we be of service?" Dr. Munroe's voice held faint traces of a Scottish accent.

"Allow me to introduce to you my betrothed, Miss Elizabeth Bennet, and her sister, Miss Jane Bennet, who is engaged to my friend Bingley, whom you already know." As the gentlemen bowed, the ladies bowed and curtsied. "The Misses Bennets' father was injured approximately two weeks ago. While talking this morning, he suddenly collapsed. He has remained unconscious since that time. Allow me to take you to him. The apothecary who treated him when the incident occurred is with him and can explain the situation to you in greater detail. It is my great hope that you will be able to help Mr. Bennet recover."

Jane and Bingley returned to the parlor to wait with the younger girls and Mrs. Annesley, as William offered his arm to Elizabeth. They mounted the stairs, leading the doctors to Mr. Bennet's room. After introducing Mr. Jones to the two gentlemen, Elizabeth and Darcy stepped into the hallway. Elizabeth showed Darcy where they could get chairs from some of the bedrooms, and they settled in to await the verdict from the two medical men.

They waited for more than half an hour, but to Elizabeth the time felt longer. When the door to her father's room opened, Elizabeth rushed to his bedside. Darcy stood behind her with his hands lightly resting on her shoulders.

"You and Mr. Jones were wise to send for us, Mr. Darcy." Dr. Munroe looked at Elizabeth and explained to her what they would need to do to help her father."

"What items do you require to perform the surgery, sir?" Elizabeth tried to keep her voice steady, but the men could hear the emotion in it.

"We shall need as many lamps as we can get to light the area. We shall also need two basins, hot water, and fresh towels. If possible, a wide board about the length of Mr. Bennet would be helpful, as well as a clean sheet with which to cover it. Lastly, I need boiling water to sterilize my tools. I shall also require several strong men to help hold Mr. Bennet still as I drill. Please make sure those who assist have scrubbed their hands with soap and hot water. They should not touch anything after doing so and should come straight to this room."

Elizabeth and Darcy left to assist in the gathering of the needed items and helpers. When all was ready, Darcy stayed to help keep Mr. Bennet still, while Elizabeth reluctantly returned to the hall to wait.

In a brogue more pronounced than his partner's, the surgeon explained to everyone what they needed to do. The young groom's eyes grew wide as he listened. "Do you think you can assist or do you feel this will be too much for you, young man?" Dr. Lennox spoke in a firm but kind voice. "I will not be able to stop and attend to you should you faint."

"I can do it, sir. I just won't be watchin'." Sam stood straighter and tried to look calm.

"Alright, then, does everyone understand what they should do?"

The men all nodded and took their assigned places. They laid Mr. Bennet's body on the wrapped board, angling it off the bed. The board supported his shoulders, neck, and lower skull, while the remainder of his head hung off the end. Beneath Mr. Bennet's head sat an empty bowl on a small table. Dr. Munroe would hold Mr. Bennet's head still. Darcy had his hands on each of the man's shoulders while Mr. Hill and Mr. Woods, the coachman, each held a hip and upper thigh. Young Sam held tightly to Mr. Bennet's feet and ankles. When everyone was in position, the surgeon placed his drill against Mr. Bennet's skull and turned it to create a hole.

Elizabeth's sisters had retired by this time, and Mr. Bingley had returned to Netherfield with Miss Darcy and Mrs. Annesley. Mrs. Bennet's last cup of tea contained a sleeping powder so that she would not disturb the operation. The house around Elizabeth was still and silent. The only sounds were the beating of her heart and the occasional muffled noise as the surgeon instructed his helpers. While she waited, Elizabeth prayed for her father's complete recovery and his return to his former self.

A half hour passed, then an hour. As it approached one and a half hours since Elizabeth had left her father's side, the door to his room finally opened. Mr. Hill passed her, carrying a bowl of what looked to be blood, though the color was not the bright red with which she was familiar. It was much darker, and there appeared to be some lumps in it.

"How is my father? Did everything go as expected?"

"Everything went well, Miss Elizabeth. Now we must wait and see. Hopefully, he will wake soon, or as it is night, his body may recognize that, and he may sleep until morning. I will stay with him for the first few hours while Dr. Munroe rests. Then he will relieve me."

"I plan to sit with my father as well."

Darcy smiled at her. "I had a feeling you would. I will wait with you, my love."

Elizabeth gave William a tired smile. "I will have Mrs. Hill send up some fresh tea for the three of us."

"That would be most welcome, Miss Elizabeth. Could you ask her for some additional boiling water so that I may clean my tools?

"Certainly, Dr. Lennox."

While Elizabeth sought out the housekeeper, Darcy moved their chairs into the bedroom, placing them next to the bed. He took a seat in the less comfortable of the two and spoke quietly with the surgeon as he waited for Elizabeth to return. The rest of Longbourn's occupants were already asleep.

The gentlemen stood when Elizabeth entered the room, followed by a servant with a kettle and Mrs. Hill, who carried the tea tray. The maid set the hot kettle on the hearth and, opening the window, emptied the bloody water onto the lawn below. Pouring in a little of the water, she wiped the dish dry with a clean rag before refilling it with the water from the kettle. She placed two clean cloths next to the bowl.

With a word of thanks to the departing servants, Elizabeth prepared a cup of tea each for herself and Darcy as Dr. Lennox cleaned his surgical tools. Placing her cup on the small table beside the bed, she settled in the chair and reached for her father's hand.

"Are there any complications we should watch for as we wait for Papa to wake?"

"There is always a risk of fever or infection for surgical patients. However, in my studies at Edinburgh and through extensive reading, I have come across several treatises regarding cleanliness in medical treatment. I am a bit tired to give you all the background information, but I have found that through the use of scalding water and frequent handwashing, as well as the cleaning of surfaces such as doorknobs or stair rails with which many people come in contact, I can keep an illness from spreading very far. I also use individual towels so that no one touches the items another used. The fact that I boiled my instruments before use should prevent an infection at the wound site, but fever is a risk with almost any illness."

"That is fascinating information, Dr. Lennox. I will remember that should I have to deal with an outbreak of flu at any time in the future."

Their voices were not above a whisper, and soon the room became silent. Neither Darcy nor Elizabeth had slept well the previous evening and soon were dozing in their chairs. Darcy was slumped over against the top of the soft, overstuffed chair in which Elizabeth slept, her feet curled beneath her. Elizabeth retained her hold of her father's hand, and Darcy had grasped the other before dozing off. Elizabeth's head rested against the back of the chair, almost touching that of Darcy's. The obvious affection between the young couple touched Dr. Lennox's heart.

---

As the first rays of sunshine peeked around the edge of the navy curtains covering the windows of Mr. Bennet's bedchamber, Elizabeth slowly stirred. Her left shoulder felt stiff and her hands tingled, but she could not think why. However, when Elizabeth felt a flutter in the palm of her hand, she recalled the events of the previous day and her eyes snapped open. She turned first to look at her father and realized that her shoulder ached because she had held his hand throughout the night. Elizabeth looked from her father to Dr. Munroe, who must have replaced Dr. Lennox while she slept. She raised her brow in question but received only a brief shake in return.

Feeling a slight breath on her neck, Elizabeth looked to her other side. William was asleep in the chair beside her, his head resting near hers. She pulled back to see him better and noted the curl that fell across his forehead. Gently releasing her father's hand, she rolled her stiff shoulder a time or two before reaching out to brush the curl from Darcy's face. Darcy did not stir, but a slight smile turned up the corners of his mouth as if his dreams were pleasant.

Elizabeth turned to look at the clock on the mantle above the fireplace. It was a little after half-past six. She stood to ring for a servant. After placing an order for tea and rolls with butter and jam, Elizabeth hurried to her room to refresh herself. Fortunately, someone had already brought a pitcher of warm water for her. Quickly stripping off her clothes, she washed with the water before dressing herself in a clean day dress. Grabbing her brush, she quietly returned to her father's room. Darcy was not stirring, and the doctor's eyes were drifting closed.

She returned to her chair and reached up to remove all the pins from her hair. Using her hands, she combed through her tresses and gently massaged her scalp. Sleeping in her hairpins always made her head itch. Next, Elizabeth took her brush and began to pull it through her long hair to return it to some semblance of order. She dropped her brush in her lap and reached around to braid her hair.

"Leave it down for a moment," a soft whisper spoke next to her ear. "I have never seen a more beautiful sight."

Turning to look at William, Elizabeth blushed at his words, which also caused a shiver to run down her back as his breath brushed her skin like a caress. "Good morning, William. How are you this morning?"

## A Matter of Timing

"I have slept better, but I have never awakened to a more lovely sight. I look forward to the time when I can see you every morning upon waking."

"I look forward to that as well, William."

A hoarse cracking voice was heard to say, "Do you not think you should ask my permission first, Mr. Darcy?"

Elizabeth and Darcy's heads whipped towards the occupant of the bed. Tears welled in Elizabeth's eyes as she spoke. "Oh, Papa, it is a pleasure to see your eyes open. How do you feel?" Dr. Munroe also awoke at the sound of a new voice in the room

"I have a bit of a headache," Mr. Bennet replied as he reached up to touch the offending appendage. Discovering the bandage around his head, he assumed a look of confusion. "Would one of you please tell me how I came to be here with a wounded head and to discover that you and Mr. Darcy appear to have spent the night together at my bedside?"

Darcy and Elizabeth blushed at her father's words. Before speaking, Elizabeth looked at Dr. Munroe, who nodded his assent. "Mr. Darcy came to talk to you yesterday morning on a matter of importance. You were not particularly kind in your response, and I came into the room to assist in resolving the matter. You yelled out, then clutched your head and fell to the floor. This is the first time you have awakened since then." Mr. Bennet could not miss the concern in his daughter's eyes, nor did he fail to notice an unusual lack of certainty in her appearance. Elizabeth continued. "This is Dr. Munroe. He is Mr. Darcy's personal physician. Along with his partner, Dr. Lennox, who is a surgeon, the gentlemen came to Longbourn upon receiving Mr. Darcy's express. Mr. Jones was called and was relieved to hear that we had requested medical assistance for you."

"That explains how I came to be here, but did I injure my head in the fall? Why is it bandaged?"

"No, that fall did not cause your injury," Dr. Monroe said in his deep voice with a trace of a Scottish burr. "It was explained to us that you took a fall about two weeks ago. You hit your head, but there was no outward swelling. Unfortunately, there was swelling inside your skull. It caused pressure on your brain and eventually caused your collapse."

Mr. Bennet's eyes widened as he listened to the doctor.

"Though the conversation was unpleasant, I was glad Mr. Darcy and I were with you when you collapsed," Elizabeth said. "Otherwise, it could have been some time before anyone discovered you."

"We rarely have unpleasant conversations, my Lizzy. What were we arguing about?"

Elizabeth did not answer right away. When she did speak, it was to ask a question. "Do you recall anything of the last several days?"

Mr. Bennet frowned in concentration as he attempted to answer Elizabeth's question. "Not really. In fact, the last thing I remember was getting a letter from Colonel Forster. Oh, dear heaven," cried Mr. Bennet, his face paling. "Lydia." The man attempted to rise, but both Elizabeth and the doctor placed a hand on his shoulder to prevent him from doing so.

"There is no need to worry, Papa. Lydia is home, safe and sound."

Mr. Bennet looked startled at Elizabeth's words. Darcy decided to take over the story. "I was fortunate enough to meet Miss Elizabeth and the Gardiners as they toured my estate in Derbyshire. We had a chance to spend a few days together before she received Miss Bennet's letters requesting her uncle's assistance. As I was present when Miss Elizabeth learned the news, I offered my help as well. Unfortunately, I have first-hand experience with some of Wickham's less-than-gentlemanly behaviors. I knew some of his favorite haunts in London and a few of his past acquaintances. It was through one of them that I discovered Wickham and Miss Lydia's location on our first day in town. It took only one visit with the couple and a well-devised plan from Miss Elizabeth to convince Miss Lydia to return home."

"I do not understand," said Mr. Bennet quietly. *I do not think I have ever heard the gentleman speak so much at one time in all of our acquaintance*, he thought.

Darcy attempted to explain further. "Miss Jane enclosed the colonel's letter, in which he indicated no one in Brighton was aware of her disappearance. I sent him an express in which I informed him of my past relationship with Wickham. I also asked him to put out the word that Miss Lydia was ill, and I requested that he also say he would return her to her aunt and uncle in London once she was a little better. He was to meet me in London on a particular day and to bring 'Miss Lydia' and her belongings in a closed carriage, which he would take to the Gardiners."

"That was a good plan, but I doubt very much my family at Longbourn managed to keep the matter a secret."

"There you would be wrong, Papa. Mama took to her bed, and Jane ensured that the girls all remained at home to attend to her."

Mr. Bennet looked impressed. "What is this plan you spoke of to convince my willful youngest daughter of the error of her ways?"

Darcy and Elizabeth took turns explaining what had occurred on the day they visited the inn where Lydia and Wickham resided. The recounting brought a range of expressions to the gentleman's face. When he heard that his youngest had attacked her former suitor upon hearing his unkind words, a chuckle escaped him. It quickly became a groan of pain as Mr. Bennet grasped his head.

Dr. Munroe eased Mr. Bennet into a sitting position and encouraged him to drink from the glass of water Elizabeth held out to him. "You must remain in bed for a few days, and I would recommend quiet and rest." Looking towards Elizabeth, the doctor continued. "I would recommend that no stressful discussions take place for at least a week."

At his words, Darcy and Elizabeth both looked crestfallen before their eyes locked in shared disappointment. Darcy reached for Elizabeth's hand and gave it a squeeze, whispering something only she could hear.

Mr. Bennet did not miss the reaction of his favorite daughter and the quiet, stern gentleman from the north. Nor did he fail to notice that the gentleman still held his Lizzy's hand. Mr. Bennet's eyes focused on the pair before he spoke.

"May I ask the topic of the discussion we were having before my collapse?"

Darcy and Elizabeth shared another look and then glanced at the doctor. He studied them carefully before nodding.

Clearing his throat, Darcy spoke in a neutral tone. "I had just asked you for Miss Elizabeth's hand in marriage."

"And we argued about this to the point that Lizzy thought she should intervene?"

Darcy nodded but said nothing.

"Papa, from the moment of my return you were not acting like yourself," Elizabeth said. "I only came in to let you know that I loved William and wished to marry him. From the beginning of our relationship, a series of misunderstandings occurred between us, but we have resolved them. He is the best man I know." This time, Elizabeth gave Darcy's hand a squeeze.

"I see," said Mr. Bennet. "Had I given you an answer?"

"No," Lizzy hurriedly replied as Darcy looked at her.

"Well, then, let me do so now. You have my permission and blessing to marry Elizabeth, Mr. Darcy. Just see that you treat her as the treasure she is."

Darcy's expression was surprised at first but quickly turned to jubilation. Lizzy cried, "Thank you, Papa," as she leaned over and kissed his cheek.

"If you will send for Reverend Carter, I will give him my permission to call the banns beginning this Sunday."

"Thank you, sir. Thank you very much." Darcy's smile was so broad, Mr. Bennet caught a glimpse of his dimples.

"I believe it would be better for you to rest a while, Mr. Bennet. Perhaps the Reverend can come this afternoon."

"I will arrange it so," said Darcy.

He and Elizabeth stood to leave the room, but Elizabeth turned back to look at her father. "Papa, do you remember giving Jane and Mr. Bingley permission to marry just two days ago?"

"Mr. Bingley?"

"Yes, Papa. He returned to offer his assistance to Jane during Lydia's disappearance and your illness. They have been inseparable since his return."

"I have no recollection of the matter, but I always thought them a well-matched pair."

Lizzy returned to the bedside and kissed her father once more. "I love you, Papa. I hope you will recover soon, as you must give us away on September sixth." Elizabeth waved from the doorway as Mr. Bennet smiled after her.

# PREPARATIONS

Darcy refreshed himself and changed for the day before he and Elizabeth took off for an early morning walk. By the time they returned, Bingley and Georgiana were sitting with Jane and her younger sisters in the parlor. When Darcy and Elizabeth entered, Jane was quick to ask, "How is Father this morning?"

"He is awake and spoke to us. We have his permission to marry on September sixth."

Jane and Bingley shared a smile at the radiant expressions the newest arrivals wore. Everyone offered their congratulations.

"We are grateful for your good wishes, but perhaps we should speak more softly. Dr. Monroe has requested at least a week of rest and quiet to aid in Mr. Bennet's recovery," Darcy said.

"I am so happy for you both!" exclaimed Georgiana. "I will finally have a sister!"

"You shall have five sisters," said Lydia with a smile at her new friend. "I know just how we can ensure the house is quiet enough for Papa's recovery." The expression on Lydia's face was a mixture of her usual forward behavior and a touch of mischief.

"And how is that?" Elizabeth's look and tone were stern as she addressed her youngest sister.

"We can all return to town and shop for trousseaus for you and Jane."

"I do not think it is necessary for all of us to go."

"But, Lizzy, if we are to continue our lessons with Mrs. Annesley, we must be where Georgiana is, and I doubt Mr. Darcy would wish to leave her behind. I am sure he does not know all the best places to shop as Miss Darcy does." Lydia's expression was both earnest and playful, causing everyone to laugh.

"Perhaps we could discuss the merits of this idea over breakfast," suggested Darcy.

The group trooped to the dining room and did continue to debate Lydia's suggestion. The biggest concern was leaving only Mrs. Bennet to care for her husband, as her manner was neither quiet nor restful.

"I would be happy to hire a pair of nurses to watch over Mr. Bennet and attend to his needs and medications. That way, your mother will be able to focus on the preparations for the wedding and wedding breakfast. In fact, I will offer to send any special items she needs from town."

Elizabeth smiled at her betrothed. "That is very kind of you William. It will also mean, Jane, that we do not have to battle with Mama over the amount of lace on our gowns." Elizabeth chuckled at her words. The others soon joined her.

When the meal ended, Jane ascended the stairs to give Mrs. Bennet the news about her father's recovery and the second engagement, as well as the date they had determined for the wedding. Elizabeth's job was to speak to her father about the group returning to London.

Elizabeth had barely entered her father's room when a loud screech came from Mrs. Bennet's room.

"Two daughters engaged. Oh, I shall go distracted. I must go visit my sister immediately."

Shaking her head at the expected reaction, Elizabeth glanced at her father to see if the noise had awoken him. Her gaze took in her father's usual sardonic grin.

"I take it someone has given your mother the good news?" Mr. Bennet raised his left brow in a question, very much like the expression his favorite daughter often assumed.

"Yes, Papa. Jane was to speak to Mother about recent events. It is my job to ask if you would allow us to return to London and shop for our trousseaus. Mr. Darcy and Mr. Bingley will accompany us, and we shall all stay at Mr. Darcy's townhouse. With all of my sisters and Mrs. Annesley for chaperones, there should be no concern for our reputations. Mr. Darcy has also offered to arrange for nurses to tend to you so that you shall be spared Mama's raptures and plans as she prepares for the upcoming events."

"I would like to talk to both Mr. Darcy and Mr. Bingley before I make that decision. Would you be so kind as to ask the gentlemen to visit me, Lizzy?"

"Certainly, Papa."

A few minutes later, Mr. Bennet heard a knock on his bedchamber door. While the family dined, Dr. Lennox had examined him, helping his patient take both broth and tea. At Mr. Bennet's insistence, Dr. Lennox had helped him into a sitting position. The doctor had been hesitant to jostle Mr. Bennet about so soon after surgery, but he could well understand the disadvantage Mr. Bennet felt at speaking to his future sons from his bedchamber. Consequently, he assisted Mr. Bennet into a seated position, surrounding him with a mound of pillows for support.

Dr. Lennox had just settled Mr. Bennet when a knock sounded at the door.

"Come in."

Darcy opened the door with Bingley at his shoulder. The two men bowed to the older gentleman and inquired after his health.

"Other than a headache, I suppose I am as well as can be expected. Not having any memory of how I felt after my initial injury, nor of my behavior over the last few days and weeks, it is hard for me to say." Having learned that laughter caused his head to ache worse, Mr. Bennet grinned at the gentlemen.

Bingley chuckled at Mr. Bennet's words, and a smile turned up the corners of Darcy's lips. "I must say, you were a bit more serious recently than I remembered you being," said Bingley. "I am glad to know you are out of danger and have returned to your usual good humor."

Mr. Bennet noticed the tightness around Darcy's eyes as Bingley began speaking. This made him wonder more about their disagreement.

"You asked to see us, sir. How may we be of help to you?" Darcy asked.

"Elizabeth has spoken to me about your desire to go to town. I am sure Jane and Elizabeth would both enjoy shopping without their mother, but are you sure you wish to be responsible for my entire gaggle of daughters?"

"As they will soon be my sisters, I am not opposed to their joining us. They should each have a new dress for the wedding as well. Also, they have joined with my sister, Georgiana, in her daily lessons with her companion. Since Miss Lydia's encounter with Wickham, she is desperate to learn to behave better. Mrs. Annesley is an excellent example for them, and they have all shown a desire to improve themselves."

Mr. Bennet looked shocked at Mr. Darcy's words. "Lydia is voluntarily taking lessons?"

Darcy nodded.

"I could not have imagined what I am about to say, but thank goodness for Mr. Wickham if it has wrought such a change in Lydia."

Darcy could not help but laugh. "It is, indeed, not something I would ever expect to hear someone say. Nor would I ever have expected his poor behavior to provide a positive outcome for anyone. Unfortunately, it cannot make up for the damage he has caused to so many other young ladies."

## A Matter of Timing

"When would you like to depart for town?" asked Mr. Bennet.

"I believe it would be best to leave on Monday. I am sure we would all wish to be here for the first reading of the banns. That would allow us a week or two in London, and we could return for the third reading. Then there would be only a few days before the wedding."

"That sounds like a good plan. I will give Elizabeth a draft so that my brother, Gardiner, can obtain the funds they will need. I know what a bill from the dressmaker here in Meryton can run for so many young ladies. I hope they will be able to purchase a sufficient trousseau for one hundred and twenty–five pounds apiece."

Glancing quickly at Bingley, Darcy nodded.

"I will send an extra twenty-five pounds for the other girls to use. Now, how do you plan to keep Mrs. Bennet from joining you?" Mr. Bennet's look and tone were teasing as he gazed at the gentlemen.

Both of the younger men blushed slightly, but Darcy stared at his future father-in-law as he replied, "I plan to offer to bring things from London for the wedding that she cannot obtain in Meryton."

Try as he might, Mr. Bennet could not contain the chuckle that escaped him. "I see you are learning how best to handle my wife, Mr. Darcy. Now, if you do not mind I will rest until Reverend Carter arrives." The gentlemen both stood and bowed to Mr. Bennet before taking their leave.

Once in the hallway, Bingley turned to Darcy. I do not know what the dressmaker here charges, but I know from the bills I see for Caroline that the amount Mr. Bennet has set aside will not buy near enough for Jane or Elizabeth. Caroline can spend that much on just seven gowns."

"That is because she does not care how much she spends and because you frequently allow her to overspend her allowance. You will need to be more careful now that you will have a wife," Darcy advised.

"However, I thought I would tell Georgiana to have Madame LaRue bill them exactly what they have and to send the balance for Elizabeth's items to me at Darcy House. She could do the same for you and Jane."

"That is an excellent idea, Darcy. Please be sure to ask her to do that for me as well."

---

Darcy and Bingley found Elizabeth and Jane working on their needlework in the parlor. Elizabeth examined Darcy as the men entered the room. She was relieved to note no trace of discomfort on his face.

Taking a seat near Jane, Bingley asked, "How did your mother take the news?"

"She was overjoyed that she has two daughters engaged. I am surprised you did not hear her response for yourself."

"Your father has agreed to our trip to London. I suggested we leave on Monday. I for one would wish to hear the first calling of the banns." Darcy gave Elizabeth his dimpled smile as he spoke.

"I, too, would very much like to hear those words." Elizabeth returned his smile with one of her own. It was the soft and loving one she reserved just for him.

"I quite agree," Jane added. "Perhaps, Lizzy, you should write to Aunt Helen to let her know of our upcoming visit. It would be wonderful to visit Uncle's warehouse for some fabric before meeting with Aunt's dressmaker."

"That is a good idea, but I believe we should use Miss Darcy's modiste. She has already begun work on four gowns for me."

Jane looked at her sister, and Elizabeth could easily read the question in Jane's eyes. Could they afford to acquire all they would need from someone like Madame LaRue?

## A Matter of Timing

Reading Elizabeth's concern, Darcy spoke. "Your father has set aside one hundred twenty-five pounds for each of you. Based on the bills for Georgiana, I am sure you will be able to get all that you need." Elizabeth looked doubtful, but Jane looked relieved. Darcy just smiled and changed the subject. "Would you ladies care to take a turn in the gardens or perhaps play cards?"

"I believe a walk in the gardens would be wonderful, William," Elizabeth said. She and Jane put away their needlework and went upstairs to get their bonnets and shawls. A short time later, the two couples were wandering through the garden. They were in sight of each other, but far enough apart to ensure that they could speak privately.

"Would you like to take a wedding trip after we marry, or would you prefer to go straight to Pemberley?"

"I look forward to returning to Pemberley, but I have not given any thought to a trip. Where did you think we could go?"

"I would take you anywhere you wish."

"And I would be happy to see anything, but as I have not been farther than London and Hunsford, I would not begin to know where to choose."

"Do you wish to view the sea or perhaps go to Bath?"

"I might like to visit the seaside next summer, but I believe I would most like to go home to Pemberley and spend a few weeks with just the two of us alone."

Darcy pulled Elizabeth from the path and behind the trunk of a large oak, trapping her body between himself and the tree. His swift movement startled Elizabeth, but when she met his eyes and saw the look of passion, her face flushed. "I cannot think of anything I would like more." Darcy leaned in, intending to steal a quick kiss, but when Elizabeth's arms snaked around his waist and up his back, he could not bring himself to let her go.

When they finally broke apart, each was gasping for breath. Darcy rested his forehead against Elizabeth's as his breathing calmed. "We shall need to be on our guard when you stay at Darcy House. You deserve all the respect I can give you, but the more time I spend with you, the greater my desire for you grows. I waited a long time for you to accept my proposal and I am afraid these next few weeks will feel longer still."

"Though I did not come to recognize my feelings as early as you, I am sure my desire is as great." Elizabeth blushed and looked away as she whispered these words.

Darcy took one of his hands and lifted her chin until Elizabeth had no choice but to meet his gaze. "Never be ashamed of your feelings for me. Certainly, the ardent feelings we share bode well for our marriage. I do not care if it is unfashionable. No one will doubt the fact that I am deeply in love with the remarkable woman I married." Darcy kissed her forehead before stepping away. He offered Elizabeth his arm, and they returned to their stroll.

"I will speak with Lord and Lady Matlock while we are in town and ask them to keep Georgiana for a time. Perhaps we could return to town for a few weeks of the little season and then enjoy a family Christmas at Pemberley."

"That sounds like an excellent plan, William."

---

The remainder of the week passed with everyone spending their days in a similar fashion. The younger ladies enjoyed lessons at Netherfield with Mrs. Annesley. They even planned a dinner party for Saturday evening, giving the girls the opportunity to put some of their learning to use.

The two engaged couples found themselves spending a portion of their time reviewing wedding plans with Mrs. Bennet. The woman bemoaned the fact

## A Matter of Timing

that she had only four weeks to plan and suggested postponing the event to allow her at least three months. Mrs. Bennet's suggestion met with four decided "nos." It took some flattery from Bingley about her abilities as a hostess and the promise of using Netherfield Park for the wedding breakfast, as well as Darcy's offer to obtain from town any items she could not find in Meryton to quiet Mrs. Bennet's concerns. She also spoke forcefully about what her daughters would need for their trousseaus as well as the best places to shop. Elizabeth and Jane were quick to conclude those conversations and whisk their betrotheds out-of-doors.

Mr. Darcy spoke to Dr. Munroe about the nurses for Mr. Bennet and sent an express the same day. Once the nurses were in place, Dr. Munroe and Dr. Lennox returned to town, though they promised to call weekly until Mr. Bennet's complete recovery. With the care of his nurses, Mr. Bennet steadily improved.

Finally, Sunday arrived. The carriage from Netherfield pulled up to the chapel just as the Bennet party approached. Mr. Darcy and Mr. Bingley stepped down, each offering an arm to his particular lady. Mrs. Bennet and her young daughters entered first and took a seat in the Bennet pew. The two engaged couples followed them inside and sat directly across the aisle in the pew designated for the Netherfield party. Miss Darcy and Mrs. Annesley joined them.

News of the gentlemen's return to Netherfield had spread throughout the small village. However, they had not been at home to receive callers, nor had anyone seen them about Meryton. Because no engagement had resulted from their first stay in the area, the mothers were all eager to reintroduce to the gentlemen their unmarried daughters. When Mr. Bingley and Mr. Darcy entered the church with the two eldest Bennet sisters, the whispers and moans began. It was evident from the looks the couples shared that the gentlemen were no longer available.

Darcy enjoyed the church service very much. It was a pleasure to have Elizabeth at his side. He could hear her beautiful voice as she sang the hymns, and their hands occasionally brushed against each other as they shared her prayer book. The minister gave a short sermon, but his meaning was clear and scriptural references backed it up. Just before the end of the service, Reverend Carter stood before the congregation, clearing his voice to gain their attention. He was a pleasant gentleman with a shock of white hair, bright blue eyes, and rosy cheeks. Having known the Bennet sisters since their births, he was delighted with the announcement he was about to make.

"I publish the banns of marriage between Jane Bennet of Longbourn and Charles Bingley of Netherfield Park and between Elizabeth Bennet of Longbourn and Fitzwilliam Darcy of Pemberley in Derbyshire.

"This is the first time of asking. If any of you know cause or just impediment why these two persons should not be joined together in Holy Matrimony, ye are to declare it."(2)

As the party departed the church, many people stopped the two couples, wishing to offer their congratulations. In spite of his discomfort with strangers, Darcy made a great effort to be more receptive of those with whom he came in contact. It was some twenty minutes before they were able to depart the church. With their ladies on their arms, the two men followed the other Bennets to Longbourn, where they would pass the remainder of the day.

After the mid-day meal, Mr. Bennet had a private interview with each of his three youngest daughters. In each case, he told them that he loved them and apologized for not taking a greater interest in their upbringing and well-being.

For Mary, it was the first time she had heard words of love from either of her parents. Realizing this nearly caused her to break down in tears. When Mr. Bennet added that he was proud of her efforts at the pianoforte and in her extensive reading, the tears flowed.

## A Matter of Timing

"You have great potential, Dear Mary, but you must relax a bit and not be quite so judgmental. You must take to heart the old adage to treat others as you wish to be treated. Feelings of warmth and compassion will improve not only your music but also the way others interact with you."

Kitty was speechless when her father called her for a visit. After expressing his love for her and his regret for his neglect, Mr. Bennet attempted to boost the young girl's self-esteem. "Kitty dear, you are almost two years older than Lydia, but you have always followed her lead, no matter the trouble it brought you. You must learn to stand up for yourself. You have a kind heart and a real talent for drawing. You must not let others dissuade you from developing that talent. It is also more important for you to learn from your elder sisters and follow their example so that you can set a better example for Lydia. I have confidence in you; now it is time to have faith in yourself and your choices rather than following blindly."

When Lydia entered her father's room, she was visibly trembling. She, too, heard words of love and regret and was surprised when her father apologized for allowing the mishap with Wickham. "Had I taken a firmer hand with your mother and you younger girls, you might have been better prepared to deal with the words of a practiced seducer. I was pleased to hear that you stood up for yourself upon hearing him disparage you. I was also proud that you could discern the need to change your behavior. Continue your efforts to grow and improve and look to your elder sisters as an example. I will try to work on improving the family situation so that your mother will not feel such a great need to rush each of you to the altar."

"I am sorry for being so discourteous to my family and for failing to think of anyone but myself. I have learned my lesson and will try very hard to make you proud of me in the future, Papa."

"I know, my child, I know. I shall try to give you reason to be proud of me as well. Now run along and enjoy your time with your sisters."

Most of the ladies' belongings were packed and ready for the following morning. Only the outfits for the morrow and the few personal items they would need to prepare for the day remained. When the gentlemen departed for Netherfield after dinner, everyone but Mrs. Bennet was in high spirits. Mrs. Bennet continued to lament being left behind and the lack of time she would have to prepare a wedding breakfast worthy of two such rich and eligible gentlemen.

Because of their excitement, the Bennet sisters found it difficult to settle for the night. They gathered for a while in the bedroom that Elizabeth and Jane shared.

"I believe Father's recent ill health has made him look at things a bit differently," said Elizabeth. "He is feeling guilty for his lack of attention to the family."

"Indeed," added Jane. "He apologized for allowing the family's behavior to scare away Mr. Bingley and his family and the pain that caused me."

Mary spoke next. "I have certainly never been more surprised in my life than I was at what he said to me earlier today."

Her feelings on the matter were evident on her face and induced Elizabeth to ask, "Do you wish to tell us about it?"

Mary did so, followed by Kitty and Lydia. Jane and Elizabeth were each impressed with the fact that her sisters could take their father's words to heart and desire to live up to the expectations he had spoken about with them. Finally, after they had each talked of their experience, they were able to find a peaceful night's sleep.

# EXCURSIONS

Two carriages appeared in the drive of Longbourn just before breakfast. The visitors stepped down and were admitted to the house, where they received an invitation to join the family in breaking their fast. The meal was a happy, somewhat noisy occasion. Excitement ran high with the upcoming trip to London. Lydia had seen little of it during her previous visit and Mary and Kitty had never been.

After the meal, the young ladies gathered the items they would take with them in the carriage as Mr. Darcy directed his footmen on where to place the luggage. Before hurrying down the stairs, the sisters each stopped at their father's room to kiss his cheek and offer wishes for his improved health. Their excitement was so high, they barely took the time to wish their mother farewell before rushing from the house.

Elizabeth and Lydia rode in the Darcy carriage with Mr. and Miss Darcy and Mrs. Annesley. Jane, Mary, and Kitty rode with Mr. Bingley in his coach. Mrs. Bennet remained on the front porch, waving her handkerchief until the carriages were out of sight.

Everyone was in much better spirits on this trip than they had been on the previous journey from town.

They took a brief break halfway through the journey to enjoy lunch at an inn along the way. The carriages pulled up before the Darcy townhouse shortly before time for tea. Mrs. Baxter, the housekeeper, was on hand to welcome everyone and direct them to their rooms. Mr. Bingley received a room near the family suites, while, to help preserve proprieties, the Bennet sisters found their accommodations on a separate floor.

After refreshing themselves, Georgiana gave the sisters a tour of the house. When they rejoined the gentlemen in the drawing room, they were delighted to see Mr. and Mrs. Gardiner in attendance. Georgiana served as hostess, and Mrs. Annesley spoke to the younger girls about the proper way to serve tea. She suggested that each girl take a turn acting as the hostess so that they might better learn the duties they would assume when they became the mistresses of their own homes.

After serving everyone, the girls made plans for the shopping that would begin the next day. Elizabeth gave her uncle the draft from her father so he could provide them with the funds they would need. The group enjoyed a pleasant evening meal and some music before retiring for the night. The knocker would not be put up on the door until after they completed the majority of the shopping and other business needs.

Before everyone retired for the night, Darcy managed to draw Elizabeth apart from the others for a few moments of private conversation. They sat on the window seat and listened to Georgiana play. "So much has happened in such a short time that I have not had an opportunity to give you something of great important."

"And what could that be?"

Her raised brow and teasing voice caused Darcy to smile. He extracted a small, square, black velvet box from his pocket. "Your engagement ring." He pulled back the lid to expose an exquisite diamond and ruby ring. The center ruby was round and the diamonds encircled it. An engraved heart, situated close to the set stones, appeared on each side of the gold band.

"Oh, William. It is beautiful."

"It was my grandmother's. I love the red highlights in your hair when the sun shines on it, and that made me think of this ring." Lifting the ring from the box, Darcy reached for Elizabeth's hand and slid it on her finger." His heart swelled with love as he looked at the ring on her hand.

When Darcy looked up at Elizabeth, he saw that tears glistened in her eyes. "It fits perfectly, and I will cherish it always," she said. "I love you, William." Her last words were no louder than a whisper, but the look in her eyes spoke volumes.

The next three days were a whirlwind of activity. The ladies of Darcy House, with Mrs. Annesley as their chaperone, spent Tuesday morning at Mr. Gardiner's warehouse. Mrs. Gardiner joined her nieces and the others to help with their selections. Two shipments of fabric arrived the preceding day. Mr. Gardiner assigned two stock boys the responsibility of unpacking and inventorying the items, then placing them in his showroom for display. He closed the showroom for the morning, allowing his nieces first choice of the new materials. It had taken several hours before Jane and Elizabeth had each amassed enough fabric for a good-sized trousseau and for the other girls, including Georgiana, to select the fabric for their new gowns. That afternoon, Mrs. Annesley met with the younger girls and discussed appropriate behavior for their upcoming expeditions. She impressed upon the Misses Bennet the importance of quiet voices and demure behavior as well as balancing that with their individual natures.

Fearing Lydia and Kitty's exuberance as well as Mary's strictures on pride and humility, Jane, Elizabeth, and Mrs. Gardiner each felt some trepidation at the outing. Bringing the three youngest Bennets sisters to the shop of London's most renowned dress designer seemed, on the face of it, to be a poor idea. However, to the women's great shock and delight, everything went very well. Georgiana had set the appointment for nine in the morning—an hour before the shop usually opened, thus allowing them time to arrive and settle in the largest of the private rooms without others seeing them.

Madame LaRue expressed her pleasure upon seeing Miss Elizabeth and Mrs. Gardiner again. Georgiana then introduced the others. Madame's eyes lit up when she realized she would be creating a much larger trousseau for Miss Elizabeth as well as an additional trousseau for the elder Miss Bennet. Looking at the differences in the appearances of the two young ladies, Madame found her mind becoming aflutter with ideas. Miss Jane Bennet was the epitome of society's perfect lady. Madame LaRue could create new styles that would grow her business, as everyone would wish to emulate this extraordinarily beautiful young woman. On the other hand, Miss Elizabeth's petite size and voluptuous figure would allow Madame LaRue to showcase her talents with other body types. She imagined creating styles that would show off Miss Elizabeth's striking figure while giving the illusion of conforming to the style of the day in an entirely unique way.

Two of the footmen from Darcy House accompanied the ladies on their excursion. Their task was to carry the fabrics the women had purchased the previous day. Madame exclaimed over several of the fabrics that Elizabeth and Jane had chosen.

"I must know where you found such beautiful fabrics!" exclaimed Madame LaRue. "I 'ave rarely seen zeir like."

Mrs. Gardiner smiled with pleasure at the modiste's words, but it was Elizabeth who replied. "They are from my uncle's warehouse. He is the owner of Gardiner Import/Export.

"I 'ave 'eard of Monsieur Gardiner, but 'ave not 'ad the pleasure of meeting 'im. Perhaps, Madame

## A Matter of Timing

Gardiner, you might arrange for ze introduction. If 'e can obtain such beautiful fabrics, I must have access to 'im."

"I would be happy to arrange a meeting between you, Madame. He received two large shipments this week and has not yet displayed them in his showroom, though I believe he may do so today. When would you be available to meet?"

"For such an exciting opportunity, Madame Gardiner, I would 'appily cancel the appointments I have zis afternoon."

"If you have some paper and someone who could deliver a message, I shall write to him immediately."

Madame opened the curtain and snapped her fingers. An assistant appeared at her side. After a whispered conversation in French, the assistant disappeared.

Two assistants waited in the room for Madame's orders. Another appeared carrying a small portable writing desk, which she placed before Mrs. Gardiner.

As Mrs. Gardiner wrote the note to her husband, Madame turned to Elizabeth. "When you were last 'ere, Mademoiselle Elizabeth, you could not tell me the name of your betrothed. I would imagine since you are back zat you can do so now?"

Elizabeth smiled and prepared to answer the question, but before she could, Georgiana burst out with, "Elizabeth is going to be my sister. They will be wed in a double ceremony on September sixth with Miss Jane Bennet and her betrothed, Mr. Bingley." Georgiana's words abruptly ended as she heard the giggles from her companions. Her face turning a brilliant shade of red, she added, "I am sorry, Lizzy. I should have allowed you to answer."

"You need not worry, Georgiana, it is a delight to know you are happy to gain me as a sister."

"I am, indeed!" This sparked another round of giggles and an indulgent smile from Mrs. Annesley.

While the assistants measured Jane, Elizabeth had the first fitting for her wedding gown and the other dresses she had already ordered. Upon the completion of those measurements, the ladies looked through Madame LaRue's pattern books. There were enough books to go around, so while Mary and Kitty perused day dresses, Lydia looked at evening gowns. Georgiana gazed at afternoon dresses, while Elizabeth looked at ball gowns and Jane at wedding dresses. The group took more than four hours, but when they departed, they had ordered more clothing for Elizabeth and Jane then the five sisters together had owned in their whole lives.

Mrs. Gardiner accompanied Madame La Rue to her husband's warehouse, while the others returned to Darcy House for luncheon. The peace of the study, where Darcy and Bingley sat discussing marriage settlements, disappeared when the sounds of laughter and feminine voices reached them from the entryway. The gentlemen set down their glasses and strolled out to meet the ladies. Bingley's face lit up at the sight of his angel and warmth filled Darcy's heart upon seeing the two women he loved most in the world.

When Wednesday arrived, the ladies from Darcy House met Mrs. Gardiner at her modiste in Cheapside. The shop did not have the elegance of the one they had visited in Bond Street the previous day, but the fabrics and patterns were of equal quality. The younger Bennet girls had initially experienced disappointment when they learned that Madame LaRue would not be making their dresses. However, Mrs. Gardiner explained that by using her modiste, they would have funds remaining to purchase some accessories they would like. As only three gowns were necessary, this outing was much shorter.

After completing their errand, the ladies split between the two carriages and drove in the direction of Hyde Park, turning in at the entrance to Rotten Row from Park Lane. As it was early in the day, they were able to avoid the fashionable crowd that usually came to see and be seen. Consequently, the carriages traveled without many delays. A newly cut track led off the main path towards the banks of the Serpentine. In a freshly created clearing sat a small restaurant, reminiscent of the cafés along the Champs-Elysees. Two horses were tied up outside, and from the carriage window, Elizabeth could see Darcy and Bingley waiting by the water.

At the sound of the carriages, the gentleman turned and moved forward to assist the ladies. Darcy placed Elizabeth on one arm and led the group to the café. He requested one of the outdoor tables overlooking the water. They placed an order for tea, lemonade, and a selection of pastries.

"Now that you have finished your shopping..." began Darcy.

All the ladies laughed.

"Am I mistaken in my thinking? Have you not finished ordering all the dresses and other clothes you need?"

Elizabeth patted his arm and tried to keep her amusement under control. "You are correct, William. We have ordered all the new clothes we needed. However, we still have many things to purchase as well as at least one or two fittings to attend."

"In any case, I was wondering what you would like to do while in London. We can certainly partake in at least one or two activities, can we not?"

"I would like to see the animals at the royal menagerie," said Lydia.

"I would like to see the new art exhibit," added Georgiana.

"As would I," chimed in Kitty.

"Jane and I would enjoy a trip to the theater or a musical evening." Elizabeth added her choice.

"A concert sounds pleasant," agreed Mary, "or perhaps a walk in Kensington Park."

Bingley felt he should contribute something to the conversation. "I think all of those ideas sound very enjoyable."

"William, have you and Mr. Bingley completed all the business you said required your attention during our stay in town?"

"We have met with our solicitors to finalize the marriage settlements and have placed the announcements of the engagements in the papers. They should appear tomorrow."

Elizabeth leaned close to him and whispered, "Have you told your Fitzwilliam relations about the wedding?"

Darcy could hear a touch of anxiety in her voice. Reaching over to pat her hand, he answered her question. "I wrote to my aunt and uncle, and they expressed their desire to attend the wedding. Apparently, Richard had given a good account of you after our meeting in Hunsford and had taken it upon himself to indicate I might have a preference for you. They plan to arrive two days before the wedding and to stay at Netherfield."

"I hope they will not judge me too harshly, as their first exposure to my family will likely be my mother's nervous excitement as she finalizes the arrangements for the wedding breakfast and orders Mr. Bingley's staff about."

"You need not worry, my love. They will be delighted with you, particularly when they see how happy you make me." Darcy's whispered words were like a caress and caused a soft blush to suffuse her cheeks.

As they finished their refreshments, they set a date for each of the desired activities. Then they returned to their homes. The first event was to be dinner at the Gardiners' home on the following evening.

---

At the same time the shopping party arrived in London, Charlotte Collins received a letter from her mother, informing her of the two engagements, the shopping trip to London, and Mr. Bennet's ill health. When Mr. Collins asked his wife about the news in her letter, she was slow to respond. The only excuse she could come up with was to claim that it was her mother's answer to a question about female matters.

The parson's face turned red with embarrassment. "I hope you are well, my dear," had been his only comment.

Unfortunately, as Mr. Collins sat at the table several days later, he noticed the announcement of two engagements. As he read them, his eyes nearly popped out of his head.

"Oh, dear. Oh, dear! I do hope Lady Catherine will not blame me for this matter."

"Is something wrong, Mr. Collins?" his wife asked.

"I believe the paper has made a mistake. There is an announcement here of Mr. Darcy's engagement to my cousin, Elizabeth. Lady Catherine will be most displeased."

"If you think that to be the case, perhaps you should not mention the matter to her." Charlotte voiced her suggestion tentatively. "I am sure Mr. Darcy will write to his aunt about the matter, and as you say, it could be a mistake. There is no need to upset your patroness if it is an error."

Mr. Collins hesitated. His wife made a good point. "Perhaps I should travel to Longbourn to speak to the Bennets about the matter. Should my cousin have overreached in such an infamous manner, it is my duty to talk her out of the betrothal. In fact, I made the family aware of Mr. Darcy's engagement to Miss de Bourgh, when I visited last fall."

"I would suggest a letter. It would be an expensive trip to undertake if the notice in the paper is a misprint."

"You are quite correct, my dear Charlotte. I shall write to Mr. Bennet directly. I believe I shall send the letter express, as well."

"You do that, my dear. I have some correspondence I should attend to, also." Charlotte finished her breakfast before shutting herself in her private parlor. Knowing that Elizabeth was in London and having the Gardiners' address, Charlotte wrote to her friend, relating her husband's reaction to the news and his plans to learn more.

*"I do not know what Lady Catherine's reaction will be, but hopefully, with foreknowledge of her probable response, you and Mr. Darcy will be prepared to deal with the lady."*

Looking over her last paragraph Charlotte signed and sealed her letter.

Knocking on her husband's door, Charlotte peeked her head inside. "I have some shopping to do in Hunsford. Would you like me to take your letter to the express office, husband?"

"I would appreciate that, Mrs. Collins, for I must finish my sermon for this week and review it with Lady Catherine." Mr. Collins rose and handed the letter to his wife, kissing her cheek as he did so.

"I shall return soon."

---

At the close of their first week in London, Elizabeth received Charlotte's letter. After a brief discussion with Mr. Darcy, he sent an express to his Aunt and Uncle Fitzwilliam. William requested his uncle's early return in case Lady Catherine decided to make trouble. By the time he received the return express, they were on their way.

Midway through their second week in London, the residents of Darcy House spent an enjoyable morning walking the paths of Kensington Park. They were enjoying tea when they heard Simmon's slightly raised voice asking someone to wait to be announced. However, Caroline Bingley had no intention of waiting.

"There is no need to announce me, as Mr.—uh, Miss Darcy and I are such old and close friends." So saying, she flounced past the butler and headed for the stairs. Halfway up, she paused and turned back to the servant. "In which drawing room will I find him, I mean them?" She did not wait for an answer, calling out, "Never mind, I shall just take a peek in each room until I find my friends."

The occupants of the room exchanged looks showing a variety of emotions. Georgiana looked disconcerted, Bingley looked embarrassed, and Darcy appeared extremely irritated. Rising to his feet, he looked at his friend, saying, "I am sorry, Bingley, but I will no longer tolerate your sister waltzing into my home as if she owned it. I hope you will not be offended, but I plan to address the matter with her."

Darcy stepped into the hall to see Miss Bingley exit the room nearest the stairs. She did not glance about before pausing to preen before a nearby mirror. As she turned, she saw Darcy coming towards her. Her usual predatory smile appeared on her face.

"Mr. Darcy," she purred. "I am delighted to see you again. It has been much too long. We stopped at Pemberley on our way back from the north. We hoped to continue our visit that had been so rudely interrupted and abruptly cut short. When you were not there, we rushed to London so that we might be reunited."

By this time, Caroline had arrived at Darcy's side and reached out to take his arm. He stepped back, preventing the lady from attaining her goal. The expression he directed at her was very stern.

"Miss Bingley, I believe it is only polite to wait to be announced when entering someone's home."

"With a friendship as close as ours, we can dispense with such formalities."

"No, we cannot. I am not at liberty to receive you today, as we are entertaining other guests."

"Then I shall take only a moment to greet Georgiana and invite her to tea tomorrow before departing." Darcy tried to grab her arm as she waltzed past him, but she was too quick. He followed her to the open doors of the drawing room. "My dearest Georgiana! Oh, how I have missed you!" Trying to make a grand entrance, Caroline Bingley swept into the salon. She was curious to know who Darcy was entertaining. She wished it might be the Earl and Countess of Matlock. She had previously failed to gain an introduction to them and was hoping to make a good impression.

She stopped abruptly, noticing a significant number of females in the room. As she focused her eyes more closely on the occupants, her face took on a decided frown.

"Miss Bennet, Miss Eliza, whatever are you doing here?" Looking more closely, Caroline almost screeched. "Oh, good heavens! All the Bennet sisters are here and the tradesman's wife, as well." Pausing for breath, Caroline noticed three children seated near Mrs. Gardiner. All of them stared at her with wide eyes. A shudder ran through her, for Caroline detested children. "Thank goodness I have arrived, Georgiana! Your brother should dismiss your companion for allowing you to receive people of such lowly status. It could damage your reputation! And that woman did not have the sense to leave her children at home. Children should not be allowed in Darcy House. Their dirty, grubby hands will ruin so much and could damage many of the precious heirlooms." She grabbed Georgiana's arm in an attempt to remove her from the unfortunate influence of the Bennet sisters.

"Miss Bingley, please release me." Fury at the rude way in which Miss Bingley spoke about her friends gave Georgiana confidence. "How dare you come into my home and speak so to my guests? Nor have I ever given you permission to address me so casually. Please desist in doing so.

"Do be quiet, Caroline!" Bingley whispered to his sister as he took her elbow and tried to drag her from the room.

## A Matter of Timing

"Stop it, Charles. I shall certainly not leave. I have as much right to be here, if not more, than these interlopers."

"That is where you are wrong, Miss Bingley."

Caroline turned slowly towards the sound of Darcy's voice. He stood in the doorway, bearing a forbidding expression. "As I stated earlier, good manners dictate waiting to be announced and to see if your hosts can receive you. Miss Darcy and I are unable to accept a visit from you today."

She moved to stand within inches of Darcy, her look pleading. "How can you be helping that fortune hunter ensnare my brother, again? You must let me save both of you from a most disastrous situation!" Caroline Bingley made little attempt to lower her voice, intending for the others in attendance to hear her insults.

Darcy's look grew even more furious. "That is enough, Miss Bingley. I never agreed that Miss Bennet was a fortune hunter. I am particularly familiar with that type, as one is standing right before me."

Caroline looked around, assuming someone must be standing behind her. She was appalled to realize Mr. Darcy was referring to her.

"You forced your way into my home, you have insulted my sister, my betrothed, my future sisters, and myself. I believe it is time for you to leave. The staff will have orders to not admit you in the future without explicit instructions from me to do so."

Caroline was flabbergasted. "Mr. Darcy, it is unkind of you to tease me so." She attempted to laugh off his words, but the sound fell flat. Darcy swept his arm towards the door, indicating she should precede him from the room. When she did not move, he gave a quick nod to Bingley, who stepped forward and again took hold of his sister's arm, pulling her from the room. Once the three of them were in the hallway, Darcy closed the doors to the drawing room, for he did not wish any further insults to reach the others.

Simmons was standing in the upstairs hallway with two large footmen. One look from their master and the footmen stood directly behind the unwelcome intruder, one on each side of Miss Bingley, though she was not aware of this.

Caroline reached out to grab Darcy's arm. "Mr. Darcy, what have they done to you? Please, you and Charles must leave with me now, before those dreadful Bennet sisters manage to entrap you in a compromise."

"Both Miss Bennet and Miss Elizabeth are far too ladylike to attempt such a thing, unlike some I can name." Darcy gave her a derisive look as he recalled the footman's words about finding Miss Bingley trying to enter the family wing before his trip to London. "Indeed, there is no need for them to take such action. Betrothals already exist between your brother and Miss Bennet and between Miss Elizabeth and myself. The wedding is less than two weeks away."

"No, it cannot be. You are mine. I have been your friend for years and have done everything I can to prove to you that I am the perfect mistress for Pemberley and Darcy House. I have patiently waited for you to make me an offer. I was sure it would be soon."

"I do not know why you would think such a thing. I have done absolutely nothing that would lead you to believe I had feelings for you. You are merely my friend's sister."

"How can you say such a thing? I am the only woman you have ever invited to Pemberley. Why else would you invite me to your homes?"

"Miss Bingley, I have never directly invited you to visit, nor would I do so. However, you have always insinuated yourself into your brother's invitations. In the past, I chose to ignore such behavior in deference to my friend's feelings. However, I will no longer tolerate your presence. You are not welcome in any of my homes. For Bingley and Miss Bennet's sake, I will be polite in public, but I recommend that you keep your distance rather than try my patience on the issue."

## A Matter of Timing

Miss Bingley could not believe what she was hearing. All of her dreams were crumbling at her feet and all because of the dreadful Eliza Bennet. Caroline's anger blazed. She pictured Elizabeth standing before her and the satisfaction she would feel upon striking her rival. The picture was so vivid in her mind that her arm reacted of its own accord. However, the satisfying sound of her hand connecting with Elizabeth's face caused an unusual amount of pain. It was the feeling of pain that returned her to her present surroundings. Her face showed horror when she saw a handprint appearing on Mr. Darcy's face.

Before she could speak to offer an apology, the footmen grabbed her elbows, lifting her feet off the floor. They whisked her away and down the stairs before she could blink. When the motion finally stopped, Caroline Bingley was staring at the closed door of Darcy House.

Elizabeth sat staring at the door, waiting for William to return. When Darcy and Bingley entered, she was out of her seat in a second, pulling the bell to summon a servant. Then she moved to stand before her betrothed, studying the mark on his face.

"Did Miss Bingley actually strike you, as it appears?"

Darcy tried to laugh it off with a teasing comment. "Indeed, she did. It is a good thing I am such a big, tall fellow, for she would have knocked a lesser person to the ground. She has an impressive strength."

His words did not fool Elizabeth. Raising a brow at him, she asked, "Does it hurt very much?"

"I have experienced much worse when sparring with Gentleman Jackson, Elizabeth."

At that moment, Mrs. Baxter entered in answer to the bell. Elizabeth looked at the housekeeper, saying, "Is there any ice available? I believe Mr. Darcy requires some for his cheek." Mrs. Baxter looked confused but hurried to carry out the request.

Elizabeth took William by the hand and moved him to a seat that kept the injured side of his face from view. Upon settling him, she walked to a small table on which sat a set of decanters. Taking a glass, Elizabeth poured Mr. Darcy two fingers of brandy. She handed him the glass before taking a seat on his injured side. It was fortunate the younger girls were engrossed in conversation. Only Jane and Georgiana had looked at the gentlemen when they returned, and both gentlemen had rolled their eyes at Miss Bingley's antics before turning away.

"Was it something you said that caused your injury or was it merely a temper tantrum?" Elizabeth's voice was so soft, only Darcy could hear it.

"I banned her from my homes and told her not to approach me in public. My patience with her would extend only so far as to not embarrassing Bingley and Miss Bennet."

"I am not surprised she did not take such a statement well. I suppose we are lucky her hand was the only weapon available to her. Do you think she will comply with your request to keep her distance?"

"I can only hope so."

Mrs. Baxter returned with a small chunk of ice wrapped in a towel. She handed it to Elizabeth, then bobbed a curtsey and returned to her duties. Elizabeth leaned closer and applied the ice to Darcy's cheek. To the others, it would appear like she was acting forward, but she did not care.

Darcy sighed in relief as the coolness soothed his inflamed skin. "Are you prepared to meet my family tomorrow?"

"Do you think they will like me?"

"Of course they will. The earl and countess will love you, just as Georgiana and I do."

"I am glad they will be dining here. Mrs. Annesley will be able to keep an eye on my younger sisters so that I will be free to concentrate on making a good impression on your illustrious relations."

## A Matter of Timing

"Just relax and be yourself. It was those qualities that made me fall in love with you and that made such a positive impression on Richard. I am sure you will charm them before the night is over."

Elizabeth bestowed a radiant smile on Darcy. This new William always seemed to know the right thing to say. Glancing quickly at the other occupants of the room, she realized no one was paying them any attention, so she lifted the ice and planted a quick kiss on William's cheek before pulling back and replacing the cold compress.

---

Richard Fitzwilliam arrived at Darcy House ahead of his parents. He needed to speak to William. Earlier that day, the colonel had received a letter from Colonel Forster in Brighton. The court martial for George Wickham had taken place two days prior, and William had to know the outcome.

As he entered the room, Georgiana spotted him first. "Richard! You are early!" she cried as she rushed to embrace him.

"Hello, Georgie. I needed to speak with Darcy for a moment and did not wish to take him away from his guests once my parents arrived." He glanced about him, greeting the others he knew. "Good evening, Miss Elizabeth, Miss Lydia, Bingley."

The others returned his greeting, Lydia somewhat shyly.

Turning back to Georgiana, he said, "When I have finished speaking with your brother, I shall expect you to introduce me to these other lovely ladies." Nodding towards Darcy, he said, "If you will excuse us for just one moment."

"I will return shortly." As Darcy bowed over Elizabeth's hand, she leaned in and whispered something to him. He nodded in return and turned to lead his cousin to his study.

"What was so important, Richard? Please tell me that Wickham has not escaped!"

"No, indeed, cousin. Wickham shall never bother you, or anyone else, again."

Darcy stared, waiting for Richard to give him the details.

"The court martial was two days ago. Wickham was found guilty of desertion and conduct unbecoming an officer. Not one mention of the attempted elopement. And though he tried to blame you for every problem in his life, the court refused to listen to anything he said. Because the losses on the peninsula have been considerable, desertion is up, so the Army decided to make an example of Wickham. The hanging was the same day."

"I know learning he is dead will cause the ladies distress, but they must be aware that they have nothing further to fear from him. Though, I shall wait until after dinner to make the announcement."

William was, indeed, correct. The Earl and Countess of Matlock were delighted with Elizabeth and her sisters. The younger girls behaved like perfect ladies. As the countess sat with Georgiana and the Bennet sisters during the separation of the sexes after dinner, she took the opportunity to ask many questions of Elizabeth.

"So, you have one last appointment with Madame LaRue on Friday and will return to Hertfordshire on Saturday?"

"Yes, Lady Matlock."

"I should love to join you ladies if you would permit it."

"We would be happy to have you, your ladyship."

"Now, none of that. You will be my niece in just under a week. I would love for you to call me Aunt Elaine."

"I would happily do so, but only if you call me Elizabeth or Lizzy, as my family does."

## A Matter of Timing

"What time should I arrive? I will bring my carriage so that we have plenty of space."

"If that is the case, perhaps the Darcy carriage could leave a little earlier and pick up my Aunt Gardiner from her home in Cheapside."

When she mentioned her aunt's address, Elizabeth watched Lady Matlock closely. She saw a look of puzzlement appear on the countess' face, but no disdain.

"Would your aunt be associated with Mr. Edward Gardiner, the owner of Gardiner Import/Export?"

"She is his wife." Elizabeth's face showed her surprise at Lady Matlock's words.

"I will look forward to making her acquaintance. I have been delighted with some of the items I have purchased from Mr. Gardiner's warehouse. He carries such beautiful and unique things. They make marvelous gifts."

"I am sure they would both be delighted to know that. I will be happy to introduce you to my aunt on Friday."

When the gentlemen joined the ladies, Lady Matlock mentioned Elizabeth's connection to the Gardiners."

"Excellent fellow, your uncle. He has a great head for business and investing. I was an investor in his last warehouse purchase," the earl said.

"You are correct in your estimation of Mr. Gardiner, Uncle. I have also invested some funds with him. He is hoping to expand again. This time he is talking about a shop to sell the many coffee and teas he imports."

The evening ended on a pleasant note. The Earl and Countess both departed for home with a very positive impression of all the Bennet ladies, particularly Elizabeth.

Just before the ladies retired, Darcy requested that Elizabeth, Georgiana, and Lydia join him and

Richard for a moment. Bingley offered his arm to Jane and led the others up the stairs to their rooms.

The ladies sat on the sofa with Elizabeth between the two younger girls. Elizabeth had a suspicion of what news he might have to impart, but Georgiana and Lydia only looked confused.

Without preamble, Darcy began speaking. "Colonel Fitzwilliam received a letter from Brighton today. Mr. Wickham was court-martialed and found guilty of desertion and misconduct." Darcy took a deep breath, looking at Elizabeth for courage. "They hung him the same day." A gasp escaped each of the young ladies, so Darcy rushed to complete his explanation. "Apparently, there have been an unusual number of desertions because of the heavy casualties on the peninsula. The army chose to make an example of Wickham in an attempt to curb the losses."

Darcy studied the expressions across from him. Tears were silently sliding down his sister's pale face. Elizabeth was obviously distressed, though he knew it had nothing to do with her feelings for the man. He was sure her distress had to do with her involvement in anyone's death—no matter how little she could have affected the outcome. Lydia's expression was hard to decipher. She had obviously cared for Wickham, but he had also hurt her terribly.

"I want you all to remember one thing. Wickham signed a contract with the militia. He knew there would be consequences if he abandoned his position. Nothing any of you did could have affected the result of his trial. Wickham was a grown man; he knew the risks he was taking. Please remember, Wickham did this to himself. You did not make him desert his post in a time of war. Please try to rest and put the matter from your minds." Darcy hugged Georgiana and kissed her forehead. "I know it is sad when someone you once cared for comes to such an end, but it was the life he chose for himself. Had he not felt so entitled, he could have accepted Father's gift and led a very useful, comfortable life." Darcy turned to Lydia. "Are you well, Miss Lydia?"

"I think so. Wickham was not a good man, but I am sorry he is dead."

Elizabeth looked at the confused young ladies before her. "No matter who you are, you have choices before you. Mr. Wickham grew up in a loving home and had an outstanding patron who tried to assist him. He allowed jealousy and greed to blind him and made choices that led him to attempt eloping with both of you. Because of that, I feel confident that Mr. Wickham's decisions and actions would have led him to the same end, whether it happened now or later."

"You are wise to realize that, Miss Elizabeth," Darcy said. "Each of you girls made an unwise choice, but you learned from your mistakes. George Wickham never did. Now, I will ask again that you put this out of your mind and find peace for the night. There are still a few outings before we return to Hertfordshire."

Darcy held out his arm to Elizabeth and motioned for Georgiana and Lydia to lead them from the room. They mounted the stairs and said good night one last time before turning to their separate rooms.

# LAUGHTER IS THE BEST MEDICINE

Mr. Collins was irritated. He was going to be late for a meeting with his esteemed patroness, Lady Catherine de Bourgh. Mrs. Collins was in the village, and a button had fallen off his coat. The parson could not present himself to Lady Catherine in such a fashion. Entering his wife's private parlor, he looked around for her sewing basket. After all, Mr. Collins had attended to such little things before having found the companion of his future life. Finding the box in the corner near a window and overstuffed chair, Mr. Collins opened the top. He was surprised to see a letter atop the other items and he lifted it out. Studying the date and return address, Mr. Collins realized it was the one Charlotte had said involved female matters. Though he was not sure, he wished to know more, as concern for his dear wife overcame his hesitation. Collins unfolded the letter and began reading. The further he read, the angrier he became. Why had Charlotte deliberately misled him and withheld this information? Lady Catherine would be beyond furious with his family and perhaps his wife should she discover the truth. Perversely, he wondered if Mr.

Bennet still lived, or if he, William Collins, was now a member of the landed gentry.

As he stitched the button back on his jacket, Mr. Collins decided how he could use the upcoming meeting with Lady Catherine to his advantage. Though Mr. Collins was not particularly intelligent and had an over-inflated opinion of himself, he had one instinct that was extremely strong—self-preservation. If it was a matter of his personal comfort, he could be rather ingenious. When his attire was again in pristine order, he hurried up the drive to Rosings Park.

Upon his admittance to the grand lady's presence, Mr. Collins set his plan in motion. "My most humble apologies for being tardy, your ladyship, but I received some distressing news just before departing. It seems my Cousin Bennet is at death's door. In fact, he might already have passed."

"Yes, well, do not allow it to happen again. You know how I dislike being kept waiting."

"Of course, Lady Catherine. My dear patroness, I wonder if I might impose upon you for an opinion. I know of no one with your understanding of estate matters." Lady Catherine preened at the compliment. "There is no other estate that could compare with your magnificent Rosings Park." The lady's smile grew.

"You are quite correct, Mr. Collins. What advice can I offer you?"

"I am concerned that Mrs. Bennet has attempted to conceal this illness from me in order to keep me from my inheritance. I am but a humble parson with no experience in such matters. What would your ladyship advise?"

"I would clearly state your expectations upon arriving and set a deadline for the ladies to remove from the residence. It cannot be too short, or you will appear heartless, but you cannot allow them to take advantage of your good nature."

"I had thought much the same and am relieved to know how much I have learned under your tutelage." Lady Catherine delighted in this new praise.

"Unfortunately, there is one rub. Mrs. Bennet is subject to fits of nerves. I am sure she will take to her bed and refuse to leave. As a gentleman, I will be unable to take any action against her and should not wish to try, for it may reflect poorly upon your ladyship."

"I know how to deal with such paltry antics. I shall accompany you, Mr. Collins. In exchange, once you have gained your inheritance and I have found you a suitable steward, you must promise to return to your duties here until I can select a replacement for you."

"You are too kind, Lady Catherine. I shall be only too happy to agree to your request. When would you wish to depart?"

"We should not dilly-dally, Mr. Collins. We must leave early tomorrow. Leave your sermon for me to review, and we can discuss it during our journey. Now, excuse me, I must make arrangements for our trip. My carriage will stop at your abode promptly at seven in the morning."

"Good day, your ladyship." Mr. Collins smiled to himself as he stepped through the doors of Rosings Park. Now, to deal with his deceitful wife!

When Charlotte returned from Hunsford Village, Mr. Collins awaited her in her private parlor, her letter in his hand.

With seeming unconcern, Charlotte addressed her husband. "I am surprised to see you here. Is there something with which I can help you?"

"You can explain to me about this letter."

"What letter is that?"

"The one that arrived from your mother last week. When I asked you about the contents, you said it was an answer about a woman's matter. That was a blatant lie."

"How dare you, sir. You forced your way into my private room, snooped through my belongings, and read my personal correspondence. I am appalled at your conduct. How can you so disrespect your wife?"

Charlotte put her head in her hands and pretended to cry.

"Now, now, my dear, do not cry. I came upon your letter by accident while I was looking for a needle and thread to repair the button on my jacket. It came off just before I was to meet with Lady Catherine. You know what a stickler she can be about appearance." Charlotte just sniffed, so Mr. Collins handed her his handkerchief. "That still does not explain why you misled me."

"I was trying to protect you." The words came out between sniffles.

"That is very considerate of you, my dear wife, but I believe protection falls under my purview as the man. How did you think you were protecting me?"

Charlotte raised her head and wiped away the tears she had managed to force from her eyes. "I know how poorly the Bennets treated you on your first visit. I did not wish for you to rush there if Mr. Bennet were not gravely ill. I would not wish him to be unkind to you again."

Mr. Collins remembered his shame and chagrin at the way Elizabeth had refused his offer of marriage. "That was very kind of you, Charlotte, but it does not explain why you withheld information about cousin Elizabeth's engagement to Mr. Darcy. You know that he is engaged to Miss de Bourgh."

"Something Miss de Bourgh said when last we had tea together led me to believe they had broken the engagement. I was afraid if you raised the matter with Lady Catherine and she had not recovered from her disappointment, she might take her anger out on you."

Mr. Collins' doubt registered on his face. "What could Miss de Bourgh have said that would give you that idea?"

"She expressed her happiness and belief that her cousin's heart was attached elsewhere. Miss de Bourgh said it was only her mother who wished the cousins to marry. She did not have the heart to disagree with her mother's wishes but Miss de Bourgh does not want to marry her cousin, Darcy. I felt sorry for her, that she might be forced to marry someone should her heart be elsewhere. Then she would never know the kind of happiness we share, dear husband." Her eyes still glistening with tears, Charlotte smiled sweetly at her husband.

"Well, we will discuss this no further, and I will make no mention of your actions to Lady Catherine."

Charlotte looked down to hide a grimace.

The next morning, Lady Catherine's coach arrived a few minutes early, but fortunately Mr. Collins was ready. The footman picked up and stowed his trunk as the parson climbed into the carriage. He held two newspapers under his arm.

"Good morning, Lady Catherine. I thank you for your assistance in this most delicate of matters."

"Yes, well, it is early yet, so I believe I shall rest in preparation for the work we will need to accomplish later."

"Certainly, my lady. I have two posts to read, as I am a little behind due to parish matters. I shall be as quiet as possible so as not to disturb your rest."

Mr. Collins began on the front page of the newer paper. If his patroness was asleep, he would be unable to make her aware of the engagement. Grabbing the post that had arrived the previous day, Mr. Collins turned the pages as quietly as possible. Nothing of importance caught his notice, so he placed the paper aside and turned his attention to the passing scenery.

Almost three hours had passed since they had begun the journey. Lady Catherine was showing signs of waking, so Mr. Collins picked up the earlier paper and turned to the announcement of Mr. Darcy's engagement. Watching his patroness in the window, he saw the lady's eyes flutter open and closed a few times before she finally woke. Keeping his eye on her reflection, he watched her pat her hair and smooth her clothes.

After five minutes of studying the woman, Mr. Collins decided the time was right. Rattling the paper as if he had just turned a page, he read for a moment before crying, "This must be a mistake!"

"I beg your pardon, Mr. Collins?" Lady Catherine's tone was brusque, as she assumed Mr. Collins had addressed his remark to her.

"Forgive me, Lady Catherine. I was startled by an engagement announcement I just read."

"Why should such a notice surprise you? Who is getting married?"

"I believe it would be best if you read the notice yourself, your ladyship." Mr. Collins handed the paper to his patroness. He pointed to the relevant paragraph on the page and sat back to await her reaction.

"This cannot be!" Lady Catherine's screech startled her companion, even though he knew she would not react well to the news. "It is good that we are already on our way to Hertfordshire. I shall have to speak to Miss Bennet and remind her that Mr. Darcy is already engaged to my daughter." Lady Catherine rapped on the ceiling of the carriage with her walking stick. "Make haste, driver. We must reach Meryton quickly!

Lady Catherine sat back in her seat and spoke not another word, though it was easy for her companion to see the lady's mounting anger.

---

It was half-past four in the afternoon when Lady Catherine's carriage turned into Longbourn's drive. Mrs. Bennet was at Netherfield and Mr. Bennet was enjoying tea in his study as he reviewed the mail that had arrived during his recovery.

When the carriage stopped, Lady Catherine waited impatiently for the footman to open the door, set the step, and assist her down. As Mr. Collins exited the carriage, Lady Catherine surveyed her surroundings. It was not a large estate, but it would be sufficient for her parson and his family. She marched to the door, her nose in the air, and knocked several times with the metal knob of her walking stick.

It was quite some time before anyone answered. When Mrs. Hill opened the door, she stared at the visitors for a moment before speaking. During his previous visit, Mr. Collins had not made a good impression on any of Longbourn's inhabitants, even the servants. As a result, she was hesitant to admit him, as the master was still recovering from his surgery. Her gaze turned to the imperious lady standing before her. The woman appeared angry and impatient.

"Yes, can I help you?"

"I am here to see Mrs. Bennet. Why was I not informed of Mr. Bennet's poor health?" Mr. Collins said.

"Never mind that now," said Lady Catherine, swatting at Mr. Collins like he were an irritating insect. "I demand to see Miss Elizabeth Bennet immediately."

"I am sorry, but Mrs. Bennet is not here, nor is Miss Elizabeth. You'll 'ave to come back another time."

"Do you know who I am?" cried Lady Catherine.

"No, I don't, nor do I care. The people you wish to see are away from home. Now, please leave. Perhaps you should send a note requestin' a visit before you return."

"This is not to be borne!"

"This is my esteemed patroness, Lady Catherine de Bourgh," said Mr. Collins. "Now, as the master of Longbourn, I demand you let me in."

"You aren't the master of Longbourn yet, sir, so you'll not be comin' in."

"What are you saying? I received word that my cousin suffered a head injury and collapsed. I heard he was not expected to live."

"Well, Mr. Collins, you were misinformed. The master is recoverin' nicely, and this is his first day out o' his room. You'll not barge in here and disturb 'im."

"I am not going anywhere until I have spoken with Miss Elizabeth." Lady Catherine advanced on Mrs. Hill, but the housekeeper held her ground.

Another voice spoke up. "I thank you, Mrs. Hill, for attempting to maintain my peace, but I will see these individuals. Since they refuse to take your word about the happenings here, perhaps I can persuade them."

Mr. Bennet stood in the open door of his book room. He had heard every word of the exchange, for neither individual made any attempt to keep his or her business private. Lady Catherine huffed as she pushed past the servant, whereas Mr. Collins' look showed that he feared for his future. Mrs. Hill matched his look with a glare of her own.

She followed the visitors into her master's study. At the door, she said, "I will send Mr. Hill to assist you, sir. Please remember what the doctors said about undue stress."

"Thank you, Mrs. Hill. Please ask him to wait outside the door; I will call for him if he is needed."

"Yes, sir."

"Mr. Collins, I will deal with you first. When you were last here, you were asked not to return. What do you have to say for yourself?"

"I was informed of your illness—though, because of their ill upbringing, not by your family. As the only remaining male Bennet relation and heir to this estate, my place was here."

"There was no need to let you know anything, as my prognosis was good. Had there been a reason for you to know of my condition, my attorney would have notified you. Now I will ask you to leave my house. You shall not be granted admission again unless I am dead and gone."

"But as a member of the clergy, I could have provided comfort to your family while you were ill."

"No, Mr. Collins, they had enough to concern them. They did not deserve to have such a punishment inflicted upon them as having your sermonizing and unending praise of your patroness bore them to death."

"Mr. Bennet! You dare to insult such an exalted personage! Perhaps the head injury did more damage than anyone realizes. You must be out of your mind to speak so of Lady Catherine."

"I will say this only once more, Mr. Collins. Leave now or I will have Mr. Hill remove you from the house by force."

As if on cue, the door opened and Mr. Hill appeared. "How can I help you, Mr. Bennet?"

"Please show Mr. Collins out."

"Yes, sir."

"Follow me, please, Mr. Collins." Mr. Hill stared at the man as if he could make the parson move by sheer force of will.

Mr. Collins glared at his cousin. "That is twice I have been asked to remove myself from my future home. I will remember this poor treatment when you are gone, sir. Your family should expect no consideration from me when I inherit!" Mr. Collins glared at his cousin before stomping from the room.

Mr. Bennet turned his gaze upon the unknown woman before him. "Now, what is it I can do for you, madam?"

"I am Lady Catherine de Bourgh," she cried in her most autocratic tone, "and you shall address me properly."

"Why have you invaded my peace, *Lady* Catherine?" Disdain dripped from Mr. Bennet's words.

"I demand to speak with Miss Elizabeth Bennet immediately."

"That is impossible, as I have already informed you. My daughter Elizabeth is from home and will not return for another few days."

"Then I shall have to deal with you." The expression she wore showed her frustration and anger. "I am here to inform you that your daughter cannot be engaged to my nephew, Fitzwilliam Darcy, for he is already engaged to my daughter."

"If that is the case, why did he bring me a marriage settlement, which has already been signed, by the way?"

"The document is not valid, for, as I said, he is engaged to my daughter."

"And do you have a marriage settlement to prove this fact? You cannot expect that I will simply take your word on the matter." Mr. Bennet had a hard time keeping a smile from his face. Darcy had told him about his aunt and her plans for his future—plans in which neither he nor his cousin wanted any part.

"Do you know who I am?" Mr. Bennet's doubting her word only increased Lady Catherine's indignation and fury.

"You did tell me your identity, but that in no way changes the need for proof."

"The engagement between my daughter and my nephew is of a peculiar kind. It was the fondest wish of his mother, who was my sister, and of myself."

"Ah, I see."

"I am glad you plan to be reasonable about this, Mr. Bennet."

"I am afraid I do not understand your meaning, ma'am."

"Now that you know of their long-standing engagement, I expect you to have your daughter break things off with Darcy."

"Why would I do that? Elizabeth and Mr. Darcy have expressed their affection for each other and clearly stated their desire to marry. I sincerely doubt that Mr. Darcy would have proposed to my Lizzy if he were not in a position to do so."

"How much?" demanded Lady Catherine.

"I beg your pardon?" Again, Mr. Bennet had to look away to prevent a smile from escaping.

"I know that your estate is small and that you have five daughters to marry off. How much will it take for you to break the engagement?"

Mr. Bennet appeared to give her question some consideration.

## A Matter of Timing

"I will give you five thousand pounds. You can add it to Miss Elizabeth's dowry, which will help to overcome the broken engagement."

"That hardly seems fair to my other daughters."

"Ten thousand, then. That will give all of your daughters two thousand pounds each."

"Well . . ."

"Fifteen thousand, but that is my final offer. "Fifteen thousand pounds would give them each a three-thousand-pound dowry, which is more than your estate produces in a year."

"I am sorry, Lady Catherine, but I cannot accept. It would break my Lizzy's heart if she lost Mr. Darcy. From what I have seen, they will be very happy together. Between him and Mr. Bingley, my eldest daughter's betrothed, I need not worry about my family's future care. I do not need your money. Now, if —"

"This is not to be borne! Mr. Bennet, I warn you, I am not a woman to be trifled with."

"I am doing no such thing. Now, if you will excuse me, I am still recovering from my injury and wish to rest until dinner. Good day, Lady Catherine."

Mr. Bennet walked to the door and through it. Lady Catherine heard his feet mounting the stairs. Recovering from her surprise, the woman raced after him. "I demand that you stop." Lady Catherine's voice rang through the empty rooms.

Mr. Bennet paused and turned. Mr. Hill and the young groom, Sam, were forcibly preventing Lady Catherine from ascending the stairs as Mrs. Hill watched.

"I will not leave until you grant me what I wish."

"And I shall certainly never give it. Goodbye." Mr. Bennet continued to his room, closing the door firmly.

"Well, I never!" Lady Catherine cried.

Mrs. Hill moved to the front door and opened it for the lady to depart. When Lady Catherine made another attempt to mount the stairs, the men each took an elbow and nearly dragged her from the house. Sam stood on the porch to ensure the carriage departed, while Mr. Hill re-entered, locking the door behind him. Mrs. Hill had climbed the stairs to check on her master, but as she raised her hand to knock, she heard Mr. Bennet's laugh coming from the other side. A broad smile creased the housekeeper's face. If her master's sense of humor had returned, he was completely recovered.

# HOME AGAIN

AS THE CARRIAGE BEGAN ITS RETURN journey to Longbourn, Elizabeth gazed at the London landscape. Watching out the window, she remembered, with pleasure, the outing with Lady Matlock on the previous day.

*They had traveled together to get Mrs. Gardiner. Elizabeth noted with satisfaction that it was not long after their introduction before the ladies were talking and laughing like old friends. At the shop, Lady Matlock had praised both Elizabeth and Jane's wardrobe choices, complimenting them on their excellent taste. Afterward, she had insisted on treating everyone to tea at her favorite shop. There, the countess had proudly introduced Elizabeth to several of her acquaintances. Elizabeth's heart filled with relief and joy as she remembered.*

"Where are you, my Elizabeth? You seem far away." Darcy's warm breath on her ear sent a shiver down Elizabeth's spine.

"I was just reflecting on my outing with Aunt Elaine. I never dreamed I would receive such easy acceptance nor earn her affection so quickly. She is a remarkable lady. I hope she will be willing to help me learn my way around the ton. She has such grace and ease of manner."

"Very much like you, Elizabeth. Your relaxed, happy manners and graceful ways were the first things I noticed about you."

"I know that not to be true, Mr. Darcy. I believe your first notice of me was that I was merely tolerable and not tempting." Her teasing smile and sparkling eyes removed any sting from her words.

"I see that you shall frequently remind me of my poor behavior."

"Of course, for if I cannot tease you, who can?"

"It is certainly more enjoyable when you tease me than when Richard does." They both laughed. The colonel had been relentless teasing Darcy and Bingley about their loss of freedom. "However, his day will come, and under your tutelage, I shall be an expert in teasing when it does." Again, they laughed softly.

"I hope my mother's requests for items from London were not too excessive." Elizabeth's expression showed embarrassment and trepidation.

"Do not worry, Elizabeth. I was happy to provide them, for you deserve only the best, my love."

"Thank you, William."

They moved on to speak of other things and the journey passed swiftly. As they prepared to turn into the inn yard where they would break the trip for luncheon, they barely avoided another carriage, which was driving much too fast for the sharp turn onto the main thoroughfare. Darcy glanced at the vehicle, intending to complain to the driver, but he caught a glimpse of the crest on the door and quickly turned away. When the carriage was again on the larger road, he glanced at it once more. The crest was that of his aunt, Lady Catherine. She appeared to be heading for London, and Darcy prayed she had not been at Longbourn. A visit from his demanding aunt could cause a setback in Mr. Bennet's recovery—or worse.

It was Darcy who was a bit preoccupied as they continued the trip after they dined. Eventually,

Elizabeth pulled him from his reverie. Though he did not wish to cause her unease about her father, he told her of his suspicions.

"I am sure Mr. and Mrs. Hill managed the situation quite capably." Though she spoke with conviction, Darcy knew she was trying to convince herself as much as him.

Just before teatime, the carriage arrived in front of the manor house. The Bennet sisters were thrilled to see their father waiting for them in the open doorway. Mr. Hill, with the assistance of Darcy's footmen, quickly had the trunks unloaded and distributed to the correct rooms.

Upon seeing her father, Elizabeth released Darcy's arm and hurried to embrace him. "You look much improved, Papa, but are you sure you should be out of bed?"

"I received permission from both Dr. Munroe and Dr. Lennox and am enjoying my second day of freedom, Lizzy. The walls of my bedchamber felt like a prison, and the light is not nearly as good as in my study, so reading was not something in which I could indulge myself."

"Were you able to comfortably rest while we were away?"

"Very much so. Your mother spent most of her time either in Meryton or at Netherfield, and Mrs. Hill took it upon herself to spoil me in her absence. With the amount of time your mother spent there, I do hope Mr. Bingley pays his staff well or he may find himself short a few servants." The grin on her father's face brought tremendous joy to Elizabeth.

Seeing the housekeeper beyond her father's shoulder, Elizabeth smiled and mouthed, "Thank you."

"Let us all go inside. Mrs. Hill has tea almost ready and has baked everyone's favorite biscuits to celebrate your return."

Lydia and Kitty moved up to take their father's arms and lead the way inside. As they walked, they took turns speaking to him about all the things they had done while in London. The bemused look on their father's face was not one of indulgent humor, but rather surprise at the polite and mannerly way in which they conducted themselves.

"He looks very well," Darcy whispered to Elizabeth. "He certainly does not appear to have been affected by a visit from my aunt."

"The quiet apparently agrees with him. We shall have to invite him to visit us frequently," Elizabeth whispered in return. "He can enjoy the peace of the library to renew his spirits."

The group enjoyed a pleasant tea. Before they could return to Netherfield to change for dinner, Mr. Bennet asked Darcy and Elizabeth to join him in his study for a brief conversation. After Darcy and Elizabeth each took a seat, the older man said, "I met a relation of yours, Mr. Darcy. She and my cousin, Mr. Collins, paid an unexpected visit."

"I apologize, Mr. Bennet, for I know the experience cannot have been a pleasant one. Allow me to assure you that nothing my aunt said regarding a prior engagement was true."

"There now, Mr. Darcy. You need not apologize, and you did warn me she might attempt to disrupt things if she heard about it. I was easily able to toss my cousin from the house, which gave me great pleasure. Not only that, my conversation with your aunt was most entertaining. It was easy to understand why she selected Mr. Collins. They are the perfect pair." Mr. Bennet's laugh was deep and rumbling, and his eyes glinted with mischief. The look was reminiscent of one Elizabeth often employed.

Darcy looked at his future father-in-law, his mouth agape. After a moment he shook his head and responded with a grin. "I have heard my aunt called many things over the years, but never 'entertaining.'" At the younger man's words, Mr. Bennet could not contain his chuckle. Soon Darcy and Elizabeth joined him.

## A Matter of Timing

Settling more comfortably into his old, worn desk chair, Mr. Bennet recounted the conversations. Elizabeth was greatly annoyed at Lady Catherine's attempted interference but kept those feelings to herself as she watched for Darcy's reaction.

"She actually offered you fifteen thousand pounds?" Darcy asked.

"Indeed, she did. However, I told her that you and Mr. Bingley would take care of any family who might need it, so her money was not necessary." Mr. Bennet grinned as he recalled the lady's look of astonishment. "She was silent for almost a full minute. I was halfway up the stairs before she recovered from her disappointment.

"We passed Lady Catherine's carriage as we broke our journey at an inn for lunch. She nearly ran us off the road. Fortunately, I noticed the crest before speaking my mind to her driver."

"I am glad you did. I would not have wished my Lizzy to have to listen to her mean-spirited nonsense."

"I am not sure my aunt would have won such a confrontation. Miss Elizabeth was well able to hold her own against my aunt's impertinence when she visited at Hunsford. We were in company on a few occasions, and Miss Elizabeth was able to deflect the worst of my aunt's rude questions."

Mr. Bennet chuckled again. "I should like to hear about those encounters when you have time, Lizzy."

"Certainly, Papa."

"Well, I am pleased to know that not only am I gaining an intelligent new son with whom to converse and play chess but an assortment of relatives whose company will undoubtedly provide many hours of unparalleled entertainment. Now, off with you both. I plan to rest before dinner. I will see all of you later. Please have Mrs. Annesley join us, too."

"Thank you, sir. We shall see you later."

The Earl and Countess of Matlock were enjoying tea together when loud voices interrupted their peace.

"It seems your sister has finally arrived, and by the sound of things, her mood is worse than I expected." Lady Matlock cast a look of resignation at her husband. "And it had been such a pleasant day so far."

"You do not have to face her if you do not wish to, my dear," the earl offered gallantly.

"Though she will not listen to a thing I say, I am happy to support you, dear husband." Lady Matlock quickly kissed his cheek as he patted her knee.

When Lady Catherine burst through the drawing room door ahead of the butler, Henry and Elaine Fitzwilliam ignored her. The butler was on Lady Catherine's heels, but the barest flick of the earl's wrist sent him on his way without the necessary introduction.

"Would you care for more tea, Henry?"

Before he could answer, Lady Catherine pounded her walking stick on the floor. "How can you sit there calmly drinking tea when our nephew is about to disgrace the family?"

The earl turned to his sister, his face registering surprise. "I did not realize you were here, Catherine, since you did not allow Winslow to announce you."

Her younger brother's voice contained a note of reprimand, but Lady Catherine was too angry to recognize it. "I could not wait for the doddering old fool you call a butler to announce me. We must stop Fitzwilliam before he makes a fool of himself and the entire family."

"William is the most sensible young man I have ever known. I cannot imagine him doing anything that would cause disgrace." The earl delivered his words in a slow, deliberate tone.

## A Matter of Timing

Lady Catherine banged her stick on the floor again.

"Please desist in damaging my floors, Catherine." Lady Matlock glared at her sister-in-law.

"You should leave, as I must discuss this situation with my brother."

"You shall not dismiss me in my own home, and if you continue in this manner, I will have you removed." The ladies glared at each other, but neither would relent.

"Stay if you wish, but you will keep your opinions to yourself. You are only a Fitzwilliam by marriage, so this does not concern you." Lady Catherine threw the words at her sister-in-law.

"That is where you are mistaken. William and Georgiana are as dear to me as my own children, and I have cared for them as such since before Anne's death. I care greatly about anything that affects either of them."

Lady Catherine opened her mouth to speak, but the earl cut her off. "That is enough, Catherine. Now sit down and tell me what has you so up in arms."

"An insignificant, fortune-hunting country girl has bewitched Fitzwilliam. She has managed to turn his head so far that he has engaged himself to her when you know he is already engaged to Anne. I went to see the young woman to remind her that Darcy was already engaged, but she was away from home. I spoke with her father in her place and even after I offered him money to break off the engagement, he refused. That family—with five unmarried daughters—will empty the coffers of Pemberley."

"That should not matter to you as long as Rosings' accounts are full," said the earl dryly.

"Henry! If he marries this girl, Anne's heart will break and the family will be disgraced. She is not of our circle, and she has connections to trade. It will be the ruin of us."

"I find Miss Elizabeth Bennet to be a delightful and intelligent young lady. She will be a lovely addition to the family."

"I agree with you, Henry. Elizabeth is precisely what Darcy needs. She will be the making of him, and the Darcy name shall shine in the years to come."

Except for the animosity in her eyes, Lady Catherine ignored the countess' words and looked at her brother in dismay. "You knew of this situation and did nothing about it. How can you allow Darcy to hurt Anne in this manner? Anne and I engaged them at birth."

"No, Catherine, it was your wish and yours alone," the countess said. "I have heard from both William and Anne that they do not desire to wed one another. I also know that William informed you at Easter that he would not be marrying Anne. The fact that you failed to believe him is your fault, not Darcy's."

"How could I imagine that he would dishonor his mother's most cherished dream? I would not have believed him capable of such disrespectful behavior."

"That is enough, Catherine! I do not wish to hear another word. You will not be getting your way in this matter, and that is the end of it. It is not William and Elizabeth's marriage that will embarrass this family but your disgraceful behavior! You attempted to bribe the bride's family. If word of this should become a topic of gossip, you will be a laughingstock."

"No one would believe such gossip about me," Lady Catherine sniffed.

"Of course they will," the countess said. "You have made no secret of your wish for William to marry your daughter. Since you rarely come to London, you do not hold the sway over society's opinions that you think you do. Your behavior will reflect poorly on Anne. People will believe she cannot attract a husband on her own, and you will have to buy her one."

Lady Catherine's eyes nearly bulged from her head.

## A Matter of Timing

"Perhaps we should invite Anne to join us for the season next year, Henry. She will have a better chance of making a match with us should there be gossip about her mother."

"That is an excellent idea, Elaine. I would enjoy the opportunity to spend more time with Anne."

"She is a dear girl," the countess added.

Lady Catherine could not believe what she heard. Finally, her temper exploded. "How dare you say such things about me and talk about me as if I were not present? This is not to be tolerated."

The earl cut short his sister's rant. "I will tell you what we will not tolerate, Catherine, and that is your selfish ways. You have no right to dictate to William whom he will marry. And though Anne is your daughter, she is of age and more than capable of making her own decisions. She is tired of your dictates stifling her. If you are not careful, you will find yourself in the dower house, to which your husband's will relegates you. Anne is aware of the terms of her father's will, and I will help her take her rightful place if you continue to push your desires on everyone around you. Now, I am ordering you to return to Rosings Park. You are not to speak one disparaging word about Darcy's choice of bride. Elaine and I will be in attendance at the wedding and will sponsor Elizabeth next season. If you do not wish to find yourself cut off from the family, you will drop this matter and wish William and Elizabeth well. As you were leaving the inn yesterday, you nearly struck Darcy's carriage. He recognized you and spoke to Elizabeth's father upon arriving at Longbourn. I received an express from him late last evening. William is furious with you, and if you were to speak ill of Darcy's wife, you would find yourself no longer welcome at Pemberley or Darcy House. By the way, I expected you last evening based on William's letter. What delayed you?"

"We had not gone far when one of the horses threw a shoe. By the time it was repaired, it was too late to safely travel farther. I was forced to spend a second night in the most dreadful accommodations."

"If you had stayed at home where you belonged, you would not have had to suffer so."

The large sniff the lady made at this remark left no one in doubt about her umbrage at her brother's words.

"Because it is late in the day, I will have a room prepared for you, but you will be returning to Rosings early in the morning.

"My parson traveled with me; he will require a room in the servants' quarters."

"I am sure we can find a place for him," said the countess. "Have you left him waiting in the carriage all this time?"

Lady Catherine nodded.

Lady Matlock pulled the bell cord. When a footman appeared, she requested that he invite the gentleman in Lady Catherine's carriage into the house.

"Now, Catherine," said the earl, "if you are prepared to leave this subject aside, you are welcome to dine with us this evening. However, at the first word against William or Miss Bennet, you will be finishing your meal in your room. Knowing this, what is your desire?"

"I shall take a tray in my room."

"Very well then, we shall see you in the morning."

As their conversation concluded, the trio had moved into the hallway. The earl and countess turned when they heard footsteps rapidly approaching. Before them, a sweaty little man with greasy hair was bowing so low, he looked like he would topple over.

"It is a very great honor to meet the relations of my esteemed patroness, Lady Catherine. My most humble apologies for the disgustingly forward behavior of my cousin. I myself made her aware of the engagement between Mr. Darcy and Miss de Bourgh. I spoke of it often during my visit last fall. She first tried to lure me into her trap, as I am the heir to her father's estate, but I was able to see her for the temptress she is. I shall do all in my power to assist my patroness in making the situation right again." The words were a bit difficult to understand, as Mr. Collins delivered them to the floor as he remained bent forward.

"Stand up, man," remarked the earl. "Am I to understand you know Mr. Darcy and his betrothed?"

"I had the extreme pleasure of meeting Mr. Darcy last fall in Hertfordshire and again at Rosings this past Easter. I met my cousin, Miss Elizabeth Bennet, last fall, also, when I met my relations for the first time. Hoping to prevent them from being homeless upon their father's demise, I intended to offer for one of my fair cousins. However, I could see that none of them, with the exception of the eldest, perhaps, was worthy of the position of my wife or to be permitted into the influence of my illustrious patroness."

The earl and countess looked at one another, unsure what to make of the ridiculous man before them. "There is no need for you to be concerned, Mr. Collins. I have given my blessing to William and Miss Bennet. We are delighted to welcome her to our family."

"But, but . . ." Mr. Collins looked between the earl and Lady Catherine. She was obviously displeased with her brother's announcement, but how was he to argue with a peer of the realm?

The man looked as if he would say more, so the earl forestalled him. "I will tell you the same thing I told my sister," said the earl. "If I learn that anyone has spoken out against Miss Elizabeth Bennet or her marriage to my nephew, I shall be very displeased and will personally ensure that the person's life becomes very uncomfortable."

Mr. Collins' face paled at Lord Matlock's words. Still, it galled him to think that Miss Elizabeth would prosper after turning down his most generous and eligible proposal.

Fortunately, the housekeeper appeared to direct the guests to their rooms. Lady Catherine and Mr. Collins followed Mrs. Reid up the stairs and down a hallway. When the others were out of sight, the earl offered his wife an arm and they ascended the staircase on the way to their suite.

"Do you think that man actually had the temerity to offer for Elizabeth?"

"Could it have been any other?" returned the countess.

They shook their heads in disbelief as they continued to their rooms.

---

The church service was a repeat of the first Sunday of the reading of the banns. As Reverend Carter stood to make the announcement for the third time, Darcy and Elizabeth sat with intertwined fingers. When they heard no objection to the betrothal, they each released a breath that neither realized he or she was holding. Their simultaneous exhalations made them both chuckle as they smiled lovingly at each other. After the service, the group divided themselves between the Bennet and Darcy carriages and went to Netherfield Park for Sunday dinner.

The next day was Elizabeth's birthday. The cook fixed all her favorite breakfast items. Later in the day, Darcy, with the help of Bingley and Jane, arranged a picnic lunch on Oakham Mount for the two couples. They spoke of their upcoming wedding and hopes for the future. The only disappointment for Elizabeth and Jane was the distance that would separate them.

Dinner was a celebration of Elizabeth's birthday. Again, the cook had fixed all her favorite dishes. After the meal, the family gathered in the parlor to watch Elizabeth open her gifts.

Her three younger sisters had saved some of the funds set aside for their new dresses and bought

Elizabeth a selection of ribbons for her hair. Many of them would match her new gowns. Jane and Bingley gifted her a set of lovely hairpins, and Georgiana bought her a fur muff and hat for the cold Derbyshire winters. Mr. Bennet gave Elizabeth a new book and her mother gave her several handkerchiefs stitched with her new initials. Darcy's gift was a set of personalized stationery and a seal showing her initials above the Darcy crest.

# THE BIG DAY ARRIVES

The two days between Elizabeth's birthday and the wedding were busy. The day after her birthday, the Gardiners, as well as Lord and Lady Matlock, arrived from town. Everyone was invited to Netherfield to dine that evening. Elizabeth and Jane both had to pack all their clothes and personal items in preparation for their moves to their new homes. Elizabeth wished to see several of the tenants, especially the children, before departing for Pemberley.

Mrs. Bennet relentlessly demanded their attention with last-minute details. It took all of Jane's talents and Elizabeth's patience to calm her when she began to second-guess the plans she had made. Fortunately for the two brides to be, Mrs. Gardiner convinced their mother to allow her to speak to the girls about what to expect on their wedding night. Though Mr. Bennet had been paying more attention to his wife since his brush with death, their relationship was still not one Elizabeth or Jane wished to emulate. The marriage of the Gardiners, however, was a different story. Mrs. Gardiner was both sensitive and sensible in her explanation and answered any questions with patience.

One morning, Elizabeth and William took a final walk to Oakham Mount, and then Elizabeth devoted an afternoon to visiting with her father in his study. They spoke of many topics—except her wedding—and played a game or two of chess.

Now the big day was here. The first rays of sunshine were creeping around the curtains when Elizabeth Bennet opened her eyes. As she stretched, the realization of the day swept over her. *I am getting married today!* She thought back to the day almost a year ago when she had first laid eyes on William. Immediately she had found herself drawn to him until she had overheard his opinion of her. The relationship had suffered from several ups and downs and misunderstandings. They had come a long way since then.

Now Elizabeth could not imagine her life without William in it. Never had Elizabeth expected to find someone she could love and who would accept her as she was. Elizabeth loved William dearly and looked forward to the life they would build together.

Checking the clock on the mantel, Elizabeth realized that if she hurried she should be able to take a short walk before she needed to prepare for the wedding. She donned an old dress and braided her hair before grabbing a bonnet and shawl. She slipped quietly down the stairs and out through the kitchen door.

The morning air was slightly cool, and little white clouds dotted the brilliant blue sky above. A gentle breeze rustled the leaves and birdsong filled the air. Here and there, flowers still bloomed, and the leaves had not yet changed their colors. Elizabeth made her way in the direction of Netherfield, stopping atop a rise from where she could view the house. She had no plans to meet William this morning, and she wondered if he was awake yet. From this distance she could not see anyone stirring, so turned towards home to begin her preparations.

## A Matter of Timing

After bathing and washing her hair, Elizabeth joined her family for breakfast. When the meal was over, Mrs. Gardiner offered to assist her in dressing, as Mrs. Bennet planned to help Jane.

Once in her undergarments, Elizabeth sat before the mirror at the dressing table while Mrs. Gardiner's maid dressed her hair. "I am so pleased for you, Lizzy," Mrs. Gardiner said. "You and Mr. Darcy are well suited and obviously very much in love."

"I have you to thank for that. If you had not invited me to join you on your trip north during the summer, I would most likely have never seen Mr. Darcy again, and Mr. Bingley might never have returned to Hertfordshire."

"Oh, I think you would have met again at some point, for you seem destined to be together."

"I am glad I do not have to wait to find out if you might be correct. William is the best man I know, and I could not be any happier than I am now. I cannot wait to marry him."

"Well, you do not have to wait long."

"What do ye think of yer hair, miss?" asked the maid.

Elizabeth turned her head from side to side, watching her reflection in the mirror. "It has never looked lovelier. Thank you." The maid bobbed a curtsey, then stepped to the closet, returning with Elizabeth's wedding dress. The maid and Mrs. Gardiner eased it down over Elizabeth's head without disturbing her hair. As the maid fastened the tiny buttons on the back of the dress, Mrs. Gardiner assisted Elizabeth with her gloves and bonnet.

They descended to the parlor to wait until it was time to depart. The three younger girls were the only ones present, but Mr. Bennet and Mr. Gardiner entered almost on Elizabeth's heels. Her sisters were already crowded around her, exclaiming over her dress.

Mr. Bennet was finally able to get a glimpse of his favorite daughter on her special day, and the sight brought tears to his eyes. "You look lovely, Lizzy."

"Indeed, you do," agreed her uncle.

Mrs. Bennet bustled into the room, practically dragging Jane with her. Again, the sisters gathered to admire one another, but Mrs. Bennet soon put a stop to it. "It is time to leave for the church. We do not wish to be late and allow the gentlemen any time to change their minds." Mary, Kitty, and Lydia groaned at their mother's ill-conceived comment, while Jane and Elizabeth merely shared a smile at her silliness. They knew the gentlemen would wait forever if necessary, but they were happy to depart and eager to see their grooms. The five daughters rode in the Bennet carriage while Mr. and Mrs. Bennet rode with the Gardiners.

As the sisters had grown much closer over the past few weeks, Elizabeth and Jane had not been able to choose one or even two to stand with them when they married. Consequently, the elder girls decided that all three of the younger sisters would attend the brides. Because of that, Richard Fitzwilliam stood up with his cousin Darcy. Bingley also had a cousin attend him, and lastly, a mutual friend from university stood up for both gentlemen.

Mr. Gardiner escorted both his wife and sister to their places. When the music began, Francis Hayward, the university friend, escorted Lydia to the front of the church. Kitty followed with Mr. Robert Bingley and then Colonel Fitzwilliam walked with Mary. Lastly, Mr. Bennet traversed with Elizabeth and Jane to the gentlemen waiting not so patiently at the altar.

The Bennet sisters looked like a bouquet of pastel flowers as they stood together before the congregation. Jane, wearing blue, stood between Mr. Bingley and Mr. Darcy. On Darcy's other side, Elizabeth, Mary, Kitty, and Lydia stood together, dressed respectively in yellow, green, pink, and lavender.

The wedding went smoothly, and before they knew it, Reverend Carter was pronouncing the couples husband and wife and saying the last of the prayers.

## A Matter of Timing

After signing the register, the two couples, oblivious to all others present, walked out to the waiting carriage and climbed in for the short ride to Netherfield Park.

Mrs. Bennet had certainly outdone herself with the arrangements for the wedding breakfast. The Netherfield ballroom looked even more spectacular than it had during the ball the previous autumn. Many of the locals were in awe at the fact that an earl and countess were in attendance. Everyone was eager to speak with the newlyweds, but occasionally there were a few murmurs questioning the absence of the Hursts and Miss Bingley.

Finally, after a sumptuous meal, many toasts, and even a few dances, the time came for Darcy and Elizabeth to depart. They would be spending the first night at Darcy House before making the trip to Pemberley. Georgiana would travel back to town with the Matlocks, who were also departing, so that Mr. and Mrs. Bingley could enjoy their wedding night without having guests to entertain. Mrs. Bennet, never one to miss a chance to show off her remaining daughters, invited Mr. Bingley and Mr. Hayward to stay the night with them before they returned to their homes. With Elizabeth's and Jane's rooms empty, space would be available for the additional guests.

---

It was late afternoon on the fourth day after their wedding when Darcy's well-sprung carriage crested a hill and pulled to a halt. He jumped down and turned to Elizabeth. His large hands wrapped around her small waist as he lifted her down to stand beside him. They walked closer to the edge of the hill and looked at Pemberley, spread out in the valley below them.

"Welcome home, Mrs. Darcy." From where he stood behind her, William whispered the words in Elizabeth's ear, his arms around her waist.

"I cannot believe I am to be mistress of such a magnificent place."

"It is a very special place to me, but before your arrival it was just a large building. Now it will be a home." Darcy nuzzled her neck before continuing, "Hopefully, the sounds of our children will soon fill the halls."

Elizabeth's cheeks flushed at his words, but she replied daringly. "Shall we go practice making those children?" She looked over her shoulder and cocked her brow at her husband.

In answer to her question, Elizabeth felt Darcy's lips descend towards hers. The next thing she knew, he lifted her off her feet and stepped up into the carriage, never breaking the kiss. Though they paused for breath on occasion, the kissing continued until they felt the carriage roll to a halt.

The footman put down the step and opened the carriage door. Darcy exited the carriage before turning towards and assisting Elizabeth. Without appearing to rush, Darcy introduced Elizabeth to the main members of the staff and promised further introductions on the morrow. Then he swept his wife into his arms and carried her over the threshold. Still holding her against his chest, he took the stairs two at a time before turning down a hallway. In the entryway below, the staff could hear the laughter of the master and new mistress float back to them. Everyone smiled and, with a word from Mrs. Reynolds, scattered to their respective responsibilities.

As she stood staring at the empty staircase, the housekeeper gave a contented sigh. "He is finally happy, and Pemberley will be a home once again."

# THE BEGINNING

# EPILOGUE

THE DARCYS GOT THEIR WISH, AS their first child, a son named Alexander, joined the family just after their first anniversary. A month and a half after their wedding, they returned to London for the little season, then spent the Christmas holidays at Pemberley with the Bennets, Gardiners, Bingleys, and Fitzwilliams.

During their brief visit to London, Elizabeth made her curtsey to the Queen and also attended several balls and dinner parties. She interspersed these duties with more enjoyable activities, including trips to the theater or museums.

The Darcys returned to London the following spring to participate in the season and present Mary Bennet to society. She made a positive impression on Mr. Hayward at their first meeting. He learned more of her from his friend Mr. Darcy and was present at every event Mary attended during her first season. The experience would be a short one for Mary, as Elizabeth's pregnancy required that they return to Pemberley before the end of May. Consequently, Mr. Hayward, who was the only son of a baronet, wasted no time in making Mary an offer of marriage, which she happily accepted.

The following year, Kitty made her debut, but in spite of receiving two offers, she remained unwed. Jane and Bingley hosted Kitty for her second season, during which she accepted an offer from a gentleman whose estate was in Suffolk.

Because of Elizabeth's second confinement, Georgiana and Lydia waited another year before they could debut. However, they made a joint debut when they were eight and ten. The girls had become very close over the years, having first bonded over their similar experiences with Mr. Wickham. Making their debut together seemed the most natural thing in the world. Neither accepted an offer during their first season, but each found their perfect match during the second one. Georgiana would marry Christopher Pembroke, the Marquis of Brookdale, son of the Duke of Devondale. The family's estate was also in Derbyshire, keeping Georgiana close to William and Elizabeth. Lydia accepted Marcus Greenwood, whose estate was in nearby Leicestershire. This decision earned Lydia her mother's disapprobation because the young man was not a peer. However, like Elizabeth, Lydia had learned to ignore her mother's more embarrassing comments.

Though Lady Catherine tried to prevent it, Anne de Bourgh did join the Matlocks to participate in the season. As it was also the first experience for Elizabeth and Mary, the three became fast friends. Anne's health significantly improved due to a new doctor whose treatment prescribed exercise and better food. Consequently, Anne took great enjoyment in her new freedom. As an heiress with a dowry of forty thousand pounds and a large estate, Anne was considered one of the belles of the season. With the assistance of her uncle, Darcy, and her Fitzwilliam cousins, the horde of fortune hunters that gravitated to Anne's sizeable dowry did not succeed in their endeavors. She eventually met and fell in love with the second son of an earl. Lady Catherine refused to recognize the relationship because the gentleman was only a second

## A Matter of Timing

son. However, having wisely invested a portion of his allowance all his life, the man had acquired a considerable fortune of his own. Due to her stubborn refusal, Lady Catherine soon found herself a resident of the dower house at Rosings Park, with a considerably smaller monthly allowance.

Charles and Jane Bingley did not remain at Netherfield Park for very long. Mrs. Bennet was far too pleased that her daughter was mistress of the largest estate in the area and, thus, visited her almost daily. Even for the long-suffering Bingleys, this was a trial. During a visit with the Darcys, they investigated several available estates within a thirty-mile ride of Pemberley. Eventually, they settled at Houghton Lodge, just over the border into Nottinghamshire. Travel between the two properties was similar to that between Longbourn and London. The Bingleys raised a large family of strawberry-blond children, each possessing his or her parents' placid temperaments.

What happened to Miss Bingley, you may wonder. She crossed paths with Mr. and Mrs. Darcy at one of the events they attended during their first visit to London following their marriage. When she noticed them, they were standing in conversation with Charles and Jane. Caroline smiled and made her way in their direction, but when she caught the look in Darcy's eyes, she remembered his threat and thought better of her actions. Eventually, she met a gentleman whose ranking in society was similar to that of Mr. Hurst. Though it was not what she thought she deserved, Caroline accepted his proposal, knowing she was close to being considered on the shelf. Unfortunately, the gentleman was not wise in handling his money and the couple found themselves selling their London home to live at the family estate in Somerset. Caroline's overbearing behavior caused a rift not only with the Bingleys but also with the Hursts. She received the occasional letter from her sister, but soon those stopped, as, in her replies to Louisa, Caroline freely expressed her bitterness with life. Circumstances prevented her from ever returning to London and the society she so craved.

The Darcys' life contained more joys than sorrows. Their family grew, filling the halls of Pemberley with the sound of running feet and happy voices.

Elizabeth stood at the window, looking out over the side lawn of Pemberley. With her hand resting on her pregnant belly, she watched her children chase each other around the yard. Darcy stood in the doorway, observing her as a sweet smile played over her lips.

"What are you thinking, my love?" Darcy stood behind Elizabeth and wrapped his arms around her, placing his hands over hers where they rested on her stomach.

"I am thinking about how fortunate it was for you to return early when I first visited Pemberley. Had you been in residence, I might not have had the nerve to accompany my aunt and uncle on the tour of your estate."

"If it had not been for my steward's letter and a growing need to be farther away from Miss Bingley, I might not have rushed back."

"It seems our reunion and our future joy were merely a matter of timing."

# END NOTES

(1) Pride and Prejudice, Jane Austen, 1813, Volume III, Chapter 1 (or Chapter 43 if in one volume)
(2) The Book of Common Prayer (as printed by John Baskerville), 1662

# OTHER BOOKS BY LINDA C. THOMPSON

## Her Unforgettable Laugh
## Book 1

Dark curls and an unforgettably sweet laugh was all he knew of his sister's rescuer. Later, a second glimpse showed her to be lovely, and he heard her melodious laugh again. Darcy wondered what it would be like to meet this remarkable, and remarkably lovely, young woman. Would the spirit that caused her to go to the aid of a stranger be able to bring some joy to his lonely life? Would they ever meet, or would he always be left wondering?

---

Little did Fitzwilliam Darcy know that his trip to Hertfordshire to help his friend would bring him face to face with the lovely young woman whose unforgettable laugh had haunted his dreams for the last several years. Would she be anything like the woman he had built up in his dreams? Would he be able to avoid Miss Bingley long enough to discover more about this mysterious young woman?

## Laughter Through Trials
## Book 2

Dark curls and an unforgettably sweet laugh . . .

In Book I of the series, Her Unforgettable Laugh, a trip to Hertfordshire brought Fitzwilliam Darcy face-to-face with the woman who had haunted his dreams for five years. Their chance meeting led to a courtship, in spite of those who wished to separate them. Now Elizabeth Bennet is traveling to London where she will be introduced to Darcy's family and the ton. How will Elizabeth be received? Will their love flourish and grow or will new trials overwhelm them?

## The Laughter of Love
## Book 3

Dark curls and an unforgettably sweet laugh . . .

In Book 2 of the series, Laughter Through Trials, Darcy and Elizabeth celebrated their courtship as Elizabeth was introduced to the Fitzwilliam family and London society. Their sojourn in town held a few difficulties, but the strength of their love allowed them to face the challenges and outwit their enemies.

Now Darcy and Elizabeth are returning to Hertfordshire for their wedding and Elizabeth worries there is still one trial to be faced—Mrs. Bennet. Her mother refuses to prepare the simple, elegant affair the couple wishes for their wedding day. Will it be the day of their dreams or a disaster?

However, the wedding turns out, Darcy and Elizabeth are excited to begin their life together. The bright future before them fills their hearts with joy. Both know they will face periods of contentment and heartache, but united they will confront whatever comes their way. Will those they have previously encountered allow them to enjoy their happiness or will there be more misfortune for them to overcome?

## The Companion's Secret

"You must marry her," the stern voice said. "I need to gain control of her inheritance before she reaches her next birthday. It need not be a long marriage, but marry her you must."

Alone in the world, Elizabeth Bennet had to rely upon herself. She knew escape was the only way to ensure her safety. With the help of Longbourn's faithful servants, Elizabeth disappeared from her home and the odious heir. She was determined to find a way to support herself and remain hidden until after her birthday.

Fortune smiled on Elizabeth when a series of events offered her the position of companion to Georgiana Darcy. In spite of her position, Elizabeth found herself attracted to her new employer. Could he ever see her as more than his sister's companion? Sometimes Elizabeth thought Mr. Darcy might care for her, too, but would his attraction—if that is what is was—survive when he learned the truth about her?

Hidden away at Pemberley, would Elizabeth be able to remain safely concealed until coming of age? What surprises did the future hold for her?